HAPPY NOW

CHARLIE HIGSON

ABACUS

ABACUS

First published in Great Britain in 1993
Reissued in 2022 by Abacus

1 3 5 7 9 10 8 6 4 2

A CIP catalogue record for this book
is available from the British Library.

ISBN 978-03491-4485-6

Typeset in Garamond by M Rules
Printed and bound in Great Britain by
Clays Ltd, Elcograf S.p.A.

Papers used by Abacus are from well-managed forests
and other responsible sources.

Abacus
An imprint of
Little, Brown Book Group
Carmelite House
50 Victoria Embankment
London EC4Y 0DZ

An Hachette UK Company
www.hachette.co.uk

www.littlebrown.co.uk

TOM

Tom Kendall was woken by the sounds of a cat killing the family of blackbirds which had nested in the creeper outside his bedroom window. The same thing had happened last year. He recognized the furtive rustling of the otherwise silent cat, then the sudden scurry as it attacked. Last time he'd gone out to try and stop it, but he'd been too late; they were all dead before he got there. This time he just lay still and hoped the panicked cheeping of the birds would soon be over.

He looked at his watch; it was half past eight, early for a Saturday. He'd wanted a lie-in, but he knew there was no point in trying to get back to sleep now, no matter how tired he felt. And he did feel tired. But then whatever time he woke he always felt this way.

He never dreamed. In fact it felt like there was no time at all between going to sleep and waking. It was like flicking a switch. One moment he'd be in bed and it would be dark, and the next moment he'd be in bed and it would be light, with nothing in between. He always woke disoriented, as if a piece of time had been stolen from him. And always tired. His body felt heavy and sluggish, worse than when he'd gone to bed. He'd been to see Dr Anthony about it, and he'd said it was perhaps a symptom of depression. But Tom told him that it'd been like this for as long as he could remember, and surely he hadn't been depressed all his life. So they both supposed he'd just have to live with it.

He got out of bed and straightened the duvet. Why leave making the bed till later? If you had a routine, everything became simpler; you saved so much time and energy.

The next thing to do was shower. The hot water falling on his neck helped to clear his head and he could start to get his thoughts together; plan out the day ahead. He hadn't meant to get to work until mid-day, but now he was up he might as well go in earlier. He didn't really need to go in at all, if the truth be told – once the presses were up and running there was little he could do – but it was a habit he'd got into. In the past he'd often spent all weekend there. He'd had a small bedroom and bathroom built behind his office; he found it relaxing lying in the narrow single bed listening to the rhythmic pounding and churning of the big machines. He was no longer closely involved on a physical level, but he liked to be there. And when it came down to it, he didn't actually have anything else to do.

After his shower he dressed in a lightweight casual suit and plain shirt and tie and had breakfast in his kitchen. He had his own muesli mix, which he remade every month, a cup of coffee, half a grapefruit and two slices of toast. Then he rinsed the plates, the cutlery, his mug and glass and put them all in the washing-up machine. Finally he checked that everything was in its place, then wiped the surfaces to get rid of a few crumbs. It was good to come into the kitchen and find it exactly the same every time. His whole flat was like that. Clean and efficient. He was very happy here, though sometimes he'd panic and feel that things weren't right, that his home lacked the personal touch. Then he'd go into Greenwich and try to find a painting or an ornament of some kind, but whatever he bought looked wrong, and after a few days' agony he'd remove it. Then peace would return. Why shouldn't he like it like this? He was responsible to no one. He could live exactly how he liked.

Satisfied that all was in order, he went through to his study and sat down at his pride and joy, a Yamaha home organ. He switched it on and doodled for a while. He'd bought the organ several years ago, and since then miniaturization and computerization had taken over. Nowadays a tiny keyboard with two buttons on it could reproduce the sounds of an entire orchestra. But Tom wasn't interested. His Yamaha was big and solid, with rows of proper stops, foot pedals, two banked keyboards (for right and left hand), and a built-in speaker. He could entertain himself for hours on it, and he found it the ideal way to clear his mind before a busy day. He sometimes composed his own songs, silly little love songs mostly, and had considered making a recording of some of them and sending them to a publisher, but he knew he never would. They were for his own private amusement.

This morning he felt like playing something from a book, so he opened the stool and sorted through his pile of music until he came to *101 Folk Songs from around the World*. He set it up on the stand and flipped the pages. 'La Cucaracha' caught his eye. Yes, that was a jolly tune. Three-four it said, so he set the internal rhythm to a jaunty waltz time. The synthetic drums popped and hissed. He switched on the autoplay for his left hand, then pulled out some brass stops for the right hand, with lots of trumpets. A couple of slight adjustments and he was ready. The chords were easy to follow, there were only two or three, and he soon had the hang of it. Second time through he felt confident enough to sing along, even though there were some unfamiliar Mexican words to contend with.

He sat there singing away for about ten minutes, round and round, filling in with the odd keyboard solo. These times of the day were his happiest, singing to himself with not a thought in the world.

Suitably refreshed, he turned off the power, returned the music to the stool, had one last look round to check that everything was in its place, then left the flat and locked up.

It was a bright but overcast day, the sky an even, pale grey. As he came down the wide stone steps to where his car was parked on the gravel forecourt, he looked beneath the creeper and saw a small baby bird lying still among the stones. He went to inspect it. It was naked and pink; a few leathery feather-tips had started to grow and it had huge purple-lidded eyes. It looked like a little monster, one of those rubber toys children were so fond of. He carefully picked it up by a soft transparent foot and took it over to the dustbins. When he got there he heard something fluttering and saw that there was another bird hiding between the bins and the low dividing wall. It was the mother, brown and drab-looking. It hopped and scuffled away from him but couldn't fly. One of its wings was broken.

'Come here,' he said gently, leaning down to try and grab it. 'I won't hurt you. Come on.'

It leapt away from him, colliding with the wall. He made a lunge for it and took hold of its good wing. Then he carefully cradled it between his hands. It was unexpectedly light and its heart was beating wildly, a hundred times faster than a human heart. The broken wing was bleeding; it looked beyond repair. One of its eyes was missing as well, and the left claw was twisted at a funny angle.

'What have you got there?'

Tom looked up to see Fiona, the girl from the flat upstairs, coming out of the front door with her bicycle.

'Blackbird. The cat got it.'

'Poor thing.'

He didn't really know Fiona. They sometimes met in the hall-way, or out here, and exchanged pleasantries, but he was happy that she mostly kept herself to herself.

'What are you going to do with it?' she asked, wheeling her bike over to him.

'It's beyond help, unfortunately. The kindest thing would be to destroy it.'

'Oh.' Fiona grimaced. 'Do you have to take it to the vet for that sort of thing?'

'No. It's all right. I know how to do it. I can do it without causing any pain.'

Fiona frowned. 'Eeugh. I don't think I want to watch.' She got on her bike. 'See you, then.' She smiled and cycled off up the road.

Tom looked at the bird. It had gone into shock and was sitting very still in his hands, as if hypnotized. He took hold of its neck just behind the head and gave a quick firm snap. He barely felt it. He opened the bin, undid the top of the black bin bag inside and dropped the two birds into it. Then he refastened the bag and replaced the bin lid.

He had to go back in to wash his hands now, which he did meticulously in a rehearsed pattern. Then he wiped the sink, straightened the towel and once again left the flat.

The drive from Blackheath to the printworks in New Cross took about ten minutes on a Saturday, and as he drove westwards the surroundings grew more and more shabby and seedy. It was surprising how quickly elegant Greenwich and the Heath gave way to run-down Deptford and New Cross. The streets were dirtier, the buildings neglected, the people noticeably poorer-looking.

Whenever Tom told someone about his circumstances, they invariably said how nice it must be to live on the Heath and how miserable to work in somewhere like New Cross. But it made no difference to him, he hardly noticed. As a matter of fact, the first time it had been said to him he'd been amazed. He'd never really thought about it. He'd bought the flat because it was large and light and handy for work. He'd never really considered that living in this area might be desirable. If there'd been a similar flat nearer to work, he'd have taken that. Once he was shut away inside he forgot what was outside, he forgot the rest of the world. Sleeping in the little room at work, sleeping in the flat, it was all the same to him.

He was always pleased to see the familiar old-fashioned sign for 'Kendallprint' stuck high up on the concrete factory building.

It had a feeling of permanence. For nearly twenty years he'd been coming here, while countless other businesses in the area had appeared and disappeared. At the moment there was a retail-fashion warehouse on one side and a laminating workshop on the other. But Kendallprint was always the same.

Except today.

As Tom pulled off the road into the car park, he noticed an unfamiliar car parked there. Frowning, he got out to investigate.

A flabby-looking man with a T-shirt and long, lank hair was getting out of the strange car with an equally flabby-looking wife and two fat children.

'Are you here for the printworks?' Tom said, smiling, but even as he said it he could see that they weren't. 'Actually, I'm sorry,' he said going over to them. 'This is a private car park ...' He indicated the building. 'For the printworks.'

The flabby man stared at him blankly, as if he'd been speaking Chinese.

'Yes ... It's not a public car park, I'm afraid.'

'We're parked now,' said the man, locking his door.

'Yes, I'm sorry, but you'll have to move.'

'What difference does it make?' the man said.

Tom took a deep breath and spoke slowly. 'The fact is,' he said, 'this is private property.'

'So what? What difference does it make? We'll only be half an hour.' The man looked to his wife and gave her an expression that said, 'Who is this wanker?' The woman shook her head and unfolded a baby carriage for one of her fat children.

'No, please. I don't want to make a scene ...'

'Then don't.' The man stared at him, daring him to push it further.

Tom felt his hands sweating. He knew he should just walk away, but it annoyed him too much. He knew he'd start to get angry if he took this any further, but it was an important matter. People had to understand that they couldn't just come in here, willy-nilly, and use the company car park. It wasn't on.

The fat family began to move towards him. But he was blocking their way out of the car park.

'You really will have to move your car, you know,' he said, his voice sounding small and strained.

'Oh, come on, mate,' the man said wearily. 'We're going shopping. We'll be half an hour at the most. The car park's empty. We're not in anyone's way ...'

'That's not the point.'

'Then what is the point?'

'The point is, this is a private car park.'

The man snorted. 'But there's nobody using it.'

'Will you just listen to me for one moment, you stupid ...' Tom stopped himself. This wasn't the way to go about it. He mustn't lose his temper. He blushed. Don't make a fool of yourself.

The whole family was looking at him now, as if he were some disgusting insect.

Tom put a hand to his temple. He could sense the beginning of a headache. The day had not started well. He couldn't think of anything more to say. All he could do was stand there impotently, humming 'La Cucaracha' under his breath and repeating to himself over and over, 'Don't get angry ... don't lose your temper ... don't make a fool of yourself.'

The man took a step forward and Tom put up a hand. 'Please ...' he said, but the effort of producing this one word robbed him of the power to finish the sentence. The man looked at him, grinned and shook his head again. 'Why don't you just piss off out of the way, mate?' he said. 'Okay?'

Tom wanted to reach out and snap his neck like he'd snapped the bird's. But he knew he wouldn't. He wouldn't do anything. He'd stand there like some tongue-tied schoolboy humming that stupid tune and staring at the man's stupid belt buckle.

'Oi!' someone shouted. Tom looked round to see Gerry, one of his press operators, coming out of the factory building. 'Is that your motor?'

The fat man gave him a long-suffering look. 'What if it is?' he said.

'You can't leave it there, mate. You'll get towed away. Cost you seventy quid to get it back.'

The man tutted and turned back. 'Come on, Linda,' he said. 'We'd better shift it.' The whole family groaned, and they returned to the car moaning and arguing with each other.

'All right, Tom?' Gerry said smiling. 'You're in early today, didn't expect you till later.'

They watched as the family packed themselves into the car.

'Not much else to do,' Tom said, relaxing. 'Thought I'd come in and breathe down your necks.'

Gerry laughed.

'No problems?' Tom asked.

'Nah. All up and running. I'm just popping out for some fags. Want anything?'

'No. Thanks.'

Gerry wandered off and Tom stood there letting himself calm down fully. He thought about the big drums inside, turning out copy after copy of the same image. Why couldn't everything be like this? Simple and organized. Then he'd be okay. Work he could cope with. Machines, employees, business. He was good at all that.

It was just when . . .

As he watched the ghastly family drive off his headache gave another little kick and he pressed his temple again.

It shouldn't be like this. Why couldn't he have dealt with the situation calmly and simply like Gerry? Instead of getting all steamed up. He hated the modern jargon, but he had to be able to take control of his own emotions. Thirty-five years old and the simplest things could reduce him to a pointless rage.

He shook his head and smiled. The whole thing was daft really.

He looked up at the flat grey sky, then turned and, humming the Mexican song, he went inside to the din, to the huge windowless room where there was no difference between night and day, and instantly his worries were forgotten.

PART ONE

PART ONE

ONE

Will Summers had a hard-on. Standing there, looking over the road at the house, he felt hot and sticky in his clothes, uncomfortable and restricted. He had an impatient rush to get on and do it, but it was exquisite, holding back, anticipating. He closed his eyes for a moment and let the heat wash over him; he felt his heart speed up, the blood thumping faster. His hands, clenched into two tight fists in his pockets, were slimy inside the thin rubber surgical gloves. For an instant he let go and fell into the darkness, then he took a deep breath and tried to clear his mind and concentrate on what lay ahead.

Her television flickered through the net curtains in the front window. It wasn't yet dark enough to pull the proper curtains, nor was it bright enough for the nets to act as efficient screens. He'd seen her come into the room a couple of minutes ago with a tray of food and seat herself on the sofa. Now that he was sure she was settled, it was time.

He crossed the road and entered the alley that ran between the small terraced houses. He walked purposefully, not too quick and not too slow.

As he came out of the alley, he turned to the right and pushed open her back gate. It was five steps to the back door. He'd been in many houses like this; they were all the same, he knew what he was doing. The back door was unlocked. Good. He didn't wait, but pushed it open. It didn't jam or squeal, and it made no sound as he closed it behind him.

He was in a small hallway between the kitchen and a bathroom extension that had been built on at the rear. He listened for any signs of movement. All he could hear was the faint muffled drone of the television. There were three or four coats hanging up; he pushed his face into them. He could smell damp, and old leather, and the woman. He pressed a hand to his crotch and gripped his hard penis.

The door into the kitchen was already open and he went through. He could hear the television properly now, the news.

He looked around the kitchen. Most of the terraces in this part of town had their kitchens further back, where her hall was, but she'd obviously had the place converted, so that the back room was now a kitchen-cum-dining-room. There were two pans in the sink, and the smell of her cooking hung in the air. Heat still rose from the electric cooker. He looked at the pans; one had a few pasta shells stuck to the edge, the other was smeared with a whitish sauce. He ran his finger round the rim and tasted it. It was some kind of fish – with the faint aftertaste of rubber from his glove.

Between the kitchen and the front room would be the stairs. He went to the door and listened. All he could hear was the television. Slowly he pressed down on the handle. There was a slight click as the door jumped open and a quick draught rustled a pile of old newspapers on the floor. He held his breath and waited. The newsreader droned on. He waited, the door on the other side of the stairs stayed shut. He let his breath out.

The stairs were always the trickiest part. There was always at least one step that creaked. He kept to the edges, gently lowering each foot, feeling for the slightest give, listening for any clicks or groans. Halfway up he found the first loose one. As he put the pressure on there was a creak. He pulled away and waited, thirty seconds, a minute, nothing. He tried the next step up; it felt solid enough. He risked it and pulled himself up.

It looked at first like a long climb to the top, but it turned out to be easy going. Then on the second to last step he got careless. He felt sure the woman must have heard the ratchet sound as the board pulled against the nails. He stayed frozen on the stairs for what seemed like an hour but was probably only a couple of minutes.

He thought he was in the clear, and was ready to go on, when he heard the door at the bottom of the stairs open. He didn't move. At the edge of his vision he saw the woman come out of the sitting-room and cross into the kitchen. She didn't look up.

Quickly he climbed the last two steps and scrambled into the room above the sitting-room. He stayed by the door, looking down the stairs. In a few moments the woman returned and closed the door behind her.

Will was soaked. He was panting quickly like an animal, his chest tight. He felt nauseous. But he was safe. She obviously hadn't heard anything. He could carry on. He hadn't dared look around yet, and he hoped that the room he was in wasn't her bedroom; he didn't want to be directly above her when he was doing it. That was the trouble with these small houses. Although you didn't have to move about too much, although everything was self-contained and closer together than in the larger places, you were always near to the owners. That was the trouble, but it was also what made them such a favourite of Will's. Knowing how close he was all the time to them.

There was still enough light from outside for him to see, and to his relief the room was full of books. True, there was a single bed along one wall, but it was covered with a heavily embroidered cloth and there were cushions along the back to make it into a sort of sofa. A spare bed. Not her bed. In the centre of the room was a low table with sewing equipment on it, and everything confirmed in his mind the opinion that she was a teacher or maybe a lecturer at the university.

This room didn't really interest him, though.

He crossed the stairs into the bedroom. He crept in, feeling the boards ahead of him. It was perfect. It was hers. Although the furniture was nondescript, possibly rented with the rest of the house, she had made it her own. And she had somehow made it very feminine. He was never sure how this was done, but you could always tell.

The room was slightly untidy, in the casual way of someone who lives alone. There were papers in the middle of the carpet, with an empty coffee cup and a pen, as if she'd been sitting on the floor, and there were clothes out on a chair. He ran his hand over them, feeling the different textures. On top of a chest of drawers, with a mirror propped up at the back, lay a jumble of make-up and perfume. He opened a couple of bottles and sniffed them. Then he selected a dark red lipstick and dropped it into one of his trouser pockets.

Stuck in the mirror frame were two photographs. One showed her and another young woman in a bar somewhere hot; they had tans and holiday clothes and smiles. The other picture was of three boys in cricket gear, who were also smiling. He took the holiday snap out of the frame.

There was a little table beside the new pine double bed, and on it was an old copy of *Elle*, an Armistead Maupin paperback, a pair of glasses and a half-full glass of water. He finished the water for her, then took out his notebook and placed it on the table with the photograph.

He stared at the bed which looked crisp and fresh. The duvet was covered with tiny blue checks.

He licked his lips and began to undress.

First he slipped off the shoes, no socks, then the tracksuit trousers, no underpants. Then his jacket, then his T-shirt. He left the gloves on. It took him less than thirty seconds.

He stretched out on the bed and felt the duvet cover cool against his hot damp skin. He closed his eyes and was again engulfed by an almost uncontrollable excitement. He gave into it for a few moments, then carefully pulled himself out of it. She was down there, oblivious to his presence. Down there, all alone, watching the television. And he was here on her bed, naked.

He picked up the notebook and the photograph.

He turned to the first blank page and began to write, first the date, and then the address. Then her.

As far as I can tell she is somewhere in her twenties, or possibly her early thirties. She has curly brown hair, which reaches just down to her shoulders. She has yellowish skin which is slightly greasy. She has a pretty face, although her nose is possibly a little sharp. She has small breasts, and has one of those bodies which looks attractive and normal in the top half, but which has wide hips and fat legs. She dresses normally, but mostly seems to go for blacks and greys.

I don't know her name, but I will call her Miss Fish, because she was eating fish while I was doing it to her.

She is watching television now, while I am up here, fucking her house.

Will looked up at the ceiling. The rest of the room had been recently decorated, but the ceiling looked old and dirty. She'd probably done it herself, and thought the ceiling too difficult to attempt.

Now, at last, he let go. He arched his back and screwed up his face. He touched himself and it was like an electric shock. He grunted through clenched teeth. In a second it was over.

Slowly his senses returned. He dried himself on his shirt and stretched out like a cat.

He'd been long enough. He ought to get going. He put the photograph between the pages of the notebook and closed it. But he still needed something else, the picture and the lipstick weren't enough. He hurriedly looked around. There was a blocked-up fireplace in one wall that still had a mantelpiece, and ranged along it was a collection of pigs. China, silver, wood, even glass. One in the middle had an ear missing; it looked older and more worn than the others. Maybe it was her first pig. It would do.

He dressed, again in less than half a minute. He'd practised enough, after all. He pocketed the pig and on his way out, as an afterthought, he also took her glasses. That was more for fun than anything else, knowing how infuriated she would be trying to find them, trying to think where she'd put them.

He remembered which steps to avoid on the way down. And when he got to the bottom he pressed his whole body against the front-room door. His aching penis was flattened against it. She was in there, on the other side of the wood. All she had to do was open it now. But he trusted her; she wouldn't open it, they never did. He kissed the shiny paint, tasting dust.

He pressed himself a little harder against the door and the pressure was enough to make him come again. It was brief and overwhelming, and for a moment he was helpless, suspended. Then it passed.

Will Summers turned from the door and left the house as neatly and as quietly as he'd entered it. Back down the alley, across the road. When he looked back briefly, the television still flickered. She was still oblivious.

He took off his gloves and put her glasses on. He couldn't see particularly well, but it caused him to stiffen again, and he knew that they would keep him that way until he got home and could relive the whole thing.

TWO

Tom was getting pissed off, which was stupid, seeing as how these meetings were supposed to help him deal with that sort of thing. But knowing how stupid his situation was only made him angrier, so that he was trapped in a tightening spiral. The 'rage spiral', Clive had nicknamed it, months ago, at that first meeting. The rage spiral, bottling anger and turning it on itself, pumping it up, until . . . Tom shook his head and smiled. It was a farce. Once again he asked himself why he was here. And once again he looked at Maddie.

He looked at the creamy strap of her bra, just visible beneath her thin shirt. That helped, took his mind off his irritation. If only Clive would shut up.

Clive Ryman, sitting there so bloody smug, spouting on about anger as if he understood the first thing about it. It was at around this point that Tom usually got up and made his excuses, left them to disappear up each other's arses. But tonight he couldn't do that; tonight it was his turn to be host. He looked round his sitting-room, looked round at these people sitting in his chairs, chairs that were normally empty. The anger started in again as he thought about having to clear up afterwards, put everything back in its exact place, hoover, wipe, make it as if they'd never been here.

Look at them. Besides Clive and Maddie, there was Jane, who was what Clive described as an emotional victim, but who Tom thought of merely as a victim. Next to her on the sofa, equally uncomfortable, was the hooligan, Ian, a young man with a history of unprovoked violence, who was about the most painfully shy and socially inadequate person Tom had ever had the misfortune to spend an evening with. Then there was old Mr Bentley, who didn't really seem to have any particular problem but who just seemed to come along because he got some kind of voyeuristic, sado-masochistic pleasure out of the whole thing. Maybe that was his problem. Lastly there were the Maxwells, husband and wife, newcomers to the group. Tom didn't really know them yet, but they probably had some depressing relationship based on violence. Tom thought ahead to all the dreary meetings and all the shared sordid secrets. Ah, what fun, getting to know the Maxwells. Sod it, he didn't ever want to know them, any of them, except Maddie. He'd had enough, stuff Dr Anthony, these meetings didn't help, they just made things worse. He wasn't like the others.

Except, perhaps, Maddie.

It was like being back at school, or something, he felt terribly self-conscious and out of place. What if one of his work force were to see him here, with these hopeless cases?

'So, Maddie, can you not see that?' Clive pressed his hands together as if praying.

Oh, do shut up, Clive.

'Can you not see that it's your own anger which is destroying your relationship with Pete?'

'Peter.'

'Peter. Sorry. It's your anger that makes it impossible for the two of you to talk, to sort out what's wrong.'

Maddie flung herself back in her chair and glared at the ceiling. 'I know what's wrong, Clive. What's wrong is that Peter won't stop fucking his students.'

A couple of the others tittered and Clive gave a little smile.

'Yes, point taken. But why do you think he does that, Maddie?'

'Are you implying it's my fault?'

'No, no, no. Not at all. Perhaps that came out wrong. But, what I mean is, do you give him any openings? It seems you're blocking him with your anger, you're excluding him. Your anger has blocked every passage.'

'It's Peter who's blocked every passage, actually, Clive, if you get my meaning.'

'Yes. Very good. Point taken. But let's take this seriously for a moment.'

But Clive had lost it. Old Mr Bentley was shaking with laughter. Jane looked shocked, Ian was smirking at the carpet, and the Maxwells were looking at each other as if wondering what they'd let themselves in for.

Tom settled back in his chair, the pressure gone. He smiled. He liked Maddie. She said what she meant, what she felt, she admitted her problems. She could make a joke about things. She was almost happy about it. But more than anything, she understood, she knew what Clive could never know, she knew what it was like to be guided by something over which you had no rational control.

He looked again at the bra strap, followed it down to the smooth curve of her breast. She shifted position and looked over at him. He jerked his eyes up just in time and smiled at her. She smiled back. They knew.

Tom realized that Clive was also looking at him, with that patient look of his. 'Tom?'

'Mm?' Had he seen him looking at Maddie?

'You've been very quiet tonight.'

As usual. Tom thought.

'Any comments?'

'Nope.'

Clive smiled. 'Okay.' Then he turned back to Maddie and his smile changed, became less professional, more personal. Why was he paying so much attention to her? And then it struck Tom. Clive fancies Maddie. The little creep.

Before Clive could say anything else to Maddie, Tom butted in. 'I don't really need to say anything, do I, Clive?' he said, a little too loudly.

'How's that, Tom?'

'Well, you've got all the answers, haven't you?'

'Not at all. I'm just here to make suggestions. I wouldn't ever presume—'

Tom cut him off by talking directly to Maddie. 'You don't have to talk to him, if you don't want.'

Maddie shrugged.

'Do you have a problem with that, Tom?' Clive asked. 'Do you not like to talk about relationships?'

'I don't know if you've noticed, Clive, but I don't have a relationship to talk about.'

'Yes.'

Yes. What did that mean? What did 'yes' mean? Yes? Yes, he'd noticed. Or yes, he was a hopeless sod who didn't have much luck with women?

'I don't think you should presume to speak to me like that, Clive.'

'I simply said "yes".'

There. He'd said it again.

Christ. Calm down, Tom. All he said was 'yes'.

'We can talk about something else, if you like,' Clive said affably. 'We can talk about what was on TV last night. But, perhaps relationships are—'

'None of your business.'

'Okay. But the whole point of these meetings is that you can discuss these things, talk about them with other people who may have shared your experiences.'

'Not everybody, Clive. Not you.'

'Yes, well, point taken. I'm just a chairman. But I do understand, I am trained, qualified.' He opened his hands. 'I'm just here to help.'

You're just here to have a go, you devious little shit. You're just here to make me feel crap. You're just here to try and get off with Maddie, aren't you?

'I vote we talk about *Coronation Street*,' Tom said, and he looked at Maddie to see what effect his joke had had on her. She didn't exactly laugh but there was definitely the hint of a smile.

'Tom, if you don't like these meetings, why do you come?' Clive asked, sounding slightly exasperated. 'No one forces you.'

'That's very true, Clive, and in fact that's exactly what I've just been thinking.'

'Share your thoughts with us, then.'

'My thoughts are that this is basically a complete bloody waste of time, sitting down every Tuesday bloody night and going round and round in bloody circles. I don't see that it helps. I mean, look at us. I get angrier, Maddie gets angrier, Jane there gets more and more miserable, Ian finds it harder to speak; as far as I can see the only person who gets anything out of it is you ... And perhaps Mr Bentley.'

'I beg to differ, Tom.'

'No, Clive, I've had it up to here. That's it, finito.'

'So you're going to quit? Just like that?'

'Yes, and it's made me happier than anything I can remember doing since I first started coming to these bloody meetings.'

'Okay, that's good. Let's talk about that.'

'Oh, for God's sake!'

'Actually, I like these meetings.' It was Jane, her voice high and wavering. 'I find they do help.'

'Good for you. I'm very pleased for you.'

'Come on now, Tom. Let's not get carried away here.'

'Carried away? Carried away? You forget, Clive, that you're talking to a man trapped in the famous rage spiral. A man "at war with his own emotions". What do you expect me to do? Eh?'

'Yes. Point taken.'

'No. Point not fucking taken!'

Tom felt like he was engaged in a battle with a giant

23

marshmallow. There was nothing to hit against. For a moment he felt genuinely furious. He ran his fingers through his hair and realized that the others were staring at him with dumb expressions, expecting him to say something. Short of telling Clive to go fuck himself he could think of nothing. The silence seemed to fill the room. He took a deep breath and put a hand to his temple.

'Are you okay?' It was Maddie's voice. The tension was broken.

'Yes. Listen, I'm sorry. Perhaps you'd all better go.'

'But we've another hour to go yet . . .'

'Clive,' Maddie said kindly. 'I think Tom's right. I think we've all had enough for one night.'

'I don't know. I really think we were starting to get somewhere here,' Clive said, pathetically eager, almost desperate. But people were getting up, looking for their things. Ian scurried out and they heard the front door slam.

'Okay,' said Clive, throwing up his hands. 'We'll call it a day.' He got up and came over to where Tom was standing near the door.

'I'm serious, Tom. I really thought that was a good session tonight.'

'Goodnight, Clive.'

'Listen, don't take everything so personally . . .'

'Clive. I know what you want me to say. That I hated my father and wanted to sleep with my mother.'

Clive laughed. 'Not at all, I—'

'Well, as a matter of fact, I did hate my father. Happy? But I'm afraid my mother died before I knew her. So bad luck.'

'Okay, Tom.' Clive was still laughing. 'We'll get to the bottom of this one day. Don't you worry.' He playfully wagged his finger at Tom and, still chuckling, he shuffled out.

Tom went to the front door to hurry the leaving process and soon only Maddie was left. As she put on her coat and stepped out into the hallway, he stopped her.

'Maddie?'

'Yes?'

'Look, it's still quite early.' He looked away and cleared his throat. 'Do you fancy a drink or something?'

Luckily she smiled. 'Lovely.'

'Great.'

They sat in the corner of the pub and for a while they didn't really speak. It was Maddie who finally got things started.

'Are you really going to quit?' she asked.

'I don't know. I just don't think it really helps, you know? I mean, do you?'

Maddie shrugged.

Tom scowled into his beer. 'It just makes me more angry.'

'Maybe that's the point, Tom, to find a way to express that anger, let it out, get rid of it.'

'I don't know. I don't know if I want to.'

'I know what you mean.'

'Yes, I think you do. Out of all of them you're the only one, Maddie. And as for Clive—'

'He's not so bad,' Maddie stopped him, and he looked at her, trying to work out what she really felt.

'It's just that he doesn't understand,' he said. 'He doesn't understand what might happen. He sees us as normal, respectable people with a bit of a problem. But—'

'Isn't that what we are?'

'It's more than that, Maddie—'

'Come off it. If we were really fucked up we'd be in hospital, not some half-arsed nouveau-hippy self-help therapy group.'

Tom laughed.

'Other people play bridge,' Maddie said. 'We have Clive.'

Tom stopped laughing. Maddie shook her head. 'Why do you let him upset you so much?' she said. 'I mean, maybe he does understand.'

'How do you mean?'

'Well, you don't like to talk about relationships, do you?'

'Relationships. That's such a horrible word.'

'You're changing the subject.'

'What is the subject?'

'You.'

'What about me?'

'Well, let's see. Tom Kendall: comfortably off, not bad-looking, respectable position, charming, polite, quiet, not exactly a pensioner, but not exactly a teenager either. You're a tough son of a bitch, really, aren't you? The strong silent type. But why no wife? I mean, you're not gay, I can tell that much. But no wife. You don't even have a girlfriend, do you?'

'You can tell?'

'I've seen your house.' She raised her eyebrows. 'And you don't seem the bachelor playboy type, screwing around a string of young dolly-birds. What is it with you?'

'You're worse than Clive.'

Maddie smiled. 'I'm better-looking than Clive, so you'll talk to me.'

'You're pushing your luck, Maddie.'

Maddie laughed. 'Maybe you're right, it really isn't any of my business. It just seemed to me that what Clive said, it hit home, didn't it?'

Tom stared at Maddie, trying not to blush. 'He fancies you, Maddie.'

'Is that such a terrible thing? I mean, you fancy me, Tom.'

This time Tom did blush.

Maddie touched his hand. 'Listen, we both know what this conversation is really about, so let's not pretend. I fancy you too, and you know it. I don't know you that well, but I know you're alone, and, well, sex is sex. I certainly know how I feel. I've got an unhappy marriage which you know about in all its gory detail;

26

we're two fucked-up people with a lot in common. So what are we going to do about it?'

'That's quite a question.'

'Yes.'

Tom felt light-headed. Somehow he'd ended up somewhere completely unexpected, and it was both exhilarating and frightening.

He cleared his throat. 'Well,' he said, seriously. 'I'm not going to sleep with you tonight, much as ... er ... much as I'd like to. I'm going to think about things, and I'd like you to do the same. Perhaps ... Probably ... Eventually we will sleep together, but it's important that we're prepared, that we both know what we're doing at the time.'

'Tom?'

'Yes?'

'Peter's not expecting me back before half-eleven ... twelve.'

'So?'

'So come on, then.'

'What?'

Maddie finished her drink and stood up. 'We've just got enough time for it to be fun.'

THREE

James Mullen, or Jimmy, as he liked his mates at the karate class to call him, was knackered. He was sweating and his body ached all over, but that was good, that was exactly how he wanted it. It meant he'd worked hard. He slumped on the bench in the changing-room, put his hands behind his head, stretched and sighed with satisfaction. He grinned to himself. He'd done it, he'd finally beaten Bob Arnell. Admittedly it was only because of a technicality, but a win was a win (despite what Mr Paxton, the instructor, said about these little contests being purely for learning purposes). Everyone wanted to win, and for the first time since he'd started coming, nearly ten months ago, James had beaten Big Bob Arnell.

He felt like he was almost bursting with life and energy; he'd certainly earned a drink. Yes, tonight he would get drunk.

Graham Prentiss threw a towel down next to him on the bench and opened a nearby locker.

'You coming to the Black Boys?' he asked, taking out a sports bag.

'Does the Pope shit in the woods?' said James, rubbing his hands together. 'Drinks are on me.'

'I'll hold you to that, sir.'

James started to change. He'd washed his hands and face. He didn't like to use the showers, they were too public, and he considered that those men who did use them were somewhat too casual about their nakedness, somewhat too enthusiastic about the whole thing.

He shrugged off his karate outfit and slipped on his trousers in one swift movement. Then he put on a sleeveless muscle vest, did up his flies and fastened his belt.

Before putting anything else on he casually strolled round to the sinks where the full-length mirror was.

A row of lockers shielded him from the rest of the changing-room, and he was alone. He stood so that he was side-on to the mirror and looked at himself.

Yes. Fifty press-ups a day, fifty sit-ups, karate on Thursdays, matches on Sundays, swimming or the gym most mornings. And it was all working, his body was slim and tight, muscular without being bulky. The vest made his chest and arms look strong and powerful. He only had to hold his stomach in slightly for the lines to be just right. No matter what he did, he just couldn't manage to get his gut really flat. Too much beer and good food.

What the hell? He was better than most men his age, better than most younger men if it came down to it. And he was certainly better than he'd ever looked before – a skinny, round-shouldered, weak-armed weed. What they'd called at school a spastic. He winced when he thought about it. But a man could change, it was Graham who'd taught him that. Graham, who'd been just another office slug until he'd got involved, first with the Territorial Army and then with these karate classes. James had watched the slow transformation, seen him grow in confidence, seen him acquire a definite physical presence, and then finally manage to shag Janet, the new secretary they'd all been talking about at Lion Insurance. That did it for James. Graham had been nagging him for weeks to come to karate classes and so finally he accepted. It wasn't as awful as he'd imagined. Mr Paxton was a quiet, intense man who took people along at their own pace and didn't encourage any macho heroics. But James had been very self-conscious about his physique, so he'd started exercising religiously. Football was the next step, first with the office team, a knockabout affair in which he could hold his own, then, as he'd become fitter, with a more competitive Sunday league team which ran its own training programme. And now he'd finally done it, he'd beaten Bob Arnell.

He straightened his back and winked sexily at his reflection. Three or four pints at the Black Boys, flirt with Wendy, the barmaid, then home to Lucy. Show off his new body to her, give a practical demonstration of just how fit he was now.

He splashed water on his hair and combed it into shape, then went back to where Graham was just finishing dressing.

'All set?' Graham said without looking up from his bag.

'Uh-huh. With you in a minute.' James sat down and pulled on his socks.

'You're getting pretty good,' Graham said, sitting down next to him to do up his shoes.

James smiled.

'You keep this up you'll be almost as good as me one day.'

James dumped his towel in Graham's lap. 'I passed you weeks ago, pal.'

'Hah.'

James jumped up and adopted an exaggerated defensive position. 'Come on, then.' He cuffed Graham over the head, messing his hair.

Graham got to his feet and took up an equally theatrical stance. 'Go ahead, punk, make my day.'

James jabbed at him and they danced around the room circling their hands and whooping, each trying to outdo the other with his Bruce Lee impersonation. Eventually Graham hit a locker with a wild high kick, swore and collapsed on to the bench, laughing and clutching his foot.

'Come on, old man,' said James, putting on his shirt. 'Let's go and get smashed.'

*

Two and a half hours later Graham dropped James off at his house on the Dereham Road, fired a parting insult and drove away.

James shadow-boxed his way up the front path, fished out his keys and opened the door.

There were no lights on inside, so he drunkenly tiptoed into the kitchen and made himself a cup of tea and some cheese on toast. Lucy, as usual, had left the place in a complete mess, but he didn't feel inclined to tidy up tonight. Tonight he was a hero. He just cleared a space on the table and skimmed through the *Eastern Evening News* while he ate his toast.

When he'd finished, he went into the bathroom to clean his teeth. He frowned when he saw that Lucy had left the top off the toothpaste again, as well as littering the place with all manner of grimy bottles and tubes. But he wouldn't let it get to him. He checked himself once more in the mirror.

Looking good. He turned out the light and crept upstairs; the last thing he wanted to do now was wake the girls. All was quiet. A dim glow came from under his bedroom door. Good, Lucy might still be awake.

She was propped up in bed reading with her glasses on. She hated the glasses but he loved them; they made her look all serious and yet still vulnerable and innocent.

She looked up and smiled dimly as he came in.

'Hello, love,' she said. 'How did it go?'

'Brilliant.' He performed a high kick and launched himself on to the bed. She shushed him but he wasn't having any of it.

'I beat Bob Arnell,' he said, punching the air.

'Well done,' said Lucy. But he could tell she didn't really know who he was talking about. No matter how often he told her, no matter how often he tried to explain, she never seemed to listen.

'You know,' he said. 'The policeman. Sergeant Bob Arnell, the most experienced guy in the class.'

'Mm.'

31

Well, that was that, then.

He got up off the bed, took off his shirt and paraded around in his vest, pretending he had things to do, but when he looked round she'd gone back to her book. So he undressed quickly and slid into bed, snuggling up against her and putting a hand over her right breast, squeezing it through the pale blue cotton nightdress. She put down the book, took off her glasses and smiled dimly at him again.

'Polly came home from school in tears again today.'

'She'll get used to it.' James withdrew his hand and sat up.

'Did you shower?'

'Didn't have time.'

Lucy glanced at the clock on her bedside table, then back at him.

'I can't shower here, can I?' said James, rubbing the back of his neck. 'It'd wake the girls.'

'Mm.'

James scratched his stomach and stared at the blank screen of the portable television at the foot of the bed. Lucy put her glasses back on and picked up the book.

'What are you reading?'

'Just a book.'

Just a book, James repeated to himself.

He could see that it was the same book she'd been reading for months. She never seemed to get to the end of it. Admittedly it was a thick book, South American, he assumed from the author's name, but all the same ... How come she never finished it when she was reading all the bloody time?

He heard her turn a page. 'Ah well,' he said, 'I guess it's late.' He leant over and kissed her, then put out his bedside light.

'I think I might read for a bit, okay?' Lucy said. James grunted and pretended to settle down to sleep, his back to his wife.

He stared at the framed poster on the wall, a reproduction of an original poster for *Casablanca*. How long had they had it? He didn't even like the film, couldn't understand what all the fuss was about.

You must remember this, a kiss is just a kiss. Or something.

He followed the lines of their new Laura Ashley wallpaper, pale pink and green. Even after they'd had the room done, they still put the bloody poster back up. Why couldn't they try something new? He thought suddenly of the Pirelli poster in Graham's office. The girl for May with the amazing knockers. Like melons. At least that was how Graham had described them. They didn't look much like melons to James, more like a pair of large breasts. 'Big knockers are coming back into fashion,' Graham had said.

James remembered the feel of Lucy's breast under her nightdress, so familiar and yet still exciting. He ground his teeth. Why did he bother? It was like this every Thursday night after karate. Why did he ever delude himself that it might be different? The more he got in shape, the better he looked, the less interested she seemed in him. What did she want? One of these nights he was going to drink one too many and throw himself on her, bugger the consequences. Perhaps that's what she wanted.

Do it.

They hadn't had a really wild night of passion since before last Christmas, and now it was May already, month of the melons. Why had she changed? He was still the same person, just fitter, healthier. Christ, that was the thing these days, wasn't it? Health. Health and big knockers. Did she really fancy him more as a skinny pot-bellied nine-stone weakling? The type of bloke who'd always hung around his own goalmouth in school football games, avoiding the ball with all the other freaks and spastics and creeps. Not any more. He'd never be the world's greatest footballer, but he could get stuck in with the rest of them, usually came home with a few bruises as trophies.

He looked better all round. He could wear better clothes, more daring stuff, didn't have to be ashamed of his body any more. I mean, they still made love a couple of times a week, maybe three times a fortnight.

Bollocks.

Who was he trying to kid? Three times a fortnight? Maybe six months ago that would have been true. Once a fortnight was more like it these days. And never, never on Thursdays. Admittedly he was usually too tired or drunk after karate, but tonight, tonight he wanted to fuck. He rolled over and put an arm across Lucy's belly, and she stroked his head absent-mindedly. He slipped his hand down on to her thigh, pulled up the nightie and felt the soft smooth skin, She carried on reading and stroking his head.

He ran through the fight with Bob again, remembering how he'd done all the right moves, not a thing wrong, dancing round him, a flurry of hands and feet. Of course there was no real contact in these contests, the odd slap, or push, perhaps, but that wasn't the point. All the right moves. And Bob had got frustrated, couldn't find an opening, eventually fucked up, cheated. And that lost him the fight.

Lucy put down the book, put down her glasses, shook her hair, plumped the pillows, switched off the light and lay down facing James.

'You still awake?' she asked quietly.

'Mm.'

She found his lips with hers and kissed him, then rolled on to her other side.

James thought about Wendy, the barmaid from the Black Boys. He'd chatted with her for quite a while this evening. She seemed to be interested in self-defence, said she'd been thinking of going herself, thought that it was a good thing for women to do, specially these days. James had agreed, encouraged her, but she had to work evenings. Graham had made some comment to James afterwards, suggested he might be getting somewhere with her. James hadn't ever really thought about it before; he'd always told himself he was happily married, wasn't really interested in anyone other than Lucy. But it seemed like there was some sort of competition between the lads from the class to see who could get inside Wendy's jeans first.

He'd never considered himself as a sex object, something that women might lust after, although he'd always had an active and satisfactory sex life. But now.

He pictured himself in his vest and favourite Next trousers.

Wendy.

He wondered what it would be like, sleeping with someone else, now, after all this time. He'd been faithful to Lucy for ... He tried to think, had to construct his usual tables, comparative facts, relative years. Polly was five, Claire was three; they'd moved to Norwich from London just after Polly was born; they'd been married for two years before then and he'd lived with Lucy for another two years before that. Nine years. Jesus. And in all that time he'd slept with only one other girl. When Lucy had gone to her father's funeral in Somerset, and he'd been too busy to make it. That was, what, six months after they'd got married? So it was about six and a half years, call it seven. Seven years of sleeping with the same woman. Well, you couldn't expect it to be plain sailing all the time, couldn't hope to never have any problems. They'd get over it. If it really was a problem. Was it really worth it, then, fucking someone else? He'd got so used to Lucy, used to her breasts, her pubic hair, what she liked, what she didn't like.

What would it be like with Wendy, a stranger? He tried to imagine her undressed, tried to picture her breasts – the others were quite enthusiastic about them – but he couldn't, he could see only Lucy's. He gave her May's breasts, but they didn't fit.

Shit, it wasn't helping, his erection wouldn't go away.

He lay there listening to Lucy's breathing, while a swirl of confused erotic images tangled in his brain, until at last it sounded like she was asleep. Carefully he got out of bed and made his way as quietly as possible to the bathroom.

Sitting on the toilet he doggedly masturbated, picturing a woman who was a sort of amalgamation of Lucy, Wendy and May.

In their bedroom, Lucy lay in the dark and waited for him to come back.

FOUR

Will Summers locked his bedroom door, removed the key, and put it on his chest of drawers. Then he went to the window and looked out at the bright spring afternoon. Clean white clouds moved across a pale blue sky.

He shivered as a gust of wind rattled the double glazing in its frame. His father had fitted it himself; he had been a keen builder rather than a careful one.

The room was in the roof, all his father's work. He'd intended to use it as an office, but he'd died before it was properly finished, and Will had claimed it for his own. His mother, the old bag, was permanently trying to make him move back down into one of the two spare bedrooms below, but he liked it up here. It was quiet, and from the window he could look out across the old tiles of the roof at the trees and houses opposite. But most of all he liked it up here in this tiny box of a room because it was right next to his museum.

He closed the curtains. It was impossible for anyone to see in without a telescope, but that wasn't really the point.

He turned on his record player and checked that everything was set correctly. First the volume, as loud as it would go without distortion, then the repeat arm, making sure that when the record finished it would start again from the beginning. The record was, as always, Vaughan Williams, Variations on a Theme by Thomas Tallis.

Although it wasn't particularly cold he lit his Calor gas heater, and waited for it to heat up before he began to undress. By the time he was naked the room was filled with a warm glow and he was ready to enter the museum.

He went to the wardrobe and pulled it aside. He'd fitted the castors on it himself, using his father's old tools, and it rolled smoothly across the polished wood floor. Behind was a small panel, papered to match the rest of the wall, just large enough for him to squeeze through. There were hidden catches at each corner which popped open as he pressed them in. He removed the panel and reached inside the opening to turn on the light.

He waited a moment, holding off, savouring the anticipation, then wriggled through, replacing the panel behind him.

He was now in a part of the loft which had been blocked off when his father had made the conversion. It wasn't really large enough to be of much use except for storage, and they had plenty of that elsewhere. It was about eight foot deep, five foot wide and five foot high, though the sides sloped inwards and met at the top so you couldn't really stand up. Will had placed chipboard over the floorboards and then carpeted it, but the rest was bare. There was no natural light.

The triangle of wall at the opposite end, exposed brick, was almost completely covered with photographs, photographs he'd taken from all the houses he'd ever been into. There were forty-seven in all, now that he'd added the one from Miss Fish's bedroom. People mostly; old men, young men, women, boys and girls. He looked over the array of faces: smiling, pensive, excited, embarrassed, drunk, oblivious. Some were blurred, some posed, some black-and-white, there were even a couple of sepia ones. He'd given them names so that, in his own way, he knew them all. He smiled at them, greeted them again.

But not only people. There was one section of 'landscapes', odd anonymous pieces of countryside that must have held some special meaning for whoever had taken the pictures. And next to the landscapes was the 'zoo': dogs, cats, a horse and a couple of rabbits.

He remembered exactly where he'd found each snap, what the room looked like, what he'd felt when he'd taken it and put it in his pocket.

Along the bottom of the wall was a low shelf on which he'd arranged his best trophies, small, mostly valueless trinkets, pieces of broken jewellery, little figurines, watches, glasses, combs and brushes, odd items of clothing, gloves and ties, pens arranged like a display of swords in a stately home, a couple of mugs, some unfinished knitting, cassette tapes and there, at one end, next to a Spanish bull and a toby jug was Miss Fish's pig with the missing ear.

He knelt in front of the display, checking and rechecking each piece, making tiny adjustments so that everything was in the best position possible. In the past he'd sometimes lit a couple of little candles on the shelf, but he'd found that after a while they made the room too stuffy. Besides, he was worried he might set fire to everything.

He could match each object to a person in a photograph. The carved wooden elephant with only one tusk he'd taken from the sitting-room of Mr and Mrs Dalmatian; there they were in the wedding photo that had become spotted with age. And here was the Nazi girl, Eva Braun, in fancy dress at a party, laughing in SS outfit and stockings. Hers was the little black diary filled with gloriously mundane facts and observations. Next to the diary was a pair of silk socks which belonged to Othello, the serious-looking black man in spectacles and university ceremonial robes, holding some kind of diploma. Just below Othello was The Bunny Girl – lizard brooch; then Old Man Rubber – a copy of *Skin Two* magazine; Mrs Maxwell House – a coffee jar full of polished pebbles . . .

Forty-seven of them. Representing, in all, thirty-nine people he now owned.

He sat and looked at them for about twenty minutes, until he heard the record finish and start up again.

Now came the best bit.

He took a new pair of surgical gloves from a box beneath the shelf, then pulled the dust cover from over his books. There were six of them, huge leather-bound tomes he'd picked up from an antiques auction for less than a pound each. He'd been ecstatic when he'd got them home and had a proper look at them, the paper was expensive, rich and creamy, not like the dry brittle stuff they made nowadays. Beautifully preserved, with marbled endpapers. The rest all blank, white and empty, ready to be filled with anything, to become anything, a whole world, a universe waiting to be born.

Soon after buying them, he'd started to fill them. That was over two years ago, and he was now on to his fourth volume. He didn't like to think what would happen when he eventually finished them, used them all up.

He opened volume three at random.

The two pages were filled with small, neat writing and various diagrams, all done with a thin Rotring pen.

He began to read.

July the seventh. Mr Lard.

Yes, he remembered him well. He didn't need to look at the rough sketch he'd drawn.

At four in the afternoon I went in. I knew he'd be there, because he never goes out, he just sits in his front room looking out. He dresses quite neatly, but the clothes never fit him properly. It must be hard to find clothes when you're so fat. I think he might be about sixty, but it's hard to tell because he doesn't look after himself very well.

It was easy to get in, the back door was unlocked. The kitchen was very small, with no fridge, and a small electric ring to cook on. He's got only one pan, and lots of cans in boxes. But he keeps it all quite clean. A small dark back room, with no carpet and no lampshade on the light bulb. It looked like he didn't really use the room. In fact, I think all his interesting stuff is probably in the front room with him.

Upstairs

One room full of junk, also unused. The bedroom has a lino floor and very old wallpaper. At first I thought there'd be nothing worth taking, but under the bed, which smelled horrible, I found an old photograph album, which didn't look like it had been opened for a long time, it looked like it might have probably got damp, and some of the pages were stuck together. There were lots of pictures of a woman, all taken a long time ago. Definitely Mrs Lard, although the name doesn't suit her, in a sort of old-fashioned way she looks quite pretty. I selected one in which she looks quite young and sort of beautiful. I had to rip the whole page out as it was too well stuck.

There's an old corner cabinet in one corner. The shelves are very dusty, and the things on them seemed at first to be no use to me. There was a bottle of pills, old elastic bands, just rubbish. But then I found a box, and inside it were some false teeth.

This is my favourite item so far.

On the right-hand page there was a general house plan, and a more detailed diagram of the bedroom, showing the exact locations of the photo album and the teeth. After that there was about half a page of impressions he'd got from the room, which ended with him sitting at the window and looking out at the world, just as Mr Lard was doing below, seeing the same view but from a higher viewpoint.

He was pleased with these two pages. The earlier stuff, in volume one, was pretty crude; the maps and drawings were amateurish, the writing over-excited and childish. His style was improving, though there was still a long way to go.

His whole technique was better. He'd take his notebook with him to the home and record as much stuff there as possible, his feelings as well as the more physical, factual stuff. And then, when he got back to the museum, he'd write it all up properly in one of the big books.

He closed volume three and opened volume four at the last entry; three pages on Miss Fish. He read it through again, imagining himself back there, feeling himself becoming aroused. The more recent the entries, the more fresh and vivid his memories.

He put on Miss Fish's glasses and peered at the now distorted, fuzzy pages, felt himself slipping into the mist, and groping his way through the haze towards her bedroom. He lay back on the carpet and was once again stretched naked on her bed.

But he mustn't peak too soon, he had to spin it out, take it all in. He must do it properly. He sat up.

The next thing was the map. Carefully he unrolled it. It was nearly four foot square and showed the whole city. Originally black-and-white, it was now spotted with red dots, and next to the red dots, names written in green: Lard, Fish, Dalmatian, Othello, Badger, Braun, Computer, De Mille, Bunny, Rubber, Maxwell House ... Forty-seven of them, spread out over the whole city. His own map, his own kingdom, all the houses he'd had. And now it was his, he'd fucked the very city itself. If he only had time, if he could only live long enough, he'd go into every house, every home, and make it his. But then he'd need a bigger museum.

If only the old bag wasn't around he could leave this little cubby-hole and fill the whole house. Mother, the one obstacle to his complete happiness. Without her he could have the whole place to himself; turn it into one huge museum. He'd draw a new map, with the house at the centre and all the red dots revolving around it. Fill the whole thing in until it was all red.

One day. He just had to wait, be patient, she wouldn't live for ever. And then . . .

He thought about how the house would look; photographs and maps on every wall, shelves and cabinets filled with mementoes. The house would become a model of his activities, a model of the whole city. How much more interesting it would be than the displays in the castle museum; the dusty stuffed animals, the paintings by people no one had ever heard of. His would be a living museum. His museum would be held together by sex.

But for now he would have to make do with this secret room.

And Mother?

That was it. She was his mother, and he had to look after her. That was what one did.

He pictured her creeping about downstairs, drifting from room to room, pointless. And him up here at the top of the house, the house like a body, him in the head, the brain, and Mother down there somewhere in the bowels, a piece of half-digested food, a piece of shit.

As he thought about the body, it became his body, he became the house, feet in the cellar, head in the roof, all the rooms in between containing different organs – heart, lungs, kidneys, liver. The front door was his arsehole, and the sitting-room, well, that was his cock.

One house in the centre of the city, ready to fuck the whole thing. He looked at the map, remembering each conquest, unaware that he was stimulating himself, descending into a trancelike, sexual frenzy until he spurted all over it, and the house crashed down, and the mist enfolded him and he disappeared.

FIVE

Tom Kendall lay in bed and listened to the sounds coming from the Heath and the busy road outside. His heart was racing slightly and he was sweating, but he knew that this wasn't entirely caused by recent exertion. Fear had something to do with it as well.

Every time Maddie left him he was terrified. Terrified that she wouldn't come back, that he'd never see her again. Terrified, also, that she would. She'd come back to him and he'd have to be with her, talk to her, understand her, even be responsible for her. The two fears fought against each other, but in the end his desire for her always won, and when she did return he felt a great rush of joy that overwhelmed everything else.

It was happening to him now, not the joy but the fear, and she'd only gone out to the bathroom. He couldn't help it, though, it was all new to him, all alien. Sometimes it would even happen when they were together and he just closed his eyes. Suddenly he'd be alone. First would come the relief, and then the fear, and then he'd force his eyes open and she'd be there and he'd bury himself in her.

But why was she being so long? How long did it take, going to the bathroom? He didn't know. He didn't know women, he didn't know other people. He clenched his fists. Thirty-five years old and he was single. And single was alone. Every relationship he'd ever had he'd broken off as soon as there was any hint that it might continue, that it might become serious.

It'd been six weeks since that first night after the meeting, the longest relationship he'd ever had. With each day the fears got stronger and the desire grew, and he felt his own personality slowly sinking under the weight of it all, disappearing. And yet whenever she was with him everything became all right again; he could stop thinking, stop worrying and simply be.

Just as long as she didn't stay away too long.

A car passing by outside sent a brilliant, gleaming reflection across the ceiling and another shiver of fear hit him, making the hairs on his arms stand up.

He rolled over and took her letter from the bedside cabinet. She'd written it a couple of weeks ago and whenever he felt lost he'd read it. He knew it pretty well by heart now, but remembering it wasn't the same as holding it; seeing her handwriting; being able to touch this thing that she had touched.

Dear Tom,

Thank you for the other day. Yeah, yeah, I know I shouldn't be thanking you – you should be thanking me – but thanks. What I mean is, I had a lovely time. Ugh, that sounds so twee, doesn't it? Like a little girl's thank you letter to her Uncle, or something. Kinky, eh? Let's play sex games, you be wicked Uncle Tom – Only kidding! Look at this letter, anyone would think I couldn't actually get to the point and say what I wanted to say. (And me a journalist! I'm supposed to be good with words.) So, what do I want to say? Not 'I love you', don't worry, nothing as Mills and Boonsy as that. But seeing you has made me very happy. There, I've said it. Just to get away from Peter and be with someone as relaxed as you. By relaxed, I mean someone who isn't part of my world. God, it gets so claustrophobic sometimes, and being with you is like an escape from all that. We don't have to worry about

*the stupid everyday things. And you're so grown up and
serious – you're different, Tom, and it's very refreshing. You're
a sort of old-fashioned, upright, decent, sort of a chap, but
you're so sweet about it at the same time, you make me laugh.
Does that make sense? God, I've just read what I've written,
I hope this doesn't sound horribly selfish, like I'm using you,
or something, but – okay, guilty, I am using you! But what
I mean is, you're welcome to use me as much as you like. So,
back to those sex games . . .*

The toilet flushed. Tom quickly hid the letter then settled back on to the pillows.

Maddie came in and walked to the window, naked and unself-conscious. He'd never be able to write a letter to her like that. His would be terribly stiff and awkward. What had she said? 'Old-fashioned, upright and decent'? Pompous, more like. Why couldn't he be as relaxed as she seemed to think he was?

He looked at her body, almost dissolved by the sun, and thought it the most beautiful thing in the world. Tall, slim, soft, rounded, so different from his own, almost as if she were another species.

A breeze passed over him and chilled his sweat.

'It's a lovely afternoon,' Maddie said, stretching and turning towards him. 'Do you think we should go out?'

'Could do.'

'We could go for a walk on the Heath.'

'We could stay in bed.'

Maddie sat down on the window-sill and shook her head. 'I've had it for today, Tom, you've worn me out.'

'Well, come back to bed at least. I'm getting lonely here.'

Maddie smiled and climbed back under the duvet, pressing her cold skin against Tom's warmth. 'Let's go for a walk,' she said.

'Okay.'

Maddie propped herself up on her elbow and frowned at him.

46

'It's just that, I mean, me and you, it's more than just fucking, isn't it? It's more than that.'

'If you say so.'

'Tom!'

'Only joking. Of course it's more than that. And besides, I've said I'll go for a walk, haven't I?'

'I want you to want to go for a walk.'

'All right, I want to. I want to go for a walk.' Tom hesitated for a moment, then put his arms round her and pulled her down on top of him. Why couldn't he ever say the things he wanted to say? Why did he always try to fuck things up? He'd lie there and listen to his voice saying things and he'd scream at it to stop but it wouldn't.

Maddie spoke into his neck. 'We get so little time together,' she said.

'All the more reason to spend it in bed.'

'All the more reason to talk. I like to talk to you, it helps. It helps almost as much as the other, the fucking.'

'I'm glad to hear that.'

'Tom, what's the matter with you today?'

'What do you mean?'

'Well, you're just taking the piss.'

'I'm not, I'm just happy. Honest.' He smiled at her. 'If you knew me you'd know that for me to make fun of someone is the highest compliment I can pay them.'

'Oh yes? And what do you do to the people you don't like? Attach electrodes to their nipples?'

They laughed.

'I like being with you,' Tom said. 'You wrote in your letter that I made you happy ... Well ... Same here.' Jesus, it sounded so stupid when he said it out loud.

'I don't know with you sometimes,' Maddie said, straddling him and sitting on his stomach. 'I think I know you, and then you can be a complete stranger.'

'I'm just not used to this sort of thing.'

'No, I realize that. But I know so little about you.'

'What's to know?'

'Everything.'

'Okay.' Tom took a deep breath. 'I'll start at the beginning. My father was a captain, proper army man.' He saluted. 'After the war he stayed on in Germany, stationed there. That's where he met my mother. She was German. I never really knew her. She died, and we, the family, we came to England. He left the army, you see? Came back to Minehead. I was only three, Lucy, my sister was one. Then—'

Maddie laughed and put a finger to his lips. 'It's all right. Don't bother. You're right. What difference does it make? As you say, I make you happy, you make me happy. What more do we need?'

A whole lot more, Tom thought and he sat up and kissed her. He'd taken the first step, trying to tell her about what he felt; he had to plough on now and take the second.

'Listen,' he said, 'I know this is going to sound corny, but, well, basically, we can't go on meeting like this.'

Maddie frowned again. 'Yes, well, basically, Tom, we don't have any choice, do we?'

'Don't we?'

'It has to be Saturday afternoon, it's the only time I have to myself. Peter's out taking his course, and I can get home, shower, change and be ready all bright-eyed and bushy-tailed so we can have a good row when he gets in.'

'I know all that, but knowing it doesn't make it any easier.'

'Who said it would ever be easy? This sort of thing generally isn't, darling.'

'Can't we try, try and make it easy?'

'I've told you, Tom, I'm not ready to take this any further. I don't know what to do about Peter. I suppose in a funny kind of a way I still love him. I'm not ready to chuck it all out.'

'I'm not asking you to. Christ, this is all new for me, too, remember?'

'I know, I know.'

'I'd just like to see you a bit more, relax a bit more. It would help us both to see things a bit straighter.'

'You're probably right, but it's just not possible, and that's the end of it.'

'Now, Madeline, as my old dad used to say, "There's no such word as impossible".'

'It sounds like your old dad was a bit of a halfwit.'

Tom must have looked pained, though he didn't mean to show it.

'Oi,' said Maddie. 'Only joking.'

'That's okay.'

'I didn't know you were touchy about your father.'

'I'm not. What did I say?'

'Nothing, but you looked all hurt like a little schoolboy.'

'That's because you're sitting on my stomach, fatso!' Tom pushed her off and sat up. 'Let's go for that walk, shall we?' he asked, and thankfully it came out all right. 'I could certainly cope with some fresh air.'

They got up and started to dress. Tom, as usual had laid his clothes out, neatly folded on the chair, while Maddie had flung hers about the room. Consequently Tom was finished first. He made the bed then sat in the chair, watching Maddie.

For a while he was silent, fascinated by her actions, almost swamped by the casual intimacy they had quickly developed. But he needed more. Yet if he pushed it, would she get scared? Would she flee from him? He didn't know. A grown man and he didn't know the first thing about women.

He watched her pull on her tights, then took the plunge.

'What about Norwich?'

'Knickers off ready when I come home.'

'What?'

'Norwich – Knickers off ready when I come home. If you spell knickers without a *k*.'

'Now who's taking the piss?'

'Well, what am I supposed to say? When out of the blue you suddenly say "What about Norwich?" I mean, what about Norwich?'

'I thought you said you had to go to Norwich for a week; some conference at the university. Something about women and cinema.'

'Oh Christ, I'd forgotten all about that. You have got a good memory, haven't you? Maybe you should be my secretary.'

'Please, Maddie, I'm being serious. I mean, you are still going?'

'Tom that's amazing. Do you remember every little thing I tell you? I'm flattered.'

'It's just that I've been thinking about it.'

'Christ, I haven't.'

'Not at all?'

'Well, to tell you the truth, I don't mind admitting that I've got less than no interest in women and the bloody cinema, but I'm always getting invited to these wretched things because ... Well, I suppose because I'm a woman and I write about films. But they're usually in London, at some bloody awful women's co-op or something. Now, a week away, on the other hand, that would be different.'

'Quite, a week away. Away from Peter.'

'Well, that's certainly an incentive.'

'Where would you stay? A hotel?'

'Fat chance. Some squalid university accommodation, I shouldn't doubt.'

'Well, listen, how would you like to stay for a week at the Wymondham Lodge? It's supposed to be one of the best hotels in the area.'

'I'd love it, of course, but I couldn't possibly afford it.'

'Yes, but I could.'

Maddie turned to Tom and crossed her arms. 'Now, hang on Tom Kendall ...'

'It's a chance, Maddie, a chance for both of us to get away for a week.'

Maddie flopped on to the bed, facing away from him. 'I don't know, Tom. It's a very kind offer. But ... Besides, you can't just take a week off to go gallivanting up to Norwich. What would you tell them at work?'

'It's my company, I can tell them what I like. I can do what I like. I could take the whole of the rest of the year off, if I felt like it. Christ, I haven't had a holiday in ten years, I think I'm due one.'

'Wealthy businessmen who haven't had a holiday in ten years don't go to Norwich, honey, lovely as I'm sure it is. They go on round-the-world cruises, or salmon-fishing in Alaska or something.'

'That's just it, my sister lives in Norwich. I've got two little nieces I've hardly ever seen. I keep promising I'll go and visit them. This would be the perfect opportunity.'

'Kill two birds with one stone.'

'You don't have to put it like that.'

'I don't know, Tom. It's all a bit sudden, all a bit much. I'll need to think about it.'

'Of course. Your conference isn't till July, is it?'

'You tell me, you seem to know more about it than I do.'

'So you've got plenty of time to decide.'

'A whole month.'

Tom went over and put a hand on her shoulder. 'I don't want to push you, Maddie. It's your choice, obviously.'

Except that it wasn't. Because he had a month, a whole month to be nice to her, to learn all about her, to understand her and plan out a strategy. He'd treat it like business. That he was good at; working on clients. If he saw Maddie as a client and Norwich as the product, things became easier.

He had to do it, because she did make him happy. His world was changing and it was for the better. They would go to Norwich, and they would be happy, whether Maddie knew it yet or not.

He put his arms around her and squeezed her tightly, and she gave a little satisfied grunt.

Knickers off ready when I come home. A man could have a worse future than that.

SIX

James flipped a pile of nine beer mats up from the edge of the bar with the back of his hand and caught them on one rotation.

'All right, all right,' said Big Bob Arnell. 'You've still got one to go.'

'No chance,' said Graham. 'The boy's peaked.'

James looked at Wendy, the barmaid. She was still watching, still smiling. He put a tenth mat on the pile and carefully straightened them.

'Ten quid?' he said.

Graham nodded. 'You've got to do it first.'

'Watch this and weep, my friend.' He snapped his hand up, lifting the mats with his finger nails. They spun and he held them … all except one, which slipped free from the pack. It sailed over the counter, flapped against the optics and fell to the dirty floor like a shot bird.

'Haaah!' Bob let out a roar and tousled James's hair.

Shit. But don't show it.

He looked at Wendy again. She was laughing now.

'Bad luck, Jimmy.'

Maybe it wasn't such a bad idea, failing, maybe she'd like that in him. Maybe if she felt sorry for him …

Maybe.

'You grab that table,' he said to Graham and Bob. 'I'll get them in.'

'I hope you're not trying to buy us off, Jimmy.' Bob wagged a finger in his face.

James took out his wallet, opened it and removed a crisp ten-pound note, fresh from the cash machine.

'There. Don't spend it all at once.'

Bob took the note and went over to the table with Graham.

James turned to Wendy. She was still there, waiting for his order, though the pub was getting quite crowded.

'Two pints of lager and a vodka and Slimline, please ... and get one for yourself.'

Wendy smiled and began to pour a pint.

James studied her; she wore no bra and her large breasts hung heavy in her T-shirt. The shirt said something about a windsurf club and there was a cartoon of a bloke on a board. James had tried windsurfing once, on holiday in Spain with Lucy and the kids. He hadn't been any good at it and hadn't tried again.

While the lager was pouring, Wendy turned and started fixing the vodka. She was wearing very tight, faded jeans and she had a full arse. It was the sort of arse that women called fat, but James didn't think of it like that. It looked like good solid flesh, shaped and moulded by the pale blue fabric, accentuated by the darker blue of the cleft where the seam cut down between the two cheeks. God, how he wanted to stroke that tight fabric, cup her buttock, feel its warmth.

She turned back, rescued the over-flowing pint, let it settle, then topped it up and passed it to him.

He hadn't cupped Lucy's buttocks for weeks. She was always tired, these days, distracted. And it wasn't just sex she couldn't find the energy for any more; the house was a mess. He'd come home yesterday and seen her through the window, sitting in the living-room, staring at the carpet as if it had hypnotized her. The vacuum cleaner was standing in the middle of the room and she was just sitting there, completely still.

He'd let himself in and gone into the living-room. Still she sat there, unmoving, didn't even seem to notice him come in. In the end he'd spoken, said hello or something and she'd looked up, dazed, like she'd just woken. Then she looked around for all the world as if she didn't know where she was.

'You're home early,' she'd said. But he wasn't, he was late. How long had she been sitting there? It spooked him when she behaved like that. And it was happening more and more often these days.

He didn't like to think about it.

Wendy passed him another drink.

He braced himself. It was now or never. But then, that's what he always thought. Every Thursday, when the others were at a table and he was alone with her at the bar. Now or never. But it was never now, and it was never never. He glanced back at Graham and Bob. They were engrossed in chat.

Maybe this time . . .

'Do you fancy going out sometime?' He heard the words but couldn't believe he'd said them.

Wendy looked up at him from the lager tap and smiled politely.

Shit. Going out. Was that the right thing to say? It sounded so adolescent. 'Going out.' What a stupid thing to say. But it was adolescent, really, wasn't it? Trying to pick up a barmaid.

'All right.' She shrugged. 'Why not?'

Good Christ, he hadn't expected her to say yes. Now what? He didn't know how to do it, he didn't know how to have an affair. An affair, that sounded even worse than going out.

'Well . . .' Why not? Why not? Why not? 'Well, can you get an evening off, then?'

'Yeah, if I give Mike plenty of notice.'

'How about next Thursday?'

'You've got your karate on Thursdays.'

'I can skip it for one week . . . It's just I'm . . . I'm busy every other night.' It's just he'd have to think up an excuse for Lucy any other night.

'I suppose Thursday would be all right.'

That was it, then, it was done.

'We could go for a meal or ... or something ... If you like.'

'If you like.'

And I could run my fingertips down that dark cleft in your jeans, down and round and under.

She gave him her phone number and that was that. He didn't write it down, didn't want the others to see. He repeated it to himself, over and over like a mantra.

He paid for the drinks and Wendy carried on being a barmaid, cheerful and friendly, and it was like it had never happened, like he hadn't just arranged to cheat on his wife. But he had done, the numbers marching round and round inside his head told him that.

He carried the drinks over to the table. Bob and Graham leered at him.

'You two getting cosy, are you?'

'Just chatting.' Why didn't he want to tell them? After all, it was their contest which had started all this, their competition to see who could get inside her jeans first. And why didn't he want to tell Graham? Graham who had quite openly boasted about shagging the secretary, when everyone knew he was married.

He knew why. It was Lucy. He felt miserable. He pictured her sitting there in the armchair, lost in her private world, and he felt desperately sorry for her. But he didn't know how to help her. Whatever he did was wrong; every time he tried to move closer to her he ended up further away. If only he could talk to her about it. It was crazy. They were living in the same house but it was like they were both encased in glass or something, unable to touch each other. And the thing was he loved her. Yes, as he thought about it, that was the bland phrase that came into his mind – he loved her. He just couldn't make her understand. Christ, why did he do the karate? So that he could be her protector, her knight, look after home and family. And now what was he doing? A bloody barmaid, for God's sake.

God's sake or his own sake?

Yes. He would be a man. He would peel off Wendy's jeans, pull up her windsurfing T-shirt and pin her naked body to the bed, and he would ... And she had Lucy's face.

'I'm just going for a slash.'

He went to the toilet and locked himself in one of the cubicles. He stared at the door, carved with years of graffiti. One phrase caught his eye: 'Debbie Stone shags coons.' Next to it someone else had written, 'Fuck off,' and next to that, 'Julian Pellow takes it up the arse.' James took out his pen. For a moment he considered writing, 'James Paxton cheats on the woman he loves,' but instead he got out his address book and turned to the P section. It was an old book, filled with hundreds of names, many crossed out over the years. He found an empty corner and wrote, 'Julian Pellow,' then he let the numbers out of his head and they lined up next to the name.

It was better now that his mind was empty. He put the book back in his pocket and idly read the rest of the garbage on the door, thinking, 'James loves Lucy.' A little heart with an arrow through it.

He got home drunker than usual for a karate night, hoping Lucy would be asleep, but she was sitting up in bed, reading. Still marooned somewhere in the middle of the book.

'Hello,' she said without looking up. 'Did you have a good fight?'

Oh, don't start, don't start straight away. She hadn't even looked up from the book. Always reading, never getting anywhere.

'Yeah, it was okay.' Just keep calm. 'What have you been up to?'

'Oh, you know ...'

No, he thought, I don't know. I don't have a clue what you get up to when I'm not there.

There was no evidence that she actually did anything. For all he knew she just sat and read that book endlessly.

'I'm just going to have a shower.'

'Okay.'

He started to undress. That was the end of it, a typical Thursday-night conversation. He didn't expect it to continue, but, lo and behold, Lucy spoke.

'Tom rang this evening.'

'Oh yes?'

'Yes, to confirm he's coming up next weekend.'

'Next weekend?'

'Yes. You hadn't forgotten, had you?'

'No, I hadn't forgotten. Where's he going to stay?'

'A hotel.'

'He's not staying here, then?'

'No. You had forgotten, hadn't you?'

'Look, Lucy, I told you – I remember. Tom's coming next weekend. I just couldn't remember whether he was staying here, that's all.'

'You will be nice to him?'

'Jesus, of course I'll be nice to him. When am I ever not nice to people?'

'You'll be here . . . ?'

'No, I'll be on the bloody moon. Yes, I'll be here. Yes, I'll be nice to him. Yes, I remember he's coming next weekend.'

He was down to his muscle vest and briefs now. He glanced at himself in the mirror, then he saw that Lucy was looking at him and he blushed.

'He's bringing a woman.'

'What? Tom?'

'Yes. You don't have to sound so surprised.'

'Well, I am surprised. I mean, come on, Lucy, for as long as I've known him he's been resolutely single. I always thought he might be queer, actually.'

'Tom? Of course he's not.'

'Evidently.'

'You won't say anything? I want him to feel at home. I hardly ever see him, and—'

James sat down on the edge of the bed next to Lucy, cutting her off. 'Lucy, it's not me.'

'What's not you? What do you mean?'

'It's not me that's difficult, it's Tom. I always make an effort, I try to be polite, to talk to him. But he's so bloody awkward with me.' He got up and pulled off his vest. 'So don't blame me.'

'Well, I think you should give him a chance.'

'But that's just what I'm saying. I'll bend over backwards. But if he doesn't give me a chance . . .'

'He's my brother . . .'

'I'm going to have a wash.'

James put on his dressing-gown and went to the bathroom. Bloody Tom, he'd completely forgotten. Oh well, at least he wasn't staying. Quite frankly her brother gave him the creeps. The kids didn't like him either, or the cat for that matter. And children and animals knew about people. He was so bloody cold and strict, just like their dad.

Old Man Kendall. Christ, he'd been a terror, a big passionless shit of a man who always looked at you like you were doing something wrong. Never a kind word, always disapproving. He'd been a tall man with very white skin and very black hair, wispy, thin, but not exactly bald. Cold, pale eyes, a lifeless feel about him.

Tom was the same. Not as bad, but he always made James feel so damned inadequate. The fellow had no feelings; nothing moved him.

James started to wash, scrubbing under his arms with a damp flannel.

They resented him. Tom and his dad. That's what it was. Neither of them had wanted him to marry their little girl. Well, sod them, he had Wendy to look forward to on Thursday, perhaps her memory could get him through Tom's visit.

*

When he got back to the bedroom Lucy had finished reading. She was turned on her side with her light off; turned away from him. He quickly got into bed and put an arm round her.

'You're still wet.'

He took his arm away, lay there staring at the back of her head. He imagined reaching his arm back round her, round her neck, squeezing her throat, crushing her head against his chest, choking the life out of her, smashing her fucking face against the fucking wall . . .

Stop it.

All he really wanted to do was just put his arm round her and hold her. That was all. He felt desperately sad again. He rolled over and turned out his own light.

Back to back, neither of them slept for a couple of hours.

SEVEN

She looks like she is probably early to middle thirties. Quite small but with decent-sized breasts. Her hair is long, she wears it sort of tied up, but it gets loose, it's a mess really. There are a few streaks of grey, which make it harder for me to guess her age. She has two children, young girls. She is married and has a husband who is quite short.

Their house is perfect. One of the bigger ones on the Dereham Road, at the end of a block, on the corner. It has a front gate, a front door, an alley through to the back garden, a back door, and a walled garden. However, it is possible to go down an alley on the side road and reach one of the back walls that way, from the side. That is safer than using their own alley. I have climbed over the wall into the back garden twice and studied the back of the house. If anything happens or goes wrong I could escape from one of the top windows on to the kitchen roof, the kitchen looks like an extension. But I don't think I will need it, their habits are regular, specially as they have children.

It is interesting to note that the windows at the front are a recent addition, double glazing – to keep the noise of the traffic out, probably. The interesting thing is that they are exactly the same type as the ones Dad put in at Newmarket Road. He got them cheap somewhere, like everything else. I wonder if they have the same problems opening them as we do. The windows are one of the things which attracted me to the house in the first place.

Every Thursday night, the short man, Napoleon, comes home from work as usual – 6:30 – probably he has something to eat, then at about 7:30 he leaves the house again with a sports bag and he doesn't come back until after the pubs shut. I suppose he does some kind of sport. This gives me four clear hours every Thursday night – two, to be really safe, from 8:30 to 10:30. I couldn't risk it with both of the couple in the house. But with the woman there – she just watches the telly mostly – and the children asleep, it is just right for me. The children are usually put to bed when Napoleon goes out, sometimes a little later, but never later than eight. Nine o'clock is the ideal time, then. Any later and it would be too dark – people are always more suspicious of other people wandering around after it gets dark.

It is a while since I have been into the rooms of a couple. It is more exciting knowing that the bed might have been used the night before, even that morning, perhaps. And then I am there, sharing it with them, invisible. A nice and cosy domestic three-some, him, her and me. Troilism I think it is called.

Will stopped writing. He was getting too excited and now wasn't the time. He had to control the anticipation, channel it, so that on Thursday night he'd be completely wired up. This writing was just the foreplay, like the watching, the sorties. Everything had to be planned, brought forward step by small step. He had to play with the house, so that he was at just the right pitch to be able to go in, keep alert and finally come in the bedroom.

But he mustn't think about that now. Now he had to keep it to hard facts. He read over what he'd written, then made a couple of additions to the neat map on the opposite page. Satisfied, he closed the book and put it in its place on the shelf in his museum.

He looked at the blank space on the end wall where he would put the photographs. He should have plenty to choose from, people with children always had their houses crammed with pictures. Then there were the objects; what would he find this time? He had a section ready in the display area. Soon the space would be filled.

He wondered what treasures this room would hold in the future. He saw himself surrounded by stuff, buried in it. He thought of the years ahead, years of secret expeditions. He was good at it now, a professional, but think how much better he would be in ten years' time; think how many houses he would have fucked by then. He was getting excited again, he had to do something to take his mind off the coming Thursday. If he dwelt on it too long he might explode. He needed to clear his thoughts. To do that he had to leave the museum.

He opened the hatch and clambered out. Took one last look then turned off the light. Then he carefully replaced the panel, rolled the wardrobe into place and went to the record player. Thomas Tallis was blasting out, rattling the cheap windows. He lifted the stylus ... Instant silence.

There was a moment of blissful quiet, then the sounds started up. He stood and listened. Eyes closed, he could see every room in the house. And there was the old bag, moving down the hallway from the front room to the kitchen, her feet clicking on the bare floorboards. He'd encouraged her on that. No carpets, Mother, he'd said, these are lovely floorboards, polished pine is much more stylish than carpets, much more fashionable. She'd put a few rugs down, though, she couldn't help it, but he knew all their different sounds now, so it wasn't a problem.

The tap in the kitchen ran. Up here in the roof next to the pipes he knew the plumbing of the house intimately. It was the cold tap. He listened ... Yes, she was filling the kettle, he knew the exact timing, the careful adjustment of the water rate in the final stages of filling. Click, click, click, over to the plug, click, click, click, to the fridge for milk and now a mug from the high cabinet, a gentle squeak as it opened, a light bang as it swung shut on its sprung hinges.

The freezer motor started up, out in the pantry as Mother called it. Oh, and now she'd put the radio on.

A babble of sounds.

Outside he could hear traffic noises; his father's double glazing hadn't been effective on any level. Cars passed, the heavier rumble of a lorry; slight vibrations in the house. Now an aeroplane overhead on its way to land at Norwich Airport. Then the alarm that was always going off in the row of shops near the roundabout.

This was no good, the city was taking him over again. Any moment now he'd be thinking of Thursday night, the sad woman with greying hair, her husband, the three of them in bed together.

Downstairs the kettle boiled. The radio went off. Click, click, click, she went back to the sitting-room. The television came on. He pressed his hands to his ears, trying to keep the sounds out, but it was no good. Perhaps if he wrote for a bit, perhaps that would do it.

He took his current notebook out of his pocket, turned to a fresh page and began to write.

I am happy now, happier than I remember being. Each day is better than the last. As long as I can keep going, as long as I can keep the energy up, then I can keep growing more happy. I do not believe that a man can be truly happy unless he fully understands what he is and can act accordingly. I have been lucky because I knew what it was I wanted, and I knew that though some people may think that what I wanted was wrong, they would be wrong to think that. How can it be wrong to be happy? I really believe that each person must go with their own feelings and urges or risk becoming unhappy, unfulfilled. We each have our own nature . . .

It was no good. He stopped and read what he had written. It looked stupid, childish. It was always the way, whenever he tried to write 'properly' it came out wrong. Whenever he thought he might be writing something that others might read, his style became stiff and self-conscious. He knew he had to write what he felt in a simple, straightforward way – he didn't have to produce something that looked like it might have come out of a 'real' book – but he couldn't find the way to do it.

He frowned, reread the page, then drew a line through it.

He started again.

I am happy now . . .

He could get no further. This was the hardest thing, to try and set down on paper how he had discovered the way to happiness. It just looked silly when he tried to spell it out. But as he looked at those four words it struck him that he didn't need to spell it out. They said all he needed to say.

I am happy now.

Maybe he should leave it at that, maybe that was all that mattered. Maybe if he tried to analyse it, to pin it down, he would break it; maybe that was the secret – not to think about it. Just be happy.

He wrote it again.

I am happy now.

And again. Until the whole page was filled with those four words. He stared at it and smiled and outside he heard a girl scream . . . No, it was laughter. A door slammed. An ambulance heading for the hospital.

The city wouldn't leave him alone.

He turned back to his book and the woman's face appeared on the page, he couldn't help it, she would possess him until it was all over.

He didn't have a name for her yet, he would wait until he was inside her room. Then he'd know. A sickening rush of excitement welled up inside him. Her room, to be in her room, to put his head on the pillow where her wild hair had lain. He always knew which side the woman slept when he entered a couple's room. He knew houses, he knew things. When he entered an empty room it was full of life. The occupants were all around him, their hair in combs, their skin in the dust, their stink in the air, their slime on the sheets.

'Shut up!'

He startled himself. He'd actually shouted out loud without meaning to. This was no good. He had to go out, get away from things.

He put on his trainers and silently opened the door. He looked down the narrow stairs at the floor below, listening. The television was still on, hymns. He crept out. He knew every inch of floor, and in his rubber-soled shoes he could move around the house without making a sound. It was good training not letting the old bag know where he was, where he was going, even whether he was in or out.

On the first-floor landing he paused again. The hymn continued. 'For those in peril on the sea . . .' He could picture the horde of shiny, singing people, mouths gaping, faces upturned, crammed together in some dreary fishing village. He continued on down. Outside the front room he paused. The old bag was in there, on the other side of the door, sitting on the sofa, gawping at the simple fisher folk. The very sofa. She hadn't even had the decency to get rid of it after. Maybe she'd kept it to mock, to mock his father. Oh yes, Will knew about the power of objects, about the life that rubbed off on to them, the life you could pick up by touching them, feeling them, stroking them. The beds writhing in orgasm, the stair carpets moving under your feet like escalators, chairs sitting, waiting . . .

He was disgusted with her.

He opened the front door, ever so slowly so that there'd be no rush of air, but not too wide to let in a flood of outside noises. When it was just wide enough, he slipped out and put his key in the lock. He turned the key, shut the door silently and released the latch.

He could never properly love this house again until she was gone from it. The times he'd thought of speeding on her departure, toyed with the idea of using the house itself to get rid of her. Electrocution, drowning, collapsing stairs, falling ceiling. But he hated the idea of taking an active part, of making things happen. That wasn't his way. He'd prayed a couple of times, prayed to the spirit of the house, begged it to devour the woman. But it never had; it, too, was waiting.

He walked along the Newmarket Road away from town. He knew all these houses here, they smiled at him as he passed. But he wanted to be alone, to have some peace and quiet, some time to himself. There was too much power here, pressing on him from all sides. The trees helped and the wide grass verges along the edge of the road, but he needed to be away from people, away from houses. He needed to cut out the constant hum, the chatter that swarmed around his head when he was in the city.

He kept walking and, slowly, as he moved away from town, things quietened down. He walked for over an hour until he was out in the country. At least it was more country than town. A small hill, with fields and trees. There were houses near by, of course, and roads, but the great mass of the city was behind him. He could sense it over his shoulder, squatting there, breathing, its heart rhythmically thumping.

It hadn't been a sunny day but it was a warm evening and the ground was dry. He sat in the long grass and looked up at the huge, grey sky.

Peace.

He went up into the sky, further and further away into the empty greyness where there was no sound but the steady rustle of the wind. And the wind didn't give a shit.

Then the four words wrote themselves in giant letters right across heaven . . .

I am happy now.

And then he felt cold. He was lonely up here; he became scared that he might never be able to get back. He closed his eyes and fell from the sky. Then he jumped up and began to run, back towards the city, back into its waiting arms.

EIGHT

Before becoming a hotel, Wymondham Lodge had been a small stately home. It had been carefully restored and modernized but still kept the feel of a fine old country house. A gravel driveway cut through the deep green lawn, clipped ivy grew up the weathered red-brick walls and two sturdy columns stood on either side of the large, wide-open doorway.

Tom parked the car, got out and smiled. This was it, this was ideal, this would surely dispel any remaining doubts Maddie had about their week away together. Ten days, actually. Ten days with Maddie. The thought frightened him, but the fear was over-ridden by a delirious excitement.

'It looks pretty posh,' Maddie said, getting out of the car. 'You sure you can afford it?'

'Of course I can.' Tom opened the boot and began to unload their bags. 'I told you, I haven't had a holiday in years. I've got a bulging bank account and nothing to spend it all on.' He turned and smiled at Maddie. 'Except you.'

Maddie smiled back, but he couldn't tell what sort of a smile it was. He was still learning these things.

'Except me,' she said.

A man came out of the hotel, rubbing his hands together theatrically. He was about Tom's age, bald, with glasses and a moustache. He was wearing a dark blue summer suit with a light blue shirt and nondescript striped tie.

'Hello there, may I welcome you to Wymondham Lodge?'

'Hi.' Tom shook his hand.

'You must be . . .' The man didn't know, he was waiting for Tom.

'Kendall, Tom Kendall. And this is Maddie . . .'

'Maddie Fisher,' Maddie said emphatically.

The man didn't bat an eyelid. Why should he? People didn't care about such things these days. In which case, why had Maddie made a point of saying it?

'I'm Phil Hollingsbourne. Head honcho. Any problems, any questions, I'm always there. Here, let me give you a hand with those.'

He picked up two of the suitcases and led the way into the hotel, chatting happily about the history of the place. Tom wasn't listening; he just wanted to get up into the room and shower after the three-hour drive from London.

The doors led straight into a large, open, reception area. To the right a few leather armchairs and sofas, little tables, carefully arranged dried flowers, a large marble fireplace with a gas-powered, fake coal fire as the centre of attention. To the left an open door through to the dining-room. Tom could see tables elegantly set with silver and crystal. Ahead was the reception desk, built from gleaming, dark wood, and next to it a stand of leaflets and maps. The place was carpeted throughout in steel-blue, patterned with the monogram WL.

Tom signed the register as Phil rattled off the facilities; swimming-pool, croquet, bowls, tennis, sauna, gym, restaurant, bar. Horse-riding, even. There was plenty of time to do all that, all Tom wanted now was a shower.

Phil unhooked a key from its peg and led them up a wide, stone-bannistered, stairway.

'No lift, I'm afraid, but you're on the first floor, so it shouldn't be too much of a problem.'

'That's fine.'

They padded down a short, windowless corridor. Little brass

lamps shone pools of warm light on to the expensive flowered wallpaper and the same blue carpet. They came to their room and Phil unlocked the door.

'There you are.' He held out an arm to show them in, beaming at them like a proud home-owner. Maddie went in first and Tom followed.

Oh, no.

It was just another tiny British hotel room. There was a narrow bed, a collection of ill-matching furniture, an undersized wardrobe, a low dressing-table with a dark, spotted mirror, a table with a kettle and a basket of tea things on it, a small old-fashioned television with no remote control ... And that was about it. The carpet was industrial, the curtains transparent-looking, the walls painted a rather unpleasant, sickly cream. Tom stood there trying not to get angry.

Phil pushed open a door by the bed.

'Bathroom's through there. Everything all right?'

'Yes, yes, that's fine, thank you ...' said Tom, briskly. He waited for Phil to leave, then let out a great sigh and stood looking out of the window at the hotel grounds.

'What's the matter?' Maddie said, opening a suitcase and beginning to unpack.

'This room's the bloody matter, that's what.'

'What's wrong with it? It's all right, isn't it?' She looked around and shrugged.

'Why don't the British understand about hotels? They spend all the money on the wrong things. All bloody set-dressing outside and the rooms are barely functional.'

'Looks okay to me.'

Tom turned around from the window. 'Look, the bed can hardly fit one person, let alone two. The furniture's crap, the room's poky ...' He stopped himself. 'Why does this always happen?'

'It's fine, Tom, honestly. It's much nicer than anything I would have got. It's a lovely situation.'

71

'I'm just disappointed, that's all. I'd hoped for something better. I mean, the amount they charge.'

'If it's the money you're worried about, I don't mind, we can just as soon find a B&B.'

'It's not the bloody money, all right? Don't worry about the money. I can afford it, that's not the point . . .'

Maddie came over to him and put her arms round his neck, smiling up at him. He caught sight of himself in the wardrobe mirror. There was a childishly petulant look on his face.

'The point is, lover,' Maddie said softly, 'we're alone for a week together, and as long as we've got a bed, nothing else matters. Okay?'

Tom went soft. She was right. What did it matter? No point in getting worked up.

Maddie pulled him down on to the bed and they kissed, and she hugged him.

'Listen, stupid, it doesn't matter what this room's like, this is our room.'

'Yes.'

'I'm the one who was supposed to be having second thoughts, remember?'

'Yes. I'm sorry.'

'Good. You behave, then, or I'm hopping straight on the first train back to London.'

'And Peter.'

'Yes, Peter. Listen, you've been great these last few weeks, no moods, no sulks. How about keeping it like that?'

'Okay,' said Tom, grinning. 'It's a deal. I'll be the life and soul of the party if you don't bring up Peter again.'

'All right. But remember, this is just a holiday. When it's over we both have to go back to reality.'

'Aye aye, skipper.'

'Right, then. Kiss me again.'

'No.' Tom jumped up. 'I've got to have a shower first. Can't do anything before I'm cleaned up and out of these clothes.'

The bathroom was usually the best test. Tom went in and a pulse of tension throbbed at his temple.

He took a deep breath.

Keep things under control, remember what Maddie said.

Yes, but a lino floor, for Christ's sake! A lino floor, a small mirror, a small sink, a rusty towel rail. There were only two consolations, a plentiful supply of towels and an enormous bath, albeit slightly stained by years of use. The shower, however, was primitive, attached to the taps by a long metal hose. The ancient plastic shower curtain was missing a couple of rings.

But it was their bathroom, that's all that counted.

Yes.

He undressed and ran the water, fiddling with the unnecessarily complex controls to try and get an even, warm flow. After a while he had something acceptable and he stepped in.

The jet wasn't too powerful and the hot and cold didn't mix perfectly, but it was better than nothing. He felt good again, his headache began to dissipate like an ice cube in warm water.

He hated long drives, they seemed designed to put him into a state of rage. Luckily the traffic hadn't been too bad getting out of London and the M11 was relatively empty. It was only on the long, dull stretch of the A11 that he'd begun to get wound up. The road was single carriage for much of the way, busy with lorries and cars driving east. He'd tried to maintain a steady fifty-five, knowing from experience that if he attempted to hurry, it only made things worse, but other drivers insisted on driving right up his arse where they fidgeted to get round him and eventually took stupid risks. With each new mad driver he'd get angrier and angrier; he felt like slamming on his brakes and having them smash into the back of him. But he was always saved by a stretch of dual carriageway, and at last they'd reached Norwich. Then, as he'd driven into the grounds of the hotel, he'd instantly relaxed. It had all seemed worth it.

And now here he was with Maddie, alone at last.

The shower suddenly became scalding hot. He leapt back with a cry and almost slipped.

'Shit-damn-bollocks-fuck,' he said quickly and lunged at the controls. He managed to redirect the flow down into the taps and stepped out on to the bath mat.

He was still covered in soap so he tried to readjust the temperature. He turned the hot right off and felt the water until it was running cold. Then he tried to bring the hot back up, but he couldn't. The sudden gush seemed to have been a last-ditch effort by the boiler to send him some hot water. Now, exhausted, all it could manage was a pathetic trickle. He clambered back in and miserably cleaned off the soap.

This is Phil's fault, he thought to himself. This is all bloody Phil's fault.

'What's it like?' Maddie asked, as he re-emerged wrapped in a couple of towels.

'I think we'd best stick to baths.'

'Suits me. I prefer baths, anyway.'

'What would I do without you?'

'Without me you wouldn't be here, honey. You've got to balance me with the plumbing . . . Which is more important?'

'Oh,' he said. 'The plumbing, definitely.'

Once they'd sorted themselves out they went for a walk round the grounds. The swimming-pool proved to be on the small side and rather shallow. It was only really suitable for children, but neither of them had intended to do much swimming while they were here so they weren't particularly bothered. Tom had relaxed enough now to treat it as a bit of a joke, and they played a game

74

in which they tried to find things wrong with the place that they could laugh about.

'What do you want to do tonight, then?' Tom asked Maddie as they sat watching a sporty young couple play tennis.

'Don't you want to see your sister?'

'Well, she's not expecting us until tomorrow. I thought maybe we could have the evening to ourselves.'

'I don't know, Tom, you haven't seen her for ages. You can't come all this way and then not meet up.'

'She's not to know. I'll see her tomorrow.'

'What if we went out somewhere and bumped into them? What would they think?'

'It's hardly likely; Norwich isn't such a small place. I mean we could just eat here at the hotel, have a couple of drinks, early night...'

'Maybe, but you should at least ring them, explain. I don't want to have to lie when we do eventually see them.'

'Okay. I guess you're right. I might as well give her a call now, get it over with.'

'All right.'

'Where will you be?'

'Oh, either here or wandering around somewhere. I can't exactly get lost.'

'Okay. See you in a minute.'

Tom went back inside and found a pay phone in reception. He was buggered if he was going to pay the extra that calling from their room would cost. He dialled Lucy's number and waited for her to answer. Phil came in from the front and waved cheerily to him. Tom nodded back.

Lucy was ages answering the phone, but just as he was about to give up, he heard her voice.

'Hello?'

'Hello, Lucy, it's Tom.'

'Oh, hello, Tom.'

'Are you okay? You sound like you've just woken up. Is this not a good time?'

'No, no, I'm fine. No, I wasn't asleep. I was, you know—'

'Listen, Lucy, we decided to come up a day early.'

'Oh.'

'Yes, traffic's always much worse on a Friday. Didn't fancy hacking down tomorrow morning, arriving all in a fluster for Maddie's introductory thing tomorrow afternoon.'

'That makes sense.'

'Now, you're not expecting us today, but I thought I'd just ring to say hello, let you know we've arrived. We'll probably just eat at the hotel tonight and—'

'No. No, Tom. You must come over.'

'Yes, but Luce, I don't want to put you to any trouble . . .'

'It's no trouble, Tom. I can just as easily cook today as tomorrow.'

'But it's not fair to—'

'Don't be silly, Tom. Anyone would think you didn't want to see us. You're only round the corner, you must come over. The girls are very excited about seeing their Uncle Tom.'

'Yes, well, okay. If you're sure?'

'Of course I'm sure, can't have you stuck out there.'

'Well, what time, then?'

'Half-seven, eight. We could aim to eat about nine.'

'Okay, sounds great. And you're quite sure?'

'I'm your family, Tom. I want to see you.'

'Half-seven, then. Right, see you . . .'

'Yes, see you later, Tom.'

Tom hung up. He knew he shouldn't have rung her. He should have waited, he really needed to spend some time alone with Maddie, get used to it. Now he'd have the added strain of Lucy and her idiotic husband, not to mention the children. He never knew what to say to children, they were alien to him. How old were they now? He had no idea. Christ, what a disaster. He just wasn't ready for this. Why had he listened to Maddie? He laughed. Maddie hadn't wanted to lie to Lucy. That was ironic, seeing as how they were going to have to lie about the central fact; that Maddie was married to someone else. He really didn't want to have to go through all this tonight.

But it was done.

Phil appeared from nowhere; suddenly he was at Tom's side, standing just slightly too close.

'Everything okay?'

No, Tom thought, the room's crap, the shower doesn't work, the pool's too small, there's holes in the tennis net, the bowling green's bumpy and the flowers need watering.

'Yes,' said Tom. 'This is a lovely place you've got here.'

'I think so, yes.' Phil smiled, then looked serious. 'I don't think the big chains can really offer the personal touch, not like a family-run place like this.'

'Must be hard work, though.'

'Well, can't complain. It's good to have work in this day and age.'

'Yes.'

'And what do you do, Tom?'

'Oh, I'm a printer, my own printworks.'

'Ah. Splendid. Interesting . . .'

The conversation fizzled out. They both stood there awkwardly for a few seconds, then Phil clapped his hands together.

'Well, no peace for the wicked.'

He grinned inanely and strode off at a brisk pace.

Tom walked slowly back outside. Maddie had gone from the tennis court. He tried the bowling green and the little walled garden, then eventually spotted her down by a pond at the edge of the grounds. She was standing looking down into the water, lost in her own thoughts.

He stood watching her, thinking she was his, thinking that

later he would be in bed with her, naked, that he would sleep with her. For the first time ever he would spend the night, wake up with her even, see her in the morning. His throat went dry. Ten days, nine nights ... He was gripped with a terrible panic. He couldn't go through with it, stuck here with Maddie and Phil. Why had he come? He was stupid, it would never work.

He turned round and looked back at the hotel. He knew what he had to do. He had to go back to the poky room, pack his things, leave a note for Maddie, pay the bill and drive back to London. To Blackheath where he'd be safe and secure in his flat. Alone. He had to be alone, he'd always known it, ever since he was a child. He couldn't cope with other people. They drove him mad.

Yes, go. Go now ...

He started to walk towards the building.

'Tom!' It was Maddie calling him.

He looked round and saw her walking towards him.

'I'm here ... Didn't you see me?' She smiled, the sun in her short light hair, her breasts moving against the white cotton of her summer shirt.

Oh God, he couldn't be without her.

He hurried towards her and threw his arms round her.

'Hey,' she said. 'Careful now, you'll break my back.'

Tom said nothing; he was fighting his way towards the light from beneath a great crush of dark water and he didn't ever want to reach the surface.

NINE

What was that Aled Jones song? From that thing with the snowman? 'Walking in the Air', something like that. Walking in the air. That was how James felt even though, admittedly, at the moment, he was driving. Driving in the air, that didn't have quite the same ring to it. He sang the line, impersonating Aled Jones's thin, high-pitched voice.

'I'm walking in the air.' He sang the line again; he didn't know any of the other words.

There was a tightness in his chest and his hands on the wheel were sweaty. Home six-thirty, out seven, see Wendy seven-thirty. That was only an hour and a half away. Ninety minutes. Five thousand four hundred seconds. James had always been good at maths. But it sounded too long, all those seconds. Ninety minutes, that was the shortest. Ninety minutes.

'I'm walking in the air.'

They seemed to show that snowman thing every Christmas now. It had become as traditional as carol services or Jesus. The love affair between a boy and a snowman. What the bloody hell was that all about?

Someone pulled out in front of him and forced him to brake suddenly. Usually this would have launched him into a fit of horn-blaring and light-flashing, but not tonight. Tonight he let it go. Because tonight he was walking in the air, and it wasn't a snowman he was going to be holding hands with, it was Wendy. A flesh-and-blood woman with large breasts. Holding hands? Would they do that? Is that what people did? The only hands he'd held recently were Lucy's and the girls when they were out walking.

Traffic was light on the Dereham Road and in fact he was home before six-thirty. Somehow, by taking things easy he'd cut his journey time by two minutes. Well, that was just another sign that today was a special day. He parked the car and another wave of Wendy hit him. He slammed his damp hands against the steering-wheel.

'Fuck!' he said out loud. 'Tonight I will fuck. Yes. Ha!' He slapped the wheel again. He got out of the car and locked it. God, this street looked so small and ordinary sometimes. He wanted to get out, get away.

Tonight.

That was a song as well, wasn't it? *West Side Story*. Ah, there was music in his soul tonight. Tonight, tonight, won't be just any night. He did a little dance step, got self-conscious and turned it into a karate move. But he still felt foolish. He shouldn't be here tonight, in Norwich, he should be in New York. On one of those steaming streets with wet sidewalks lit by neon and iron fire escapes climbing up crumbling tenements. Not on this dreary, pathetic road, with its identical terraced houses. Brickwork and pointing, neat front gardens and Aled Jones on the CD player.

Yes, well, tonight he was a Jet. He carried out a high karate kick. This one never had been a dance step. I am a fucker, he thought. I am sex.

He pushed open his front gate and walked up the path to the house. The tiny lawn needed mowing, there were weeds scattered all over it. The lawn was his concern; Lucy did the flowers and stuff. Work to be done. Maybe this weekend, maybe next. What difference did it make?

He unlocked the front door and went inside. Sounds of activity came from the kitchen. It was unusual for Lucy to be doing anything constructive at this time of day. He went down the hall past the stairs and through to the back. The kitchen was a mess, a confusion of pots and pans, open recipe books, food, knives. Why couldn't Lucy ever do anything in an orderly, organized fashion? There she was, standing over the stove peering into a pan, her face moist, her hair falling over her eyes.

'What's up?' he said.

Lucy looked round. 'Oh, you surprised me.' She tried to smile, but she was guilty about something, anxious.

'Well, this is all rather surprising. What are you doing?'

'Tom rang.'

'Oh, yes?'

'He's come up a day early.'

'What do you mean, "Come up early"?'

'He's here, in town, now. He came up today rather than tomorrow.'

'And ...'

'James, you don't mind missing your class tonight, do you? Just one night?'

'What do you mean?'

'Well, I invited him over, him and his girlfriend, for, you know, for dinner.'

'Tonight?'

'Yes. It's just one night. You don't mind, do you? Missing your class ...'

'But, Lucy, you know Thursday night's my karate night. I mean, it's the only night of the week I do anything. Any other night. It's not unreasonable that I can have one night a week to myself to do the one thing, I mean, the only thing I do without you.'

'But you go every week. To miss one week won't matter, will it?'

'Yes, but it's the principle. I mean, why couldn't we stick to the original arrangement?'

'I didn't think. He just rang up and I didn't think.'

'No, you didn't think, did you? Christ, Thursday night, Thursday night, how could you forget?'

'I told you, I just didn't think. I was so excited and ... You're not angry, are you?'

'No. Yes. Yes, I am angry. I'm bloody angry. It's bloody stupid of you. Christ, I know you don't like me doing karate, but the least you could do is respect—'

'He's my brother, James. I haven't seen him for two years.'

'And that's my fault, is it? All of a sudden it's my fault that you can't—'

'No. Of course it's not. I wasn't saying it was. All I'm saying is that it can't be so important that—'

'Christ, Lucy, I don't believe this.'

'Why? It's just karate. If it means so much to you, then go. Go on. I'll just tell Tom you couldn't get out of it. Just ... Just ...'

Lucy stopped. James looked at her. There were tears in her eyes. Good. It was the least she deserved. What the hell was she thinking of?

'Yes. Tell him that,' James said angrily. 'Because I'm not going to be here, all right?' He felt like telling her he'd rather be out every time her creepy brother decided to come round.

Lucy said nothing. She stared into the pan as if it contained all the secrets of the universe. A tear rolled down her nose.

'I'm doing your favourite,' she said quietly. 'Crispy duck.'

'Well, I hope Tom likes it.'

He slammed the door behind him as he went out. The bang seemed horribly loud. He paused for a moment, almost turned back. But tonight was Thursday night. He moved away from the door, carried on moving while his anger still fuelled him. He stomped down the hall and up the stairs.

Polly was playing on the landing. She looked up and grinned at him.

'Uncle Tom's coming for dinner, Daddy. I'm going to stay up and see him, but Claire's going to bed.'

James couldn't think of anything to say, so he just smiled at her and went into the bedroom. He closed the door and slumped on to the bed feeling utterly desolate. He saw Lucy standing there in the kitchen with her tears falling into the saucepan. Why had he been so cruel to her? He couldn't believe it was him. He banged the balls of his palms against his forehead.

'Arsehole.'

But it just wasn't fair after watching the clock all day, counting the days all week, planning it, planning his every move. It wasn't fair to be fucked up now by bloody Tom.

He got up.

Well, he wasn't going to be fucked up. What the hell, Lucy would relax more without him around, anyway. She'd enjoy herself. It was only a meal, after all.

He went to the cupboard, slid the door to one side and took out his kit bag.

All he was doing was going out to his karate class, then he'd come back later and Tom would still be there, and . . . But he wasn't going out to karate, was he? He was going out to see Wendy. To try and have sex with her. He slung the kit bag against the wall and it flopped to the carpet.

How could he come back after seeing Wendy and face them all? Lucy, Tom and whoever this woman was he had with him. That was beyond a joke. He'd tried not to think about Lucy before, whether he'd be able to look her in the face afterwards. He knew one thing, he'd have to make up with her first, apologize for losing his temper and acting like an idiot. Yes, if he could just do that, get things straight between them, then he'd be fine, free to do what he liked.

Because he had to go through with it.

He had to.

Tonight.

Tonight, tonight. Tonight he was walking in the air with Wendy.

He fetched the bag, put it on the bed and unzipped it. He carefully took out his karate stuff and laid it out on the duvet.

He undressed, stripping off his stale work clothes until he was completely naked. He looked at himself in the bedroom mirror, compact and tight, the muscles well-defined. He took up a pose, made the muscles stand up on his forearms.

'Don't fuck with me,' he said. 'Don't fuck with me.'

He relaxed the pose and stretched, then put on his dressing-gown and went to the shower room. He showered quickly and efficiently, a pure act of cleaning, then returned to the bedroom to get into his karate gear. First he had to draw the curtains, though, and when he got to the window he looked out and saw Lucy. She was coming out of the kitchen, walking very slowly, with her head bowed.

The back garden wasn't very big; it consisted mostly of a raised patio area paved with concrete slabs, which was reached by a couple of steps leading up from the back of the extension.

But Lucy didn't climb the steps, she sank down on the top one with her head in her hands and just sat there. He wanted to go to her, hold her, tell her it was all all right. Everything was all right. But how could he? How could he approach her, lie to her?

He spun away from the window and let fly a punch at the wardrobe door. His fist shattered the flimsy wood and went straight through. He cut his knuckles pulling it free. Slowly he let out his breath and sat down on the edge of the bed. He could just see Lucy from here, the top of her head, looking at the ground, not moving. There he was, naked, his hand bleeding, and there she was, alone.

'Arsehole,' he said again.

He had no idea how long they both sat like that. In the end he got up, packed his kit away in his bag, put it back in the cupboard and got out a set of casual evening clothes, the sort of clothes he wore every night other than Thursday.

Then he went down to her.

It was a warm evening, though overcast. Lucy looked dark against the grey concrete slabs.

'Luce?'

She didn't look up.

'It's all right, Luce. I won't go.'

'Go if you want,' she said flatly.

'I just said, I'm not going. I'll stay. You're right, it doesn't matter if I miss one week. I'm sorry I lost my temper.'

Lucy slowly looked up. 'Do what you want, James. Do what you want.'

Why did she have to make it so hard always? He felt like telling her to go fuck herself. It would be so easy to just turn around, leave her there and go ravish Wendy, pop her breasts from under her T-shirt.

Then Lucy got up, walked to him and put her arms around him.

'Thank you,' she said, and he looked over her shoulder and smiled. He didn't need Wendy. He was happy. When Lucy held him like this he was so happy. He squeezed her tight against him, felt her soft, warm body through her cotton dress. He squeezed her tighter and she didn't complain. He tilted her head back and kissed her cheeks. They were salty from crying. Then he kissed her mouth for a long, long time.

'Darling,' he said, his lips still against hers.

'What?'

'Let's go upstairs.'

She smiled at him. 'Okay.'

He led her inside by the hand. Upstairs Polly was still playing on the landing.

'Go down and play with your computer, honey,' Lucy said and Polly thought about it for a moment before jumping up and running downstairs.

Then they went into the bedroom and locked the door.

I don't need Wendy, James thought. I don't need anything but Lucy.

In their hurry they made love with their clothes on. Lucy's dress was pulled up to her breasts, James's trousers round his knees. It was quick and intense and exhausting. Afterwards they undressed properly and lay on the bed holding each other without talking.

James stared at the ceiling and thought about Wendy. It was a relief, really, not to have to go through with it, not to take the risk, but he had to let her know somehow. There was no way he could phone her from the house. It had to be a public call box.

'Is there anything I can do?' he said, stroking Lucy's tangled hair.

'Mm?'

'For tonight ...'

'No, it's all right. It's all done, really.'

'Why don't I go and get some wine or something?'

'That'd be nice. And get yourself some beers.'

He dressed and went back out to the car. The street had got him again. He wasn't a Jet, he was a jerk, plain old James Mullen with a lovely wife and two lovely kids, and he mustn't ever forget it.

He drove down the road to the off-licence and bought a couple of bottles of German wine and a four-pack of Samuel Smith's bitter.

The phone box outside was occupied so he waited for a few minutes, watching cars bustle past, picturing dull lives of routine and repetition. Well, he'd had his chance and thrown it away.

Bollocks, it wasn't thrown away. All he had to do was rearrange it. It wasn't the end of the world. It wasn't the end of his chances. Wendy would understand. Wendy was easy-going. Wendy was relaxed, uncomplicated. So different from Lucy.

And when he rang her, Wendy did understand. She said it was no problem. She said, yeah, make it next week sometime, just ring.

No problem.

She probably hadn't even been expecting to fuck him; it was

just a drink as far as she was concerned. Why had he got so wound up about it?

Grow up, James, don't be an arsehole all your life.

He left the phone box and got back in the car, set off down the road he knew so well. As he drove slowly along, the bottles of wine clinking in the carrier bag, he tried not to let his earlier depression slip back and take hold of him. He had to be reasonably together to cope with Tom. But it was difficult, in the back of his mind was the constant thought that tonight was ruined. He'd failed again.

When he got back there was nowhere to park, and, as he drove miserably round the side-streets looking for somewhere, he remembered that everyone died in *West Side Story*.

And the snowman; didn't he melt at the end of the film?

TEN

'No more arguments?'

'No more arguments.' He kissed Maddie quickly on the lips and rang the doorbell. No more arguments. Be happy.

The evening hadn't started well for Tom. He should never have rung Lucy, he should have waited until he was properly prepared. But Maddie had convinced him that it would be all right.

Then Maddie was the next thing to go wrong.

Tom was always punctual. If he said he was going to do something he would do it – at the exact time and place he'd arranged. But Maddie obviously wasn't like that. Maddie obviously had a completely different way of doing things.

First of all she'd insisted on having a bath just as Tom was starting to get dressed to go out. He'd had it all timed, he knew how long it would take him to dress and how long it would take him to drive to Lucy's place and now Maddie wanted a bath.

'You don't have time,' he'd told her.

But she'd just laughed at him. 'Don't be so anal,' she'd said. 'I can get dressed in no time.'

'But why couldn't you have had a bath before?'

'Oh, shut up, you old granny.'

She'd been ages in the bathroom. He'd finished dressing and was sitting on the bed watching television when she came out. He had no idea what it was he was watching, but by concentrating on the screen he could blank the impatience from his mind.

'See,' she'd said, standing dripping on the carpet. 'I wasn't long.' But before he could say anything she'd given him a disarming smile and kissed him.

'Now, don't blink or you'll miss me dressing.' She threw off her towel. 'Wonder Woman strikes again.'

As it turned out she'd forgotten to bring her favourite dress.

'But I'm sure I remember unpacking it,' she'd said, furiously sorting through the stuff in the wardrobe. 'I'm positive.'

'Well, you can't have done, can you? Because it's not there, is it?'

'Oh, bugger it. Bugger it to hell. This is just typical.'

And so she'd sworn at herself for five minutes until Tom had told her to calm down, at which point she'd started swearing at him.

'Just wear something else, can't you?' Tom had snapped angrily, and for ten more minutes she'd flung things out of the cupboard, flung them on, flung them off, flung them at the bed and flung them at Tom.

'For God's sake,' Tom had said at last. 'Just bloody wear anything, will you? It doesn't matter. We're twenty minutes late as it is, and there's still a twenty-minute drive.'

'Okay, so why don't you just go without me, then? Hm?'

'Don't be stupid. They're expecting you.'

'Don't call me stupid.'

Tom had looked at her, standing in the middle of the room wearing just her underwear and he'd smiled. 'Come on, let's calm down.'

She'd thought about it.

'If you're going to argue, put some clothes on at least. You're distracting me.'

She'd looked at herself in the mirror and started to laugh. 'Okay. Give me five minutes.'

It had taken her ten, but Tom didn't say anything.

They'd driven over to Dereham Road in silence. But once Tom had finished parking, Maddie leant over and gently bit his ear.

'I'm sorry, okay?' she'd said. 'I'm sorry I made us late. Now let's just try and enjoy this evening, shall we?'

'Good idea.'

'No more arguments.'

James answered the door with his arm round Lucy, and he shook Tom's hand – a real bone-crusher – without releasing her. Tom said hello to Lucy, and moved into the cramped hallway. When it was obvious that James still had no intention of letting go of his wife, Tom kissed her awkwardly, nearly tangling with his brother-in-law. It was an uncomfortable moment and to hide his embarrassment Tom automatically said to Lucy. 'You smell nice.' At which Lucy blushed and looked away.

'What is it?' Tom asked. 'What have I said?'

'That's James,' she explained. 'I'm not wearing any perfume.'

'Oh . . . ha!'

Luckily at this point Maddie stepped in, greeting everyone profusely. At last James let go of Lucy to kiss Maddie and the little knot broke up.

Tom clocked straight away that James fancied Maddie. He'd noticed it with a lot of men; they turned and looked at her in the street, they stood too close to her when they talked. Tom didn't mind. He quite enjoyed it, really. She was a very attractive woman with a powerful, magnetic energy about her. But what they didn't know, the men who homed in on her mesmerizing life force, was how much of it was really anger.

He was glad that James fancied her. He knew it would make their visit go that much smoother and he relaxed a little.

'I'm sorry we're so late,' he said as they went inside.

'That's okay.' Lucy led them through to the kitchen. 'I'm running behind, anyway. It's a good thing you didn't turn up on time.'

Before anyone could say anything else they heard excited little footsteps coming down the hallway and one of the two girls came hurrying into the room. Tom had no idea which one it was, it was so long since he'd seen them.

'Uncle Tom,' she yelled and grinned at him. Then she held back, shy, as if she'd been expecting someone else.

Tom didn't know what to do or say. He didn't know her name and he didn't know whether he was supposed to kiss her, or pick her up, or what.

'Hello there,' he said lamely.

'Give your Uncle Tom a kiss, then,' James said, and she sheepishly came forward. Tom leant down and turned his face slightly to the side and she gave him a quick dry peck on the cheek.

Again Tom felt that something was expected of him and he stood self-consciously in the middle of the kitchen, smiling stupidly at the little girl. Then Maddie swooped in and the child shrieked with a mixture of surprise and delight as she was picked up.

'And what's your name, then?' Maddie asked, swinging her around.

'It's Polly.'

'Hello, Polly, my name's Maddie.'

'Hello, Maddie.'

Tom felt relieved that his part was over, but then Maddie passed Polly to him and he held her inelegantly. He was sure it was uncomfortable for both of them.

Tom didn't like children, they frightened him.

Polly was wearing a loose dress and she wrapped her thin, naked legs around him and hugged his neck. Tom didn't know where to put his hands. He felt like he was molesting the girl in front of James and Lucy, and they just stood and smiled.

Tom had kept himself so completely cut off from any form of physical intimacy for so long that all contact now felt sexual. When strange women kissed him instead of shaking hands he blushed. To him the physical was erotic; he couldn't think in any other terms. And now this small girl was twined around him, her skirt pulled up, her knickers visible.

'Look at you,' Lucy laughed. 'You look like you're worried you might break her.'

Didn't she know? Didn't she realize?

Tom clumsily put the girl down and in so doing she seemed to forget all about him.

'Can I stay up for dinner, Mummy?'

'No. Five more minutes, then bed. I told you you could stay up to see your Uncle Tom and that was it.'

'Oh . . .'

They had no real chance to talk about anything while the child was around; she took up everybody's attention. Tom was relieved when James eventually took her up to bed and the rest of them could go out into the back garden for drinks.

The evening sun was low in the sky and it filtered through the trees, giving a soft, broken light. Lucy had brought out a bottle of wine and she poured them all a glass.

'I don't know what this is like,' she said. 'James got it.'

'It's fine,' Tom lied. It was rather too sweet and fruity for his tastes, but he took a couple of sips out of politeness.

'It's good to see you again, Tom,' Lucy said, shuffling her feet nervously. 'It's been too long.'

'Yes.' But that was all he could think of to say. Rather than give them a lot to talk about, the long separation seemed to have made them almost strangers and with Maddie there it made things that much more difficult. She was a spectator at the family reunion. But in the end it was Maddie who saved them. She started chatting to Lucy and they all finally relaxed.

After a while James came out with a second bottle of the wine. 'You all all right for drinks?' he asked, bouncing on to the patio with unnecessary vigour, and before Tom could say anything he refilled his glass.

James looked different to Tom; he'd always been a rather weedy, skinny little bloke before, but now he looked stocky and he walked with a sort of swagger, somewhere between John Wayne and a child with wet nappies. He had a thick neck and his shirt looked tight around the shoulders. The extra bulk didn't suit him. He was too small for it.

'What do you think of the garden?' James asked once he'd done the rounds with the bottle.

'Very nice,' Tom said without really looking.

'Don't suppose you remember what it was like before.'

'No . . .'

'It's a hell of a transformation, I'll tell you. Not that I can take any of the credit. Lucy does it all, really. She's got the proverbial green fingers.'

Tom politely followed James around as he pointed things out. It looked just like any other small town garden to him, but James was obviously proud of it, so Tom nodded and tried to make the appropriate sounds.

The whole of the back wall was covered with a lush green creeper with heart-shaped leaves and large, white, trumpet-shaped flowers.

'This is my favourite,' James said. 'Lucy's piece of resistance. I love these flowers, and the green of it. There was nothing here at all, before. She's grown this from nothing, and now look at it. Fantastic. I can never remember what it's called. What's it called again, Luce? This creeper.'

'*Calystegia sepium*.'

'*Calystegia sepium*. That's it. Never remember these Latin names. I just call it Lucy's vine . . . Right! Any nuts or anything out here, Luce? Any nibbles? I'm starving.'

'There's some stuff inside. I forgot to bring it out.' Lucy made a move to go in.

'That's all right, I'll go. You stay and talk to Tom.'

James smiled genially and put an arm round Maddie's shoulders. 'Now, Maddie, you must come and have a look at what we've done to the bathroom.'

The two of them went off indoors together, and Lucy came over to where Tom was standing looking at the creeper.

'It's bindweed, isn't it?' he said.

'Yes.'

'We used to get it at home, didn't we? Got everywhere. Drove Dad up the wall.'

'It's a terrible nuisance. Once it's established you can't get rid of it. You can dig it up, but any tiny bit left behind and it grows again. It just chokes everything out. I fought it for the first couple of years, I was a very dutiful gardener. Then I thought, sod it, at least it covers the wall. Trouble is, it's still spreading everywhere. If I turn my back on it for a minute it takes over the whole garden. It's evil stuff ... But James likes the flowers ...'

'Yes ... I remember Dad used to spend hours following the roots, he was obsessive about it. Hated it.'

'He hated all gardening, really, didn't he?' Lucy said distantly.

'He hated everything, I think, the miserable sod.'

'Yes.'

They both laughed and somehow they were together again. Alone out here with the bindweed, Tom felt like they were back home in the garden at Minehead, playing together, children. He smiled at his sister and she smiled back at him, and they knew they didn't need to say anything else. She just took hold of his hand and held it, and that was enough.

'Tom, you have to see the bathroom.' Tom quickly let go of Lucy and looked round to see Maddie and James coming back out. 'They've got mirrors everywhere, it's wild.'

'It was James's idea,' said Lucy.

'Makes the room look bigger,' James explained. 'Terribly poky it was before.'

And so they talked about bathrooms, and carpets, and the price of children's clothes, and schools, and traffic ... and absolutely nothing. And as they talked, clouds came up from nowhere and the sky grew darker and darker, until big black spots of rain began to form on the pale grey concrete and they were forced back indoors.

They stood around in the overly formal front room for a while, stiffly listening in reverent silence while James played selected tracks on his new CD player, and it was a great relief to everyone when Lucy finally announced that dinner was ready.

ELEVEN

By the dim orange glow of the child's night-light, Will began writing a new entry in his notebook ...

> *8:52 p.m. I had to change my plans. I think it is important and necessary to be flexible and to be able to adapt to changes. So it is not a problem that I had to change my plans.*
>
> *First of all Napoleon didn't leave the house at his normal time for a Thursday night. I was waiting across the road as usual, at the bus stop, and at seven-thirty he didn't come out. At the time I thought of cancelling the attempt and felt a bit disappointed, because I had prepared for this night for a long time and was in a very keyed-up and excited mood. As it turned out he was just late, he came out eleven minutes after his usual time. I thought about it and thought that this was not too much of a problem. Anything could have happened to delay him for a short time, the important thing was that he was going. But I still thought that it was best to wait and see for certain that he wasn't coming back. I waited for about fifteen minutes, and when he had still not returned I carried out the rest of my usual surveillance. The front of the house was quiet, and it looked like there was nobody in the house at the top of the side alley. Everything looked good.*
>
> *After this I had two hours to kill, and I didn't want to hang*

around, so I went for a walk. I went about the streets, checking out future homes. There are so many of them and in my excited state I felt like an Arab must feel in his harem. There are so many homes to go into, so many secrets to discover, so many people's rooms to have sex with. I can spend the rest of my life doing this. I am careful, if I stay careful I will not be caught. Only the careless make mistakes.

It was while I was walking around the city that I had to make my second change of plan. It began to rain so I had to quickly change my schedule. I couldn't go into the house wet, there would be too much danger of leaving evidence of my being there. And, anyway, I didn't want to get wet in the first place. And so, even though I was half an hour early, I decided that I had to go into the house there and then. I quickly returned to Dereham Road, staying as dry as I could by using any shelter along the route. I scouted the front and there was a light on in the front room, and I could hear music, which was good as it meant that the woman was in there and the back of the house would be quiet. I checked that Napoleon's car wasn't back and went round to the side.

I went down the side passage quickly as if I was going somewhere and came to their side wall. I know it's best not to risk waiting about so I jumped up and climbed over quickly. I carefully went and looked in through the kitchen window – the kitchen was empty, so I went in.

There was evidence in the kitchen of cooking, there was something in the oven and some pans on the top. The rest of the kitchen was a bit of a mess. I have no idea how the woman usually cooks, or how much Napoleon eats when he comes in, but I found this a bit surprising. But I didn't want to spend too much time downstairs then investigating, I wanted to get safely upstairs. I will look into the meal and stuff later.

There was still music coming from the front room, so, while the way was clear I went down the hall to the stairs and went up, *taking care on each step, but not being over careful as the noise of the music would drown out most sounds I made.*

The layout of the house is pretty much as I expected. There are many houses like this in the area with only small differences.

It was originally a quite largish terraced house, two up two down, with the stairs up one side. However there is an extension on the back with the kitchen and then at the back of that a bathroom, and upstairs there is an extra bedroom and a small shower room with a toilet.

The room at the front upstairs is a child's bedroom, with a smaller utility room next to it not much bigger than a cupboard. Then there is the main bedroom and the extra bedroom is for the second child.

Will carefully drew a map of the two floors, with all the rooms neatly labelled. Then he carried on writing.

I looked in the front bedroom. The older girl sleeps in it. She was sleeping in a little bed with her mouth open, all sprawled out, with the covers half thrown off. I couldn't investigate too closely as the sitting-room where the woman is is below. I shall wait until I hear her move to another room downstairs.

I am saving the main bedroom for last, in a few minutes I will be in there having sex. But for now I want to get my book up to date and get down all my feelings at the present moment.

I am sitting in the younger girl's bedroom. She is lying on her side on her bed looking at me and sucking her thumb. When I came in she was asleep, I woke her up looking around the room.

She has a light, she must be scared of the dark, something I never was as a child. There are posters on the walls, a mobile of circus things, clowns and horses, elephants etc. There is a frieze of alphabet figures and lots of neatly arranged toys, dolls and soft things.

When the girl woke up she looked surprised to see me. I smiled at her and put my finger to my lips to say shhh, and she settled down.

If she did say anything to her parents I doubt if they would believe her, and anyway children's descriptions are never very accurate. So I am safe. It is nice sitting here with someone to keep me company. And she stares at me, interested in what I am doing.

When I sat down to write she said 'What are you writing?' and I told her it was a secret. That seemed to satisfy her and she hasn't said anything else.

Having these children here adds a whole new level to this house entry. I feel more excited than ever before. This is a proper family.

My whole body is sort of tingling and I feel very alive. My ears pick up any sound, even the smells of the place are very powerful. The smells of the different rooms.

Now I am ready. I shall go into the main bedroom and finish this.

Will put the top back on his pen and put it in his pocket. Then he closed the book and stood up. As he did so the girl sat up.

'Where are you going?'

'I'm going away.'

'Will you read me a story out of your book?'

'No, it's late. You best go to sleep now.'

'I'm not tired.'

'Yes, you are, you're very tired. Now close your eyes.'

The girl did as she was told.

'Goodnight,' Will said.

'Goodnight, Uncle Tom.'

Will smiled, wondering who Uncle Tom might be, then gently pulled the door closed behind him, holding the handle down so that the catch wouldn't click. Then he moved along the landing to the main bedroom.

It was perfect. Not a man's room, not a woman's room, it was a couple's room. A man and wife. There was a poster of *Casablanca*, an untidy dressing-table with a clutter of woman's things, a pile of discarded male clothing and a wall of fitted cupboards. There was a hole in the door of one of them, as if something had smashed into it. He looked at the carpet; there were splinters of wood on it. The damage had obviously been done recently. He made a mental note to be sure to put it in his book, but he didn't want to stop and write it now. The time for writing was over. Now was the time for doing.

The bed was rumpled and untidy, as if it had been made in a hurry. He pulled back the covers, pushed his face into the bottom sheet and breathed in deeply through his nose. He could smell bodies. It had been used recently. A debilitating pulse of pleasure throbbed inside him and he shivered involuntarily. He had to do it quick now.

In a moment he was undressed. Naked but for his surgical gloves, he stretched out on the bed, imagining the bodies of the man and woman with him there on the sheet. He was inside them, they existed around him as phantoms and he possessed them. He writhed luxuriously like a cat, rubbing himself against their warmth.

And then he froze.

Downstairs the front-room door opened and he heard voices spill out. He listened hard. Yes, it was definitely voices. More than one. He could hear a man, two men, as well as the woman. Footsteps. He looked at the window; it was part open. He could be dressed and out of there in about ten seconds. It was a bit of a drop, but if necessary he would risk it.

He tensed, fixed his eyes on the door, ready to move if need be.

Ten seconds. Was that enough?

The voices and footsteps passed below and entered the room beneath, and he was safe for the moment.

It was all changed. It had gone wrong. The kitchen, the cooking stuff ... They were having a dinner party. How could they? Every Thursday was the same, how could this happen? He felt cold all of a sudden, vulnerable without his clothes. His erection, which a moment ago had been hard as iron, was now shrunk to nothing.

He carefully got off the bed and looked out of the window. Light from the room below spilled out into the backyard. Then the curtain was drawn. Well, that was a start, but now he had to get out.

He crept towards his clothes, but halfway there he stopped and his body flushed with warmth.

Why did he have to go?

This didn't change anything. This just made it better. While they were downstairs entertaining friends, he would be up here, fucking them. This was the best. This was further than he'd ever gone before.

He returned to the bed and grabbed his penis. Yes. He heard the voices, then more music came on and the voices became muffled and indistinct.

Yes. Here I am.

This was an orgy, husband, wife, two little girls and dinner guests. Yes.

He didn't care if they found him now, his sex had taken over, he was helpless. The energy of the whole city was here, focused in his balls. He felt the pressure building up, pulsating within him.

Yes.

He felt incredibly light, like he was slipping away from his body, and then it hit him.

As he came he gasped and his semen splashed over the wrinkled sheet.

TWELVE

Downstairs, on the portable tape machine in the dining-room, Pavarotti warbled away about love, or death, or whatever it was opera singers sang about, and Tom wished he would shut up. There sounded like there was something wrong with the tape machine, the speed kept slipping, giving a sort of sea-sick quality to the music, and Tom was starting to get another headache.

He wished James would hurry up carving the duck. The pause in the eating had caused everyone to stop talking. They all watched in reverent silence, as if at some religious ceremony, as James stuck the long two-pronged fork into the bird's crispy skin and clear juice poured out like water.

The first course, a cold spinach soup, had gone reasonably smoothly, the only dangerous moment had been when James had asked Tom how he and Maddie had met. Tom had lied about meeting her in a pub with some friends. Lucy and James didn't know about his therapy sessions. Nobody knew except the sad fucks who attended them. And that was how Tom intended it to stay.

'Well, Tom,' James had said with a little smile. 'I'd always thought you were a confirmed bachelor.'

'Me too. But Maddie's changed all that.'

'Is marriage on the cards, then?'

'It's a little early to say, I think. We're just enjoying ourselves at the moment.'

'Do you think we should get married, then, James?' Maddie had asked him.

'Ah, well, what you have to understand, you see, Maddie, is that us married men don't approve of single men. We think everyone should be married like us.'

'You're jealous?'

'Jealous? No. Far from it. Superior. Having a family, it's like being in the best club in the world. And till you try it, you can have no idea what it's like.'

'I thought all married men had affairs,' Maddie had said pointedly.

'Not all of them,' James had said and he'd squeezed Lucy's hand and given her a most sickly smile.

Tom had remembered his handshake, James's small hand exerting all that pressure. And the smell of him in the hallway, some sort of musky scent. He'd felt slightly queasy. The queasiness had remained with him, and what with Pavarotti, James pawing Lucy, the sweet German wine and now the duck oozing fat, he was developing a real killer of a headache.

Once the food was served, however, and they could begin to eat again, things loosened up, and soon the four of them were making quite a din as they held various fragmented conversations around the table.

At first, by concentrating on his food and trying not to say too much, Tom hoped he could get through to the end of the evening without disaster. But it wasn't to be. He didn't normally drink much, and the wine – James insisted on topping him up after almost every sip – soon got to him. He found he was losing concentration, speaking a little too loudly, losing control.

He made his first mistake when James served himself a second helping of the duck.

He foolishly attempted to make a joke.

'You want to watch yourself, James,' he said, gesturing with a fork. 'You're putting on weight.'

'What do you mean by that?' James asked, a little sharply.

'I just mean you look, I don't know, bigger.'

'You're saying I'm fat?'

'No, no, as I say, you just look ... bigger.'

'That's muscle, Tom.'

'Ah.'

'And as a matter of fact, muscle does weigh more than fat. So, you were right, I have put on weight. But not in the way you implied.'

'I didn't mean to imply anything, it was a joke.'

'Training does this. I've really worked at it.'

'Yes, I can see.'

'See these hands?' James said to Maddie, holding them out for inspection. 'Registered lethal weapons.'

Tom laughed, then James looked at him, and Tom realized it hadn't been a joke.

'James does karate,' Lucy said flatly.

'No?'

'It's a damn good sport, Tom.'

'Is it like judo, what they say, the little squirt can overthrow the big hulk?' Tom said it without thinking. 'I don't mean little, I mean—'

'It's like any other sport Tom, whoever's best wins.'

'Right,' Tom nodded seriously.

'You do any kind of sport, any kind of physical activity?'

'Not really, not as such ...'

'You know what they say, James?' Maddie interrupted. 'A good fuck's as good as a five-mile run.'

Tom looked at Lucy and blushed. Lucy looked down at the tablecloth. James laughed.

'They do say that, don't they? Ha. I'd like to be the scientist testing that one out in the lab.'

'I thought you married men didn't go in for extramarital sex?'

'No I meant watching ... No, I mean. Anyway, I meant with Lucy.'

104

Tom suddenly had a horrific image of James in bed with Lucy, wired up to scanners, checking a stop-watch. 'Only another two miles to go!' And he felt an acid twinge in his stomach.

'Perhaps sex isn't the best topic of conversation for the dinner table,' he said, hoping it came out lightly.

'What else is there?' Maddie asked and James sniggered. 'Here, here.'

'After all,' Maddie said. 'Adultery is the hobby of the middle classes.'

'Ah, now, we've already been over that,' said James raising a finger. 'There's no adulterers here.' Maddie looked at Tom and raised an eyebrow. James went on. 'I'm happily married to Wendy.'

'Who's Wendy?' Maddie asked.

'I meant Lucy.'

'So who's Wendy?'

'No one. I don't know why I said that.'

'Ah,' said Maddie. 'James's mystery woman.'

'Not our James,' Tom said. 'James is far too well-behaved for that. What did Dad used to call him, Lucy?'

'I don't remember.'

'St James. That was it. St James, the original non-sinner.'

'Yes, well, we all know that your old man was a bit of a twit, don't we, Tom?'

'Really, James,' Maddie laughed. 'He doesn't like people to talk about his father like that.'

'No, it's all right,' Tom said. 'I mean, he obviously had his faults.'

'To put it mildly,' James said, half-winking at Maddie.

'Look, James, I see no reason . . .' But James was laughing now.

'What is it?' Tom said.

'When you went all serious like that. You looked just like him. I had an awful flashback to all those ghastly family dinners, with him playing the stern patriarch at the head of the table. You want to watch it, Tom, you could turn into him.'

'Come on, you two,' said Lucy. 'Be nice to each other.'

'*Nice?*' said James sarcastically. 'We are being *nice* to each other.'

'You're like two roosters with their feathers all ruffled.'

'Well, I don't agree. I'm having a perfectly *nice* time. Are you having a *nice* time, Tom?'

'Yes,' Tom said quietly.

'There we are then, we're all having a nice time. More wine, Tom?'

'No, no thanks.' But James poured it anyway.

'Please, James,' Lucy said. 'I haven't seen Tom for ages. I just wanted tonight to be nice ...'

'Nice, nice, bloody nice! Why does everything have to be nice all the time? I mean, for fuck's sake, darling, we're adults, aren't we?'

'Come on, James,' Tom said, seeing the look on Lucy's face that usually preceded tears. 'There's no need to talk to Lucy like that.'

'That's right, Tom, you don't see us for two years and then you come round and tell us how to run our lives.'

Pain pulsed between Tom's eyes and he pressed two fingers to the spot. Why had he let himself get wound up and drawn into this stupid conversation? He stared at the piece of fatty duck congealing on his plate and wished he was somewhere else. Anywhere else.

Why didn't somebody say something? Change the subject. They surely couldn't expect him to? He couldn't speak. His throat was constricted, his mouth dry. If he tried to say anything it would come out wrong.

In the background Pavarotti's pure, light voice carried on trilling, oblivious. Tom tried to clear his mind. He remembered the moment of still happiness in the back garden with Lucy, standing by the bindweed. He remembered the big, white flowers ...

His headache was getting worse.

At last Lucy spoke. 'So Maddie,' Tom heard her say. 'How do you like Norwich?'

'I haven't really seen that much of it yet.'

'It's very *nice*,' said James. And Tom exploded.

'Oh, for God's sake, James!'

'What?' James turned to him with an expression of mock innocence. 'What?'

'Nothing. I'm sorry.'

'No, what is it, Tom? Share it with us . . .'

The tape ended and the silence was impossible. They heard the floorboards creak overhead, as if the very house itself was shuffling with embarrassment.

Tom saw the bindweed again, strangling everything in the garden, saw its evil white flowers.

'Do you have a problem, Tom?'

Please, James, don't push me. Leave it. Leave me be. Please.

He felt the roots inside him, worming their way up through his body, long and pale in the darkness. Digging into the lining of his stomach, squeezing the air out of his lungs, putting out groping, wiry tendrils which snaked round his throat and reached up into his brain. He was tied to the chair by them, fixed to the floor, held rigid, unable to move a single muscle as they tightened.

'Share it with us . . .'

And then the flowers began to open.

The huge white flowers began to open in the back of his mind like exploding flares. His whole head was being filled up with whiteness. He had to do something, he had to break the hold. He had to break the tension.

'Go fuck yourself, James,' he said at last, his voice sounding horribly loud in the small room.

THIRTEEN

For a long while Will had lain on the bed, utterly exhausted, floating in a kind of limbo land of disembodied senses. A world of colour and light and pleasure, a world without form. But it couldn't last; reality had slowly fought its way back, the music downstairs had stopped and now he realized he had to get out of there.

He rolled over on the sheet and wiped himself dry. Then he got up and, moving as stealthily as possible, slipped back into his clothes.

Tracksuit trousers, sweatshirt, trainers.

Ten seconds.

Then he picked up his notebook and went to the head of the stairs.

There was silence from the dining-room. But he had to push on. He'd already stayed far too long.

He started downstairs, trying not to race, not to forget all his caution and training, all his rules. But his heart was ahead of him, trying to get out and run.

He got down safely and crept along the hall. What were they doing? Why weren't they talking? He came to the dining-room door, he was only a couple of feet away from them. Despite himself, he felt another erection growing. But he forced himself on into the kitchen.

Once in the kitchen he looked out of the window at the drawn curtains of the dining-room. He slowly let out his breath; he must have been holding it since he left the bedroom.

He was safe.

The back door was there and then the night and home.

Then he stopped. He hadn't taken anything. In the excitement he'd forgotten to pick up an exhibit for his museum. He cursed, he knew he should go, but it would all have been wasted if he had nothing physical to remember it by. He glanced around the kitchen. There was nothing, just clutter.

Bollocks. Did he have time?

'What?' James said, looking at Tom. 'What did you say?'

'I'm sorry ...' Tom was still looking down at the table, his face flushed and red, as if he was drunk. He probably was. James certainly was; wine wasn't his usual drink and it always made him light-headed. But there was really no excuse for Tom's behaviour.

All right, perhaps he'd gone a little too far in teasing Lucy. But he still couldn't quite believe that Tom had told him to go fuck himself. It was extraordinary. He wondered if perhaps he'd misheard, but the reaction of the others assured him he hadn't.

'It's not good enough,' he said, his voice sounding whiningly thin and strained; he tried to control it but he was too emotional. 'Jesus, I'm not going to sit here and be talked to like that in my own house.'

'I'm sorry. It just came out. I didn't mean it.'

'But you said it.' James wished he didn't sound so pompous. He looked at Lucy; this was all her fault really, the whole horrible evening, he should have been with Wendy. 'Your family,' he said to her. 'Your family.'

He couldn't stay in the room with these people any longer. He wanted to make a point, show his contempt for the whole sorry affair.

He got up from the table and picked up the tray with the duck on it. The carcass lay forlornly in its dish, the fork sticking out of its tattered chest.

'Well, what a bloody good fun evening this has been,' he said.

'Leave that,' Lucy said anxiously. 'Don't do that now, we haven't finished.'

'I have,' he said, and he left the room, slamming the door with his foot.

Outside, he hesitated for a moment. Was he overreacting? Would they all think him a fool? Would they talk about him behind his back?

Well, sod them. Let them talk. They could do what they liked as far as he was concerned. He'd had enough.

He went towards the kitchen.

Will was disoriented; the bathroom walls were covered in mirrors. It was like a nightmare room, everywhere he looked he saw his own startled face. He had a terrible panic that it was a trap, that he would never be able to find his way out again. But then he told himself to calm down.

He was careful. He was successful. He had nothing to fear, it was just a bathroom, a badly decorated bathroom. There was bound to be something in here he could take, a child's toy, a monogrammed towel, a favourite old flannel ...

He got his bearings and went over to the sink. There was a mug of toothbrushes on a narrow glass shelf. There were four of them; one relatively new-looking, one old with the bristles splayed and flattened, and two small, brightly coloured ones with Mickey Mouse and Donald Duck moulded on the ends of the handles. He grabbed all four of them and crammed them in his pocket, then he hurried out.

Napoleon was in the kitchen.

He was standing there holding a food dish. He looked at Will, amazed.

A burst of adrenalin fired Will and he darted for the door. But Napoleon moved with uncanny speed and cut him off.

'What the fuck do you think you're doing? What is this?'

Will said nothing. He licked his lips and fixed his eyes on Napoleon.

'Fucking burglar, are you? Are you? Eh?'

Will tried to move but felt his head ring and his jaw jar. Napoleon was leaning back on one leg, with the other up in the air like something out of a kung fu film. Will realized he'd been kicked in the chin. Luckily the blow, though accurate and beautifully executed, lacked any real power. Will was shocked but still upright.

Napoleon still held the dish and was watching Will with visible excitement.

'Well, come on, then, eh? Come on, then.' He kicked Will again, and this time he was knocked back into the table. Napoleon took the opportunity to put the dish down and adopt another fighting stance, forearms up, legs bent.

Will was truly frightened now; there was something manic and crazy about the little man. Although his attacks were more elegant than dangerous, it was only a matter of time before he'd be beaten down with no hope of escape.

He realized he would have to fight back.

Napoleon did a little dance and spin, but Will saw it coming and ducked to one side. He grabbed for the first thing he could on the table and found the food dish. Napoleon spun back and this time connected. In the flurry and confusion Will felt cold, moist flesh and sticky fat, then his fingers closed on something hard.

Napoleon came in close and jabbed Will in the side. Will gasped and furiously whirled at him with the weapon in his hand. Napoleon grunted and fell away.

Out of the corner of his eye as he raced for the door Will saw the little man slump against the cooker, dazed. But he didn't wait to see what had happened, he was out of the house and running.

He sailed over the wall and landed awkwardly, bruising his knees, but he hardly noticed, just got up and set off again.

He ran and ran for as long as he could until his lungs were on fire and his legs turned to jelly. Then he stopped, took control of himself and slowed to a walk. He was well away from Dereham Road now, and the mad little man. He was up near the university on the edge of town.

He'd come out. He'd got away. He was free. He allowed himself a smile and headed for home.

He checked his pocket; the toothbrushes were still there.

Yes, he'd done it. His smile widened. There was a tremendous feeling of life surging through his body.

He raised his arms in a gesture of triumph, with clenched fists, and then with a terrible, sickening shock he realized that he didn't have his notebook with him.

FOURTEEN

James sat on the floor, unable to move. He was rigid with fear. He stared at his hands at his sides, the fingers curled into claws, and saw that he was holding an exercise book. It was the sort kids used at school. It was bright blue with a photograph of somebody skiing on the front. It was held tightly in his right hand, distorted by the force of his grip. He must have taken it off the burglar. It was stupid: what was he doing here on the floor, holding a child's exercise book? As he stared at it, it started to vibrate. It was a fast, almost imperceptible trembling, and he watched it spread from the book into his fingers, into his hands, up his arms and into the rest of his body. He was completely taken over by it. Spasmodic waves surged through his flesh, causing him to shake and twitch uncontrollably.

He felt moisture pour down his face and drip off his nose and chin. At first he thought it was blood, then he saw that it was only sweat. He was oozing sweat and he was freezing.

It wasn't fair.

None of this was fair. The world had gone crazy. Everything was fucked up. How could you sweat and be cold at the same time?

Crazy.

And how could he have lost the fight? He'd trained, he was prepared, and yet he'd lost. Well, the burglar had cheated.

It wasn't fair.

He'd used a weapon. He remembered now, he ran through it in his mind. He'd kicked the burglar twice, two perfect attacks. The burglar had dodged his third blow and gone down against the table. Then, as he'd spun in for his final attack, the burglar had come at him with something in his hand. Something in each hand. He'd gone for the most obvious weapon, the one that was easiest to see, the leading hand ... And it must have been the book, the stupid, bloody kid's book. He'd gone for the wrong hand and the burglar had got him with the other ...

He'd cheated and now the thing was sticking out of the side of his neck. He could see the dark handle and a slight glint off the metal. It was there, embedded in him, and he couldn't move, couldn't force himself to put his fingers to it and touch it. He couldn't do anything, he was too scared. He felt that if he shifted his position, even slightly, he would fall apart.

It wasn't fair. He was St James, the man who'd never done anything wrong in his life.

The man who'd never done anything.

He was numb. He felt his senses receding and he knew that he was going into shock.

There was a ball of sticky saliva in his mouth but he couldn't swallow, because the two thin tines of the carving fork were in his throat. He could feel the points of them poking through his windpipe, and he could taste the blood which was slowly trickling down into his stomach. It wasn't right; the fork wasn't meant to be there, it wasn't part of him.

Oh God ... Oh God ... The vibration was getting worse, like there was another body inside his own wrestling to get out. But he had to hold still, he had to hold things together.

This wasn't happening, it couldn't be. He couldn't be lying on his own kitchen floor with his own carving fork stuck into the side of his neck. No. If he could only go back to sleep, then he could wake up all right.

Please God, please dear God, don't let this be for real. Don't let this be fucking happening.

He was all alone. He could hear music from the other room and voices. They would just leave him here, leave him here to die. They don't care, they wouldn't find him. He'd die, here on the floor, and they'd do nothing. Nothing.

And yet he couldn't call out, he couldn't, not with the thing in his throat. And he couldn't move, couldn't crawl to where they were. Because that was the important thing. Not to move. Hold still and it'll all be all right.

Oh God.

Tears mixed with the sweat now. His eyes were burning.

Please come to me, please, Lucy. Please come and make it better. Just hold me. Hold me now and everything will be all right. That's all I want, to feel your arms around me . . .

Shit. He couldn't die now, not without seeing her again. He didn't want their last memory to be of an argument.

Please, Lucy, come and find me. Come and make me better.

Yes. That was it. Make him better.

An ambulance. Somebody had to call an ambulance. If he could only hold on until the ambulance men arrived, with their strong capable hands . . . They'd know what to do.

He looked up at the kitchen phone where it hung on the wall. It was red. It was a long way away.

He mustn't die.

Right, come on, you fucker, save yourself. Less of the self-pity. You're a man, remember? You can do it. Yes. Yes . . .

He forced his eyes round, to look down at the fork handle. He could see his shoulder now. To his relief there was no blood. Good. Good. He was going to be okay. As long as the fork stayed in, he was safe. It was plugging the wound. Good start.

Without thinking he swallowed, and the tines dug into him. He couldn't scream, but he hissed as spinning bolts of pain shot out from his neck and rattled around inside his head. He closed his eyes, squeezing out more tears, and nearly blacked out.

Not that; he didn't want to drift away now. What if he never woke again? What if the last thing he knew was sitting here on the kitchen floor, looking at the dirt under the cupboards where Lucy never cleaned?

Oh God, oh please, Lucy. Please, come. I'll never again worry about dirt under the cupboards. It's not important. I understand now what life is for; life is for living, not hoovering. Life is for being happy. I'll make you happy, I will, I'll really try . . . If you just don't let me fucking die!

His vision became blurred; objects started to swim in front of him. He blinked and it held for a moment, but then it slipped. The picture was breaking up into thousands of dots of coloured light, like a badly tuned TV set.

His body was shutting down.

Fight it. Fight it.

He'd only ever fainted once before. It was at his wedding. It had been a scorchingly hot day, and in his heavy morning suit he'd been terribly uncomfortable. He'd got drunk the night before and hadn't been able to eat anything that morning. He'd got through the service all right, though the church had been almost unbearably stuffy. Then, as he'd stepped out with Lucy into the bright sun, everything had gone yellow and the next thing he'd known he was lying on the ground looking up at a ring of faces, some laughing, some concerned. Lucy's father had given him a look of utter contempt, and then Lucy had knelt down and smiled at him and everything was . . .

Lucy.

It seemed so vivid now. But this time he was fainting in slow motion, by degrees, a little at a time . . .

Those had been the happiest times, before the children.

Oh God, the girls. He wanted to see them now, have them

116

around him, have the family together. That was what was important. He didn't care what Tom thought, Tom could go to hell. He didn't want to be part of Tom's family, he had his own family. Him and Lucy and the girls, their own family. The Mullens. The Mullens of Dereham Road.

How long had he been here now? It was hours. What were they doing? Maybe they knew. Maybe they were just sitting out there, waiting for him to die. Maybe the burglar had been put there by them, to get rid of him. Tom hated him, after all.

But not Lucy. Despite everything he knew she still loved him. He was glad he hadn't spoiled it all by going out tonight and seeing Wendy . . . And yet, if he had gone out he wouldn't be lying here now with a fucking carving fork in his neck.

For fuck's sake, somebody come and rescue me!

Please.

God.

And then he heard the dining-room door open, and footsteps, and he knew that everything was going to be all right. It was Lucy. She was coming for him.

FIFTEEN

Tom was still consumed by embarrassment. He wanted to weep. Why had he done it? Why had he opened his stupid mouth?

In the horrible silence that had followed James leaving the room Maddie had got up and turned the tape over. Thank God for Maddie, always practical, always knowing what to do.

Over the singing they'd heard James angrily clattering about in the kitchen.

Maddie'd said maybe they'd better leave, but Lucy'd said no, everything would be all right, James just needed to calm down.

Tom hadn't been able to leave it at that. 'God, I'm sorry, Lucy,' he'd said. 'I didn't mean—'

'It's okay, Tom.'

'I'd better go and apologize.' He'd stood. He'd be grown-up. He'd do things properly. But then Lucy had stood up as well.

'It's all right,' she'd said. 'It's not your fault. James has been on edge all evening. I'll go.'

'No, Lucy. I really think I ought to say something. This is all my fault.'

'But I know what to say to him, Tom. I know how to bring him out of one of these moods.'

'No, I feel responsible. I wouldn't be able to look him in the eye again.'

'Please, Tom, I know him. Just leave him. He'll be all right.'

Tom had waited. Pavarotti had reached a climax, then fallen silent. There was no sound from the kitchen.

But they'd expected it of him; the two women sitting there, looking slightly shell-shocked. So he'd made up his mind and gone to the door.

Lucy had just looked at him.

'I'll sort this out,' he'd said.

'No.'

But he knew he'd done the right thing and now, as he made his way to the kitchen, he tried to work out what to say to James. 'Sorry' seemed a bit inadequate. Maybe he could just punch him on the shoulder, man to man, no hard feelings, eh, old chap? Maybe make a joke of it . . .

Then he opened the kitchen door and that was when everything really started to go wrong.

James was lying on the floor, half-propped up against the oven. He was curled into a semi-foetal position, his arms pressed into his sides, his knees bent. He stared at Tom with a weird, frightened expression on his face. His eyes wide and very bright, his face slick with sweat, his hair dampened against his forehead.

He was holding a notebook in one hand and the carving fork from dinner was sticking out of his neck.

His whole body was trembling and every now and then a part of him would jerk.

For a moment Tom stood and just gaped stupidly. He was trying to take in the scene, but it didn't make any sense, he wasn't prepared for it.

He looked again at the fork. There were two small drops of blood around each prong as it went into the neck.

'Jesus Christ, James . . . What . . . ?'

James just looked at him. The sad, pleading look on his face got worse.

'Jesus, I mean . . . Jesus . . .'

Tom knew he had to do something. But what? It wasn't a position he'd ever been in before. He knelt down and his hands hovered over James's body, not knowing where to go.

He looked at the fork and looked at the book. James was holding it up, as if he was offering it to him. Tom took it. He opened it, it was full of neat writing and diagrams. He flicked through the pages, then he realized he was being a fool, he was acting like a startled little kid.

He braced himself and tugged the fork from James's neck.

It was like unplugging a wine barrel. Two thin jets of blood squirted from the wounds. The blood didn't pump or sputter, but came out in a long steady stream. James gasped and went very white. He looked at Tom with the most hopeless expression Tom had ever seen and one hand went feebly up to try and cover the holes.

The gush lasted a couple of seconds then settled down into a lightly pulsing trickle, but in that short time the floor had become covered in blood.

Tom quickly grabbed a tea towel, pressed it to the side of James's neck then pulled it round and knotted it.

He stood up.

James slumped over to one side and lay very still.

'Lucy! Maddie!' Tom yelled and he heard running footsteps.

'What is it?' Lucy hurried in, followed by Maddie. 'Oh my God. Oh my God. What's happened? What's happened?'

'I don't know. It doesn't make any sense.'

Lucy dropped to the bloody floor and hugged James, holding him to her chest. 'James, darling, James, James . . .'

Tom looked round for Maddie and saw that she was already at the phone, dialling. And all he could do was stand there. Useless.

The rest of the evening was a blur.

The ambulance came and the police. The house and the street outside were filled with a swarm of people. It was all bustle and noise. Questions were asked, photographs taken. They drank a lot of whisky. None of it seemed real.

At last they left the house. They took Lucy and the girls to the hotel and checked them into a room. Room service brought more whisky up and finally, three hours after finding James on the floor, Tom stood in the dreary little bathroom and looked at himself in the mirror, garishly lit by the neon light above.

He looked at his bloodstained jacket and shirt. He looked at his tired, sagging face and felt nothing. He was washed out, blank.

'What happened?' he said to his reflection. 'What the fuck happened tonight?'

But the reflection didn't answer.

Next door the ancient bed creaked and groaned as Maddie got into it.

Tom wearily took his jacket off and threw it on to the floor. As he did so something fell out of the inside pocket. It was the blue notebook. In the confusion and the panic he'd forgotten all about it; he must have just put it into his pocket without thinking.

He knew he had to tell the police about it. He knew he had to go and phone them immediately, it might be important.

But what was it?

He opened it and looked once more at the neat handwriting. For a while he couldn't focus, couldn't see what it was. Then his eyes fell on four words written in capitals repeatedly down one page.

I AM HAPPY NOW

He turned back to the first page, sat down on the side of the bath and began to read.

PART TWO

SIXTEEN

Maddie watched as a big white carp loomed up from the depths of the hotel pond and snatched a struggling insect from the surface of the water. Then it slowly sank down into the darkness like a disappearing ghost.

It was a warm day but she felt cold. She pulled her suede jacket tighter about her body.

'Are you sure you want to stay?' she asked.

Tom just grunted.

'But what can you do here?'

'I can look after Lucy and the girls. I can ...' Tom drifted into silence.

'Come back to London with me, Tom.'

'No, Maddie, not now. I can't ... I feel responsible.'

'You can't blame yourself.'

'If I hadn't pulled the fork out—'

But Maddie interrupted him before he could say anything more. 'You don't know what would have happened, nobody does. They don't know if they could have saved him or not. He was in deep shock. His whole artery was ruptured.'

'But he'd have had a chance. The poor bastard. I can't stop seeing his face, when I did it ... He looked so—'

'Don't talk about it.'

'I'm sorry.'

Maddie turned and looked at him. He was standing staring into the distance. His face showed no expression, but she knew that inside he was fighting something. If only he was able to let it out sometimes. He kept it in, and kept it in, and then it erupted in some unexpected manner. She felt terribly sorry for him. James's death was the last thing he needed right now.

He had so much going for him. He had a successful business, he was well-off, intelligent, in very good shape compared to most businessmen of his age, and he was terribly handsome; not that he knew it. He had no concept of himself as a person, his mind was so preoccupied with other things. It wasn't fair; he had all that and should be happy, but didn't know how. Instead he was desperately unhappy all the time. But if asked he'd probably have no concept of that either, except, perhaps, now. But then they were all unhappy now.

Last night still seemed like a nightmare. She still expected to see James come strolling out on to the lawn asking everyone why the long faces?

If things weren't quite so tragic, she might have laughed at her situation. She'd not been at all sure about coming to Norwich, for various reasons; being with Tom, the boring conference, leaving Peter to his own devices... And now this had happened, something totally unexpected, something that couldn't possibly have been on her list of doubts. Well, life was like that, wasn't it? You thought that everything would go on as normal from day to day. You made plans, you dreamt about the future, and then were hit by a car, or got cancer, or went blind or something. Just like that. It only took a second to change your life completely.

It was like thinking you were happily married and then coming home and finding your husband in bed with one of his students.

Terrific.

Thank you, God. You must really like me. What's next? A plague of boils?

Thinking of which, she thought she might have thrush. She was itching when she woke up this morning. She'd got it before, when she'd first slept with Tom; they must have incompatible yeast, or something.

Big problems, small problems, somehow they were all the same. James was dead and she was pissed off about having thrush.

'I'm sorry, Maddie,' Tom said out of the blue.

'What?'

'It wasn't much of a dirty weekend, was it?'

'Don't be silly. That's the last thing you need worry about.'

'I don't know, everything's just—'

Maddie put her arms round him and hugged him. He felt stiff and unyielding, like he was made of wood. He kept his arms at his sides and made no attempt to hug her back. But she persevered.

'Try not to think about it. You mustn't brood.'

'Yes,' he said flatly.

She hugged him tighter and he softened. She felt him stroke her hair.

'Have you talked to the conference people?' he asked.

'Yes. I rang them earlier. "I'm very sorry, but I've got family problems and have to return to London."'

'Family problems,' Tom said bitterly. 'My family.'

'It was just an excuse, Tom. You don't have to read anything into it. I could hardly tell them that I was up here with my lover and his brother-in-law was murdered, could I?'

'No, I suppose not.'

'I didn't really want to go to the conference, anyway.'

'God, what a disaster. I should never have come.'

'Stop blaming yourself, Tom. You tried to save his life. Can't you leave it at that?'

'No. Because I killed him.'

'You didn't. Whoever stuck the fork in his neck killed him. Not you. Not you!'

'You say that, but—'

'I say that because it's the truth,' Maddie shouted angrily. 'What is the point? What is the fucking point of making yourself miserable like this? What good does it do?'

'I'm not doing it on purpose,' Tom said petulantly.

'Aren't you? You sound to me like you are. You sound to me like you almost want to have bloody killed him.'

'What? How can you say that? What do you mean?'

They were glaring at each other now. One of them had to back down. The trouble was, Maddie liked a fight and she knew Tom didn't. But at the same time he wouldn't apologize, that was his problem. He didn't know how to diffuse these situations; he didn't realize that if he just let things go they wouldn't be a problem. She knew. She knew how to make things better, but she didn't want to. To her a fight was pure pleasure, pure release. But this was stupid, there was nothing to fight about. They were just on edge. She didn't want it to be like this. One of the reasons she was attracted to Tom was that he was different to Peter. She didn't have to fight and argue with him the whole time, because there was nothing to fight about, and because they both knew it would lead to disaster. Being together was an escape for both of them. Nothing important. Nothing serious. But fuck it, that's how all relationships began, didn't they? It couldn't last; sooner or later all the old problems and tensions would creep into it. This trip to Norwich had just accelerated the process.

'Come on,' Tom said. 'What did you bloody mean by that?'

'Oh, shut up. Leave it, okay?'

Peter never fought back. Peter would remain passive, as if it would let him off the hook if he didn't respond to her accusations. And that just made her worse, drove her into a fury, a fury that usually ended in violence. She would hit him, bite him, pull his hair out, anything to get a response. And his response would always be the same: sarcasm. He would belittle her, mock her emotions.

That was why she'd started going to the meetings. Because if she could control her anger she wouldn't get in the fights and she wouldn't give Peter ammunition. Wouldn't give him a chance to feel superior, when he should have been squirming and apologizing. Tom's withdrawal wasn't the same as Peter's; it wasn't tactical, it wasn't a form of aggression, it was based on fear.

So who was going to back down?

Tom looked like a little boy. He reminded her of girls she'd known at school; the quiet, weird ones. The ugly ones. The fat ones with glasses who kept to little groups and only talked to each other. The ones everyone took the piss out of until one day they'd be pushed just a little too far and they'd explode; they'd become madwomen, screaming harpies. They'd be turned from shy inadequates into flailing, spitting, scratching demons and would batter into the ground whichever bully was unfortunate enough to have been the one who went too far.

A little boy.

Then she realized. That's what he was. A serious little boy. A boy surrounded by adults, acting grown up, acting the man. He didn't know the first thing, really, did he? He certainly didn't understand her, never could. He'd lived alone too long. And as she looked at him in this new light, all her desire for him disappeared.

Poor Tom.

She smiled at him. 'You should see yourself.'

'What?'

'All flustered and uppity.'

'Maddie, I—'

'Come on, Tom, let's not fight. I'm sorry.'

'You're right,' he said. 'I guess I'm sorry, too. I've got to get on the end of this.'

'You sure it's going to help? Staying here in Norwich?'

'Yes, I think so. I can help Lucy, maybe help the police. I don't know . . .'

'Help the police with their inquiries.'

'You know what I mean.'

'Yes, I was just joking.'

'Mm.'

'It's funny,' she said. 'When I was younger and they said on the news that somebody was helping the police with their inquiries, I always used to think it was very nice of them, very public-spirited, to help the police like that.'

'Maddie, do you have to go?'

'Yes.'

'I love you, Maddie. I need you, you hold me together.'

'You've got on perfectly well without me for thirty-five years, lover.'

'I don't know how.'

'If you need me so much, then come back to London.'

'You'll be with Peter.'

'Tom, I can't stay here. Not after what happened. I'm completely freaked out. I've got to get away and get my head together. And I really think you need to do the same.'

'I've got responsibilities.'

'You're not responsible.'

'I didn't say that. I said I've got responsibilities. To Lucy. I can't just abandon her.'

'She must have friends.'

'But I'm family. Family's different.'

'All right. Stalemate. I go, you stay. But you will drive me to the station, won't you?'

'Sure.'

'I'll go and get ready.'

As they drove into Norwich, Maddie looked out of the window at the town she would now probably never get to know. It had all seemed strange and new to her yesterday and she'd looked forward to exploring it, finding her way around. But now she knew she never would. She was leaving as she'd come, a stranger.

You can't escape, she thought, you can try but you'll be brought back. In a couple of hours she'd be back with Peter and it would be like she'd never been anywhere. The events in Norwich never would be real for her. The only reality was her dead marriage, her sterile, tasteful little maisonette in Camberwell. Even if she left Peter, what would change? She'd still be the same, trying so hard to make everything work and always ending up back in the shit. It wouldn't be any different with Tom; you can change your partner but you can't change yourself. It was probably over between them already. You'd have to have a pretty strong relationship to go through something like this and come out on top.

And neither of them were strong. They were both fucked up. Everything was fucked up.

'You realize you'll have to keep in touch with the police,' Tom said matter-of-factly.

'What do you mean?'

'Well, you're a witness. If it comes to court you may have to appear.'

'Oh, brilliant. How can I explain that one to Peter?'

'He'll have to find out sooner or later.'

'About us?'

'About James.'

'Well, let's hope it's later rather than sooner.'

'Maddie, why do you put yourself through this? Why don't you just leave him?'

'That's why I was coming to Norwich, to think things over.'

'But—'

'I guess in a funny way I still love him. That's the whole problem. Even after all he's put me through.'

'But if he treats you so badly, why can't you tell him what you've done?'

'Because it would give him too much satisfaction. It would give him an excuse for everything he's done.'

'That's crazy thinking. It doesn't make sense.'

'Oh yes it does, it makes perfect sense.'

'Not to me it doesn't.'

'That's because you haven't been married, darling. You haven't even been in a relationship. Relationships have a twisted logic all of their own. They're based on pain, they're based on lies and deceit and double-thinking. And, yes, probably they don't make any sense to people standing on the outside. But when you're in there and fighting, then it makes perfect sense. Everything you do has a perfect reason. You can follow a clear, simple path of thought, you can follow it and reason it, and say, I'm doing this because of this, this and this, it's the only possible thing I can do, and at the same time it's always a mistake, whatever you do. That's relationships, lover. That's marriage and, let me tell you, you're better off without them.'

'So why don't you ditch yours and get out?'

'Because it's the best thing that's ever happened to me.'

SEVENTEEN

As the waiter laboriously poured the wine, Lucy had the overwhelming impression that everyone in the hotel dining-room was looking at her. But she couldn't turn her eyes away from the slowly filling glass to see whether she was just imagining it. Besides, she knew perfectly well that if she did try to catch them at it, they'd all look away just in time and pretend they were engrossed in their conversations.

How long did it take to pour a glass of wine? And now he was going to fill Tom's. This was deliberate torture. She knew that even the waiter was looking at her. She felt like raising her head, staring them all down and shouting, 'What are you looking at?' But they had every right to look, really. She'd do the same in their circumstances. She was a curiosity. A freak.

'Thank you,' Tom said to the waiter, who wiped the neck of the bottle and put it on the table.

There had been reporters in the lobby this afternoon. The manager, Paul, or Pete, or something, had sorted them out, but she could tell that he would rather she wasn't staying here. She probably wasn't the sort of publicity he wanted for the place.

At last the waiter went away and Lucy could speak.

'I can't stay here, Tom.'

'I know. It's only till you're sorted.'

'I need to hide for a while.'

'Yes. I know. How's the wine?' Lucy was surprised, she hadn't been aware that she'd taken a sip.

'Fine ...' She put her glass down. 'To tell you the truth I can't really taste it. I can't taste anything. I eat, I know I'm eating, but afterwards I can't remember it.'

'You're holding up okay.'

'I'm numb. I guess it'll take a while to really sink in ... I'm on autopilot at the moment. But the thing is ... I don't want it to sink in. Oh, Tom, where can I go?'

'We'll think of somewhere.'

Reliable Tom. He'd always been good at giving her advice, helping her. Of course that had all changed when she'd met James.

'Oh.' She put her spoon down, a tear dropped into her soup.

'What is it?'

'I can't stop thinking about him.'

'You don't have to stop.'

'But I think about him as if he was still alive. As if he was still here. I think, "James will say this, James will think this ..." And he won't, will he? He won't ever say anything ever again.'

'You'll weather it ... And there's the girls.'

'Yes, but if only last night had been better. If I'd only been able to talk to him, remember him as being nice, not like when he stormed out.'

'You can't prepare for something like that. It was a terrible accident and it happened, and it ... Oh, I don't know what I'm trying to say.'

'Who was it, though?' Lucy said, putting her spoon down next to her untouched bowl of soup. 'That's the frightening thing. It just seems so senseless. Why should someone come into the house and ... and ...'

'It must have been a burglar, and James must have surprised him, and—'

'They will catch him, won't they?'

'I should think so. A small town like Norwich ...'

'But they say they've got nothing to go on at the moment.'

'They'll find something. Something's bound to turn up. They know what they're doing.'

'Oh, what a mess.'

'Everything all right?'

Lucy looked up to see the manager leaning over her with a caring smile.

'Lovely,' said Tom.

'If there's anything you need ...'

'We're fine. Fine, thanks.'

'Good ... good.' He moved on to another table, said something to the people eating there and they laughed.

Everything seemed to be happening in slow motion, like the whole dining-room was under water. There were no clear sounds, just a general, dull mumble. It was airless and stifling in here. It was a dead place, buried under hundreds of years of history. There was a stink about it, the stink of countless people passing through. She looked down at the pattern of letters in the carpet, the W and the L ... The W and the L intertwined. She looked harder and could see right down into the weave of the carpet, see each individual tuft of wool. Then she went deeper; it went down very far, there was a whole world inside the carpet. It was dark and blue and deep.

She grunted and jerked her head up.

Tom was looking at her seriously. 'Are you okay, Sis?'

'Sis.' He hadn't called her that for twenty years.

'You're tired.'

'God, Tom, I've been tired for as long as I can remember. I am sick and tired of being sick and tired. This isn't new for me, feeling like I'm on autopilot. It started when I had Polly. Up every night, it drives you round the bend. And then Claire ... I thought once they started sleeping it'd be all right. Well, eventually they did start to sleep and so did I. The sleep of the dead. For hours on end, and when I woke, no matter how long I'd slept, I'd still be tired. Then I started to dream, and that was when it got really bad.'

'Nightmares?'

'Nightmares would have been fine. I started to dream while I was awake. I'd be walking down the street and I'd sort of drift off, like daydreaming, but it would take over. I'd imagine being a kid again in Somerset, and then I'd be there. For hours on end I'd be walking the streets in Minehead. I'd go to all the old places, I'd talk to people ... And the next thing I'd know, I'd wake up in the middle of Safeways or something, just standing there, and I'd have no idea how I'd got there. It was terrifying; it got so I was too frightened to go out.'

'Did you see the doctor?'

'Said I was stressed, run down, gave me pills, Valium and stuff ... It didn't help. In the end I just learnt to control it. If I hold on to things, if I don't lose concentration ... I don't know, I guess I'm okay now, but it's scary, thinking that you're going mad.'

'Christ, Lucy. What a family we are.'

'You're okay, Tom.'

Tom said nothing, just shrugged.

'And I'm okay, now,' Lucy said, and she did feel okay. Why shouldn't she? Tom was here, they were talking, the wine was nice. She didn't have to worry about getting drunk, she wasn't driving, and there was something else ... Oh yes, James was dead.

It hit her like a slap round the face and she started to cry again.

'I'm no good, Tom. I'm no good to anyone.'

'You'll pull through, Sis, you're a survivor. You were always the tough one, really. I mean, I pretended, but without you ...'

'I couldn't talk to James. I lost him. Even before last night I'd lost him. All I had to do was talk to him, just talk, open up to him. But I couldn't. And then last night ... He looked so pathetic, sitting on the floor like that. Just like the old James.'

'What do you mean?'

136

'He'd changed lately, Tom. He wasn't the same. It's all this karate and training he's been doing, he's obsessed by it. He ... Not any more. I don't know why he did it. You know, in a funny way I think he thought he was doing it for me. But I couldn't tell him.'

'What?'

'Tell him that the main thing that attracted me to him was his weediness, his helplessness. I mean, you can't tell someone that, can you? He was so different when I first met him, eager and innocent and vulnerable ... and weedy.' Lucy laughed, and then she cried. Her throat hurt. She had to hold herself together, not crack up here, in front of all these people.

'But then he began to change, in the last year or so ...'

Lucy looked away from the table and caught the eyes of a middle-aged man wearing steel-rimmed glasses. He was staring straight at her, blankly, as if oblivious to what he was seeing. He was chewing with his lips slightly parted. He paused a moment, his tongue working around inside his mouth, then looked down at his food briefly before looking up at his companion, a woman, probably his wife. She, too, was chewing. They didn't say anything to each other.

'He started getting more self-assured,' Lucy said, remembering James in his underwear, prancing around the bedroom. 'Cocky, even. He started complaining if things were wrong, you know, in shops and restaurants and things. But I couldn't tell him to stop, could I? I couldn't tell him I wanted him to be hopeless and pathetic.'

The man and woman were now both staring out of the window, silent as two fish.

'You know, Lucy, I always thought ...' Tom paused, considering what he was about to say. 'I thought what attracted you to him was that he was so different to Dad, so unlike him in every way.'

'That's exactly it. He was warm and open, he made mistakes. So you can imagine how I felt when he started becoming more ... Trying to be tough, trying to be a proper man. I got scared. Poor James ...'

Tears formed in her eyes, and Tom must have seen because he came to her rescue.

'How about putting some thought to where you're going to stay?'

'I've got some friends in town, but I'd rather get away.'

'What about my place? London?'

'Tom, I couldn't. You don't have room.'

'I could stay at the works for a bit, you and the girls could have the place to yourselves. You'd fit.'

'No, Tom, I can't put you to the trouble.'

'Come on, Lucy, what are brothers for?'

It was the old Tom again. But as she looked at him she saw something else, something in his eyes she'd never seen before. Something unsettled and wild. It passed before she could pin it down and she put it out of her mind. Last night had shaken them all up. After what they'd been through it was understandable that they should be feeling some extremes of emotion.

Tom put his hand on hers where it lay on the white tablecloth.

'I'm the one,' he said and she smiled at him even though she didn't know what he was talking about.

EIGHTEEN

Will sat on the rafter in the darkness and pressed the cold metal of the gun barrel against his cheek. He smelled the old familiar smell of the oil and perhaps, very faintly, cordite and gunpowder. But that may only have been his imagination, the ghost of a smell, because the gun hadn't been fired in years. After his father's death it had lain neglected up here, padlocked in the box that was bolted against a beam. It had stayed in the dark, another sad memory of the failure that his father had been.

Neither Will nor his mother had a licence – not that they'd ever had any desire to use the gun. Will thought it should probably have been handed in on his father's death. Well, there was no way the old bag was going to be organized enough to get that sorted out.

This part of the loft hadn't been converted; it was the same layout as the museum, ending in a flat wall with the roof going up to a point. He hadn't switched the light on and he felt safe and secluded in the darkness.

The gun gave him extra reassurance.

His father's gun.

He remembered all those Sunday mornings when Dad had gone off shooting with his friends. 'Just clay pigeons, Will,' he'd say. 'Just clay. Never knowingly take a life. Even if it's the smallest bird. A gun's a thing of great power. If a man can handle a gun, he can handle himself. But there's no need to kill a living creature.'

If only the old fool had learnt how to handle a power drill properly he might still be alive today.

He wondered what sterile pleasure Dad had got out of it, shooting at little clay discs on a cold and drizzling Sunday morning. He thought he probably only really did it for social reasons, to be in with the other men who went, the other local chemists, and the drug reps and even a doctor or two. Though Dad never went with them on their annual trip, when they got to blast away at real birds on some overpriced shoot.

'It's just for sport, Will. Never knowingly take a life. Hurt no living thing, ladybird, nor butterfly, nor moth with dusty wing.'

Yes, and it was a handy way of getting out of the shoots without having to admit that he couldn't actually afford it.

'If a man can handle a gun, he can handle himself.'

And what about his wife? What about handling her?

Maybe that was another reason he went, because he couldn't stand to be alone with the old bat. Maybe he'd known what she was up to. Certainly, towards the end, they hardly spent any time at all with each other. The house had become a cold, dead place.

And now he was gone and all Will had to remember him by was an old shotgun and a lot of bad DIY.

The sad, silly idiot. He'd drilled straight into a wire, straight into the ring main. He'd blown himself up trying to put up yet another set of shelves which probably wouldn't have been level.

No, he could hardly forget him, he was built into the house; in the double glazing that wouldn't open, the doors that wouldn't close, the wallpaper that didn't line up, the cupboards that weren't wide enough for the hangers ... And the gun.

'Never knowingly take a life, Will.'

But he hadn't meant to do it. He hadn't meant to kill Napoleon ... Or James Mullen as he now knew the little man was called. He'd just been trying to protect himself. He felt ashamed; frightened and ashamed. He couldn't sleep. Well, obviously he

could sleep; at some time during the night he would drift off ...
But then there were the dreams and he'd wake again. The nights
were an eternity of half waking, half sleeping and dreams. Dreams
in which Napoleon was still alive, and everyone would apologize to
each other and shake hands and say how sorry they all were for the
misunderstanding. And then he'd wake and know that Napoleon
was dead and he wouldn't sleep and he couldn't sleep and he felt
like he was going crazy.

The first night had been the worst. That night he really hadn't
been able to sleep. He'd lain there in his bed, his ears straining
for every sound, every car that passed, every footstep on the pavement outside, imagining that it was the police. They were coming
to take him.

Then there was the second night. And now he came to think
about it, the second night was the worst, not the first. Because
the first night he only thought he was wanted for house-breaking.
When it became murder, it got really tough.

It had been front-page news the next day, right across the top of
the Eastern Daily Press.

NORWICH MAN MURDERED

That was it, he knew he was done for when he read that. There was
no point in running, no point in trying to get away, because they
had the notebook. They must know who he was.

That second day he'd just sat in his room, miserable, waiting.

But they hadn't come.

Why not? They had the book. Maybe it wasn't enough. He
tried to remember what he'd written. Certainly not his name and
address, nothing as basic as that. But still, surely, there were enough
clues in it. After all they had scientists, he'd seen them on the television. They were clever, they could track you down from a piece of
fluff found at the scene of the crime.

So, surely a bloody notebook . . .

And yet they hadn't tracked him down.

On the third day there was still no sign of them, and the papers were saying, 'No motives, no clues.' It didn't make sense.

That was when another thought had struck him. What if he hadn't dropped the book in the house? What if it was when he'd jumped the wall, or after?

He'd gone back. He'd known it was dangerous, but he hadn't been able to just sit around and wait. So he'd gone back to look for the book. He'd retraced his escape route, gone over it three or four times, his eyes scouring the ground. Nothing. He'd even darted up the alley – once he was sure no police were around – nothing there, either.

So he'd returned home to wait.

Maybe they were waiting too, building up a case, or just trying to make him sweat. If that's what they were doing, they were being very cruel. He wanted it over with, one way or the other.

One way or the other.

That was when he'd thought of the gun. He'd resisted the idea at first; it had seemed too silly, too melodramatic. But once the thought was there he hadn't been able to get rid of it.

Now it was a week later, the police still hadn't come and he was sitting here in the loft, cradling the shotgun.

He could be ready for them when they came, hold them off in some heroic siege, finally take his own life rather than face prison. Yes, all right, it was silly. It was melodramatic. And above all it was childish. But it was something. Something to hold on to.

Even before he'd got the gun out of its box, as he was undoing the padlock, he'd known he would never fire it, certainly not at another human being. He could never knowingly kill anyone.

It had been an accident. He hadn't meant to do it. He hadn't even known what it was he was hitting the bloke with. He could tell the police that, couldn't he? It was the truth, after all. He could tell them that he'd just wanted to be in the house. He'd gone in and been surprised by Napoleon, by Mr Mullen, there'd been a fight and in self-defence, in pure self-defence, he'd accidentally stabbed him.

That was what had happened. He had to tell them that, for God's sake. He'd only get a small sentence then. But even a small sentence meant time in prison; they wouldn't let you off something like this. And how could he go to prison? A prison was a dead place, and he'd die there. It wasn't a home. He had to be out where people lived, he had to be in the very heart of the city.

If he could just show them his books, his museum, they'd understand what he was doing, that he'd never meant to harm anyone. What he wanted was life, to be with people, to share their lives, not destroy them. If he could just . . .

No.

Nobody was allowed to see his museum. How stupid of him to think even for a moment that they would understand. It was his private place; he couldn't face anyone else ever going in there.

And since the killing he couldn't face going in there himself. Somehow it all seemed so pathetic. It was just a pathetic collection of crap, and a shelf of pathetic crap books. It was all just crap. Because now a man was dead because of it, stabbed to death with a 'kitchen implement' as the papers put it.

No, the museum offered him no happiness any more, it was just a reminder. And the shotgun offered him no protection; it, too, was just a reminder. A reminder of another man who could never have fired it, another man who fucked his life up.

He put the gun back in its locker and snapped the padlock shut. It would stay in there, now, just as his exhibits would stay in the museum. Unseen in the dark.

The exhibits.

He felt pain, actual physical pain as he remembered the toothbrushes. The four of them, a family of brushes.

The man's brush, Napoleon's brush, with the bristles flattened and splayed. He wondered how many times the wife had nagged him to get a new one. And now it didn't matter any more, you don't need a toothbrush where he'd gone. The woman's own brush, neat and new ... And the other two, the girls' brushes with the Disney characters on the handles ... The girls who would never see their father again.

The brushes were on the shelf in the museum, he hadn't had the heart to mount them properly. The reminder hurt too much.

The little man was dead. He'd been so full of life, bouncing round the kitchen like a miniature kung fu ninja, jumping, spinning and kicking. And now he didn't exist any more, and the wife had no husband, and the children had no father, and none of them had any fucking toothbrushes, and it was his fault.

He deserved to go to prison for it; he deserved to die for it. He should have let Napoleon kick him to death rather than fight back. He had no father, he knew how sad and lonely you could be. Christ, that was why he'd started going into people's houses in the first place, to share their lives, to borrow their families, steal their happy holidays, their loves, their secrets, and what had it led to? The death of a man, the destruction of a family.

'I'm sorry,' he shouted and slammed the side of his fist against a rafter. Several tiny splinters embedded themselves in his skin.

'I'm so sorry,' he said again, quieter now, almost a whisper. Then he crawled out of the loft space and went to his room to wait. That was all there was to do.

What can I do? he thought. What can I possibly do but wait?

For the rest of my life, wait.

He felt a great black hand hanging over him, filling half the sky, a huge fly-swatter of a hand. No, not a fly-swatter, a person-swatter. A Will-swatter. It was waiting to fall on him, crush him.

If his father had lived, if he hadn't drilled into that fucking wire ... No. No, it was too late, even by then. Because the old bag had screwed everything up. It was her fault, it was fucking Mother's fault, why couldn't the hand swat her?

He remembered coming home from school that day, creeping in quietly through the back door. Creeping because he never wanted his parents to know he was there, because they acted differently when he was around.

He'd come in silently and started up the stairs when he'd heard the sounds coming from the front room. The door was open. He'd gone over and seen her, his mother, on the sofa with another man. It was Alan, a friend of his father's, and the two of them were fucking. Right there on the family sofa.

He should take the gun to her. That would be the best thing all round. But he couldn't; even though he'd plotted a thousand ways to kill her, he knew they were all just daydreams.

Because he could never knowingly take another life.

He shouldn't have fought back. He should have accepted his punishment.

When they came for him the next time, when the fist fell from the sky, he'd take it, he wouldn't flinch, he'd be good.

Next time he'd do things properly.

NINETEEN

Tom stood at the top of the iron staircase on the small platform outside his office and looked out over the mass of machinery below. It roared and thundered as the big rollers churned out the shiny printed sheets. He looked at his watch; it was half past four in the morning. The presses would run all night and the next day, they couldn't stop. While one machine was being set up another would be working. Never stop, never think about stopping. There was always something new to print.

He thought of all the stuff he'd turned out over the years, page after page of it, millions upon millions of words; there was no beginning to them and no end. But what did they say?

He had no idea. He'd learnt early on – when he'd first started working here for his Uncle Willy as a know-nothing sixteen-year-old – he'd learnt how to check whole proofs without actually taking anything in. You could ask him a question about it afterwards and he wouldn't have a clue what any of it had said. Yet each word would be spelt correctly, set correctly, placed in exactly the right position on the page.

He was good at his job, he'd turned the stuff out all right. Mile after mile of it, and he'd never asked what any of it meant. A picture to him was simply three different layers of colour; red, yellow and blue. He could look at it and tell whether it was properly registered, whether the colours were true, whether the image was sharp, but the image itself ... He never saw it. He could never see a picture for what it represented, only what it was made of.

But that was changing, he was changing. He'd been reading lately for the first time since he was a child. Because he'd found a book he understood. He'd found a book he wanted to read, to study. Even now he was thinking about it, thinking about getting back to it and finding something new within the pages. It was almost an erotic longing, and he was deliberately holding back. That was something he'd learnt from the book, to hold off on a pleasure, let it ferment and grow within him.

The presses didn't interest him any more, he saw them for what they were, machines. Mindless things turning out countless words and pictures without meaning. The only words that spoke to him were neatly handwritten, in a notebook. They were personal, not mechanical, and they were real.

He pictured four of the words now, written repeatedly down one of the pages.

I AM HAPPY NOW

Who had written that? Who could know what that meant?

Tom intended to find out. And when he found the writer he would ...

What? He didn't know.

He had all the time in the world to do it, though. There was no way the police were going to get to the owner of the book before he did. How could they? They had no clues. They had nothing to go on.

Because he'd taken the book.

That was all that interested him now. He was using the works simply as somewhere to sleep. He remembered when he'd first got back from Norwich, the panic it had caused. 'Oh Mr Kendall, we didn't expect you back until next week!' They were actually shocked to see him. It had unnerved him at first; he'd always thought they'd have terrible problems coping without him. He thought they'd have been relieved to have him back before time. But no, instead it had thrown them into disarray. He realized he'd become nothing much more than a figurehead at the company, a desk man, remote from the everyday running of things. For a couple of days he'd gone through the motions, made the pretence of doing useful work, but his heart wasn't in it so he'd stopped. 'Bugger it,' he'd told them, 'I'm still on holiday. Don't mind me. Act as if I'm not here.' That had confused them even more but they'd get used to it. The hell with them if they didn't; he wasn't responsible to them any more.

As it was he only came in in the evenings. They probably thought he had trouble at home or something, but what did he care what they thought? He wouldn't be here for much longer. He was already making plans.

Yes, this place was now just a bed for him. Not that he slept any more. Last night he'd been awake all night, and he didn't feel at all tired tonight. He'd lie on the bed and look at the book instead.

Thinking of the book again finally forced him to turn and open the door to his office. He could hold back no longer.

He stepped inside and shut the door behind him. It was quieter in here, but you could still hear and feel the thump, thump, thump of the machinery.

In the bedroom behind the office it was quieter still. There were no windows; it was like being inside a huge warm beast. He turned on a lamp by the bed and it lit the pale blue walls with a vibrant yellow light. Everything looked vivid, humming with colour. The surfaces of objects swarmed with countless coloured dots, as if they were alive with a sort of electric energy. Maybe things had always been like this and he was only now seeing them for what they were. Maybe he had only now awakened from a form of blindness. The book had opened his eyes. The book had shown him all this. Either that, or he'd been without sleep for too long and it was messing up his eyesight. But either way it was beautiful and exciting and new, and it was all because of the book.

He locked the door and opened the cabinet beside the narrow bed.

He felt a guilty twinge, as if the book were something forbidden. But that only made it more thrilling. He took it out and ran his fingers over the smooth card of the cover, tracing the outline of the skier.

Why had he done it? Why had he taken the book, and not given it to the police?

The simple fact was he didn't know. He'd tried not to think about it. It had just seemed right somehow. The book was meant for him; it had been left for him. He felt almost as if it had been written for him. There were mysteries within it, secrets for him to unravel. Nobody else would understand it, he knew that much. To the police it would just be a clue, the only clue, to be fingerprinted, analysed, taken apart. They'd look at it like he had looked at the stuff he printed, as an object. They wouldn't actually read it.

Since James's death they'd interviewed him twice in person and once on the phone, and they were coming down to London to talk to him again in a couple of days' time. He'd noticed, each time they'd talked to him, that their attitude had changed. They seemed suspicious of something, less mindful of his feelings, but they wouldn't say what was bothering them. Oh, they appeared polite enough, but behind their professional smiles there was something else.

Well, it didn't bother him because he knew all the time that he was ahead of them, one up. Because he was the one the killer had given the book to. If they thought he was holding back on something, hiding something from them, it didn't bother him. The book gave him strength and it offered him a future.

He loved to read it, to feel close to the man who'd written it, and he'd given the unknown writer a name, just as the writer had named everyone whose house he went into.

Tom had named him the Intruder.

In a way Tom felt jealous of the Intruder, because he had done something Tom had never had the courage to do. He had seen his problem, acted on it, and found a sort of happiness.

That was his impulse, his sole impulse.

In his own clumsy way, the Intruder had tried to spell out how he had become happy. It was obvious that his writing skills weren't up to the task, he admitted as much himself, but behind the words Tom sensed an urgent truth.

'I AM HAPPY NOW.' That was all the Intruder had needed to write, and it was all Tom wanted to be able to say. He wanted to throw off his great weight, the baggage he'd been carrying around since childhood, and say, 'I am happy now. I am free.' But he couldn't.

Each day is better than the last.

What a good feeling that must be, instead of feeling that each day was a fresh ordeal you had to get through one way or another. Instead of feeling every night, as you went to bed, that tomorrow would be no better, that it would go on like that for ever, stretching away into the whiteness.

I do not believe that a man can be truly happy unless he fully understands what he is and can act accordingly ... How can it be wrong to be happy?

He sat on the bed and once again tried to form in his mind an image of the man. He'd read the notebook over and over again trying to get some sort of picture. It was written in a rather stiff, formal style, and even when it described passion, which it did quite frequently, it was at a distance. As the Intruder made clear, the real passion was in the experience, not in the telling of it. He was a young man, that much was evident, but that was about it. He didn't have a face.

Not yet.

Tom would give him a face. One day and one day soon, Tom felt confident, that grey area would be filled by a live human being. Because Tom was going to find the Intruder and he was going to make him explain things to him. Because the writer knew. The writer had cracked it.

It wasn't all here in the book. This was just notes. The Intruder wrote of a museum, a secret place where the proper truth was kept. This was just sketches, but all Tom had to do was find that museum, find the writer. And he knew how to do that because he had the book. The book would show him the way. Just as it would have shown the police if they'd had it.

Well, they didn't have it and he wasn't going to let them make him feel bad about that.

It was his book and he wanted to find the Intruder for different reasons to theirs. He flipped through the pages, looked at the flat yet evocative descriptions of people's houses, people's lives, and he could picture the Intruder sitting alone, writing these words. He could picture the rooms, picture the people and he knew what it was the Intruder wanted from them. It was the same thing he wanted – their ordinariness, their simplicity.

Their happiness.

So when Tom found the Intruder, he would be able to make everything all right. He'd be able to sort everything out, for himself, for Lucy, for Maddie.

Maddie. Yes. Tomorrow, Saturday, he'd be seeing her again. He trembled when he thought about her. She'd changed since Norwich. That was understandable, it had been a terrible shock, but she'd soon be over that and they could start again from where they'd left off. Except it would be better this time. He wouldn't be so frightened of the whole thing. Maybe he'd tell her about the book, about ... No. Not yet. She wasn't ready for it. She wouldn't understand. First he had to find the Intruder and straighten all that out, then he could tell her about it.

So tomorrow afternoon, then, he'd be with her, just like before. He'd get her some flowers. Wasn't that what people did? Or was that only when they'd done something wrong? No. Don't worry so much about things. He was a new Tom, now, a new relaxed Tom.

Flowers. Take her out for lunch, and then ... ? He couldn't take her back to the flat with Lucy and the girls there. He'd have to bring her here. It wasn't ideal, but shut away in this room no one would ever know.

Yes, he'd make her happy. He'd show her that he could be everything she wanted. He could make her happy; he could make everyone happy.

He lay flat and looked up at the ceiling. Out of the swirling colours he formed a picture of her face, of her whole body, naked and alive. She moved and pulsed above him, offering him endless pleasure.

I will be happy, he thought. No matter what it takes, I deserve it.

TWENTY

'What, exactly, did they argue about?' The tall policeman asked her. Maddie tried to think. What was it? It hadn't really seemed to be about anything at the time. She sucked her lower lip and stared at a scratch on the glass-topped coffee table. That hadn't been there before. What a pain in the arse.

'I don't know,' she said finally. 'It was kind of ... men. You know?'

The policeman didn't know. 'I'm afraid you'll have to be a little more specific, Mrs Fisher.'

'Well, surely the others can remember. I mean you must have talked to Tom. He must remember.' Maddie sounded tetchy and put upon. She was nervous. She'd been nervous ever since the police had rung that morning. So far she'd managed to say nothing to Peter about what had really happened in Norwich. She'd made up some story about fighting with one of the conference organizers and he'd well believed it.

She'd tried to put it all behind her, but she'd been sleeping badly and was even more touchy and argumentative than ever. The last thing she needed right now was two policemen in her sitting-room.

The senior officer, Detective Inspector Hapworth, was sitting uncomfortably on the grey sofa. It was rather low and he was sunk back in it with his knees sticking up in the air. He had unusually long hair for a policeman, it seemed to Maddie – not that she knew any other detective inspectors. It was untidily streaked with grey and came down over his ears.

The other man, Detective Sergeant Snack (he'd said it twice, 'Snack', probably always had to), was trying not to poke around, but couldn't resist the force of habit. He'd studied the painting above the fireplace for a long time, probably surprised at the number of genitalia in it. And now he was looking through a pile of magazines on the black bookshelves.

'We have talked to the others, obviously,' said Hapworth, 'but we need to talk to everyone concerned. It's amazing what details people can forget, and it's amazing what details can be important.' Hapworth had a mild East Anglian accent. Maddie had heard it parodied so often as a yokel accent that she couldn't help thinking of Hapworth as stupid, although she knew this was probably unfair. 'So, if you could cast your mind back ...'

Maddie sighed. What if Peter came in now? How would she explain it to him? If only she'd thought of meeting them elsewhere, a pub or something instead of at home, but she'd been pressured when they rang and hadn't had time to think.

'I remember we talked a bit about married men having affairs,' she said with exaggerated boredom. 'James had been going on about Tom and me, and—'

'Could I just stop you for a moment, Mrs Fisher?' Snack said, turning away from the bookshelves with a smile. 'Can you just clarify for us what exactly is your relationship to Mr Kendall?'

'I met him on a ... on a course. Got to know him a bit. Then it turned out he was going to be in Norwich visiting his family at the same time as I was up there for this conference.'

'Women and film?' Hapworth said, looking at his notebook.

'Yes. And anyway, he invited me round for dinner.'

'At his sister's?'

'Of course at his sister's.'

'I see. So what do you mean when you say Mr Mullen was going on about you and Mr Kendall?'

'He was just stirring it.'

'Trying to start an argument?'

'Trying to spice up the dinner-table conversation, I suppose.'

'Right. I see. And this started the argument?'

'Not really, no, that was earlier. It was when James said something about Tom's father. I think there're some family tensions. I don't think James was overly fond of his father-in-law.'

'So it was a family row?'

'Well, sort of. I mean, that's what set them off. Then James started taking the piss out of Lucy. And that was when Tom lost his temper with him. I mean, it was hard to say, it came up out of nowhere. A combination of things.'

'Was it the sort of argument that could have led to a fight?'

'Jesus, it was a dinner party, men being men, a bit of family argy-bargy, not bloody all-in wrestling.'

'But it ended with Mr Mullen leaving the room?'

'Yes. Tom told him to go fuck himself.' Maddie laughed quickly, a brief snort.

'That seems quite extreme,' said Hapworth, with a look somewhere between amazement and amusement.

'You don't know Tom. He has some problems, moods. He doesn't really like situations like that.'

'Like what?'

'Social occasions, formal things, groups. He tries to avoid them.'

'And in this instance he swore at Mr Mullen?'

'James backed him into a corner and he sort of snapped. He's like that.'

'Violent?'

'No, not violent. As I say, he has a few problems . . .' She stopped. The two policemen were looking at her intently.

'Look. What are you getting at?' she asked.

'Nothing.'

'No? Why are you so interested in Tom?'

'You were both staying at the same hotel, weren't you?' Snack said amiably. 'The Wymondham Lodge.'

'Y-yes. It was, it seemed more—'

'The same room.'

'All right. I forgot I was talking to detectives. I suppose it had to come out sooner or later. Yes, I was in the same hotel as Tom. Yes, we were sharing a room. Yes, we were having an affair. But there's no law against that, is there?'

'No. Of course not.' Hapworth smiled at her, pleasantly.

'I can't see what possible relevance any of this has to the fact that James is dead,' Maddie said. 'And I'd appreciate it if my husband didn't find out.'

'You haven't told him?' Hapworth raised an eyebrow.

'Of course I haven't.'

'Well, I suppose that's your concern.'

'Yes.'

Peter had been almost pathetically pleased to see her when she got back. He'd gone out of his way to be nice to her. There were flowers in the kitchen. They ate out three evenings in a row. He made love to her every night. He even made an attempt to curb his sarcasm. She'd been a bit nonplussed at first, then she realized it was just guilt. He'd been fucking someone else while she was away. That made her turn really sour. Hypocrisy didn't come into it – Peter was a cunt. She'd confronted him with it in the end, and they'd had a proper row. Peter had even lost his temper, joined in, which told her that he must be really, really guilty, and in the course of the argument she got it out of him that this girl, another bloody student predictably, had even moved in, had been intending to stay for the whole time Maddie was away. She'd had to move out speedily when Maddie rang up and said she was coming back.

Good.

She hoped there had been a great deal of panic and rushing about.

She was happier after the row; the status quo was restored. She could happily hate Peter again. Which was why the last thing she needed now was something like this to upset their equilibrium.

She looked at Hapworth and wondered if he was married. Probably. Decent policemen ought to have decent wives. He probably told her all about his day, while she massaged his neck.

And was he happy?

Probably not.

'So James left the room?' he said, doggedly returning to the meal.

'Stormed out in a huff.'

'And Mr Kendall followed?'

'Yes. Lucy was going to go and see if James was okay, but Tom stopped her, said he'd go.'

'What mood was he in at this point? Was he still angry?'

'No, well, perhaps angry with himself. He was embarrassed more than anything, I think.'

'How soon after was this?'

'Oh, I don't know, couple of minutes.'

'How long, exactly? Two minutes? Three?'

'Two or three minutes.'

'And in the meantime did you hear anything?'

'No, I remember I turned the tape over. So there was music on. All we heard was what sounded like James stacking pots. I suppose in retrospect it could have been—'

'And after Mr Kendall went out, did you hear anything then?'

'No.'

'So how long was it before he called you?'

'The same, couple of minutes.'

'As long as that?'

'Maybe shorter, I don't know.'

'What state would you say he was in, when you found him?'

'Terrible. There was blood everywhere. And ... You see, the thing is, he blames himself.'

'How do you mean?'

'He feels guilty. Almost as if he killed James himself.'

'He's told you this?'

'Yes. He thinks that if he hadn't pulled the fork out, James might not have died.'

'Yes, it perhaps wasn't the wisest thing to do.'

'Give him a break,' Maddie said, in an attempt to sound withering, but ending up whining.

Snack cleared his throat and sat down on the arm of a chair. 'These meetings you met each other at?' he said.

'What about them?'

'They're for people with psychological problems, aren't they?'

'You have done your homework, haven't you?'

Hapworth shrugged.

'It's not what you think,' said Maddie wearily. 'It's not all loonies and strait-jackets. They're therapy sessions. For people who are victims of their own emotions, for—'

'It's all right, Mrs Fisher,' said Hapworth, 'we've already talked to Mr Ryman. He's told us all about the sessions.'

'Clive,' said Maddie dismissively.

'Yes. He's been very helpful.'

'I'll bet he has.'

'He's explained the nature of Mr Kendall's problem.'

'Tom doesn't have a "problem"!' Now Maddie was getting angry herself. The two policemen were sitting on her furniture looking horribly superior. She pushed a hand back through her hair and twisted a strand round her fingers. Then she took a long, deep breath and let it out very slowly and noisily.

'Problems,' she said. 'Not *a problem*. There's a difference. Christ, you think he's some kind of a nutter, don't you?'

Mind you, he had been behaving more and more oddly since

that night. First he'd argued with her about not coming down to London, then, the very next day, there he was on the phone, 'Hi, it's me, I'm back,' with the bloody sister and kids in tow. Then he'd ring her at every opportunity: 'Please, Maddie, I have to see you, it's important.' In the end it seemed the only way to get him off her back was to meet him and explain that it was over, that it couldn't possibly work between the two of them.

He was staying at his printworks. In a tiny airless room which reverberated with the sound of the presses. He'd been strangely manic, couldn't sit still for a moment, even though he'd looked desperately tired. He'd gone on about finding happiness and changing his life, like he'd got religion or something. She'd wanted to talk to him, let him down gently, but in the end she'd gone to bed with him, just because it had seemed easier than resisting.

Afterwards, lying in the cramped, single bed, he wouldn't shut up about his plans. She hadn't really listened, just wondered how she'd ever got involved with him. He bored her now. He'd kept saying he was going to put everything right, he was going to solve everyone's problems.

She'd left him and gone home feeling more depressed than ever.

Hapworth was turning pages in his little book. 'If we could just backtrack slightly to the argument,' he said. 'Would you say that Mr Mullen was in any way flirting with you? The wife says he was paying you rather a lot of attention.'

'He might have been. It happens.'

'Did Mr Kendall notice?'

'To tell you the truth, he seemed more protective of Lucy than me. That's what really set him off, James having a go at Lucy.'

'So you don't think perhaps Mr Kendall might have been jealous?'

'Tom? Of James? Ha! You've got to be joking, Tom hated James. I mean . . .'

The two men were looking at her again.

159

'Oh, for Christ's sake. What is the point of all this? What is the bloody point? Why are you giving Tom a hard time when you should be out trying to catch whoever attacked James?'

'The thing of it is,' said Sergeant Snack, getting up off the chair and resuming his idle snooping, 'we don't have anything to go on. There was no evidence left at the scene of the crime.'

'Oh come on,' said Maddie. 'There must be something.'

Hapworth held out his hands in a gesture of emptiness.

'And there's no sign of a struggle,' said Snack. 'You heard nothing. Somebody just walked in there and stabbed him. Why?'

'Well, obviously James surprised a burglar and the burglar attacked him.'

'And what sort of burglar breaks in during a dinner party?'

'A very stupid burglar.'

'Quite,' said Hapworth. 'And most burglars aren't stupid. They do it during the day when there's no one around. But in this case . . . small house, music playing, guests . . . it makes no sense.'

'There isn't any other explanation,' Maddie said.

'Isn't there?'

'You're the policemen, you tell me.'

'The only prints on the fork belong to Mr Kendall,' said Snack.

'Well, I'm not bloody surprised. He took it out, he . . . Wait a minute. You're not suggesting . . . ? Oh come on.' Maddie laughed again. 'Are you telling me you think Tom did it?'

'I didn't say that.'

'No, but you implied . . . Jesus, is that what all this has been about?'

'I didn't say anything, I was just going over the facts. It was you who said—'

'That is the most ridiculous thing I've ever heard,' said Maddie, shaking her head. 'You're telling me that in the middle of a dinner party Tom gets up, goes out to the kitchen and calmly stabs his brother-in-law to death with a kitchen fork? Is that what you're saying? Well, let me tell you, Mr Policeman Plod, you're barking up the wrong bloody tree.'

Maddie got up and before she knew what she was doing she found herself stalking angrily about the room. She stopped herself.

Come on, Maddie, methinks the lady doth protest too much.

Stupid.

After all, it was only what she herself had begun to suspect in the last few days.

TWENTY-ONE

Lucy held Claire's arms and looked very seriously into the child's face. 'Who was the man?' she asked. 'It's important you remember who the man in your room was.'

'It was Uncle Tom,' Claire said with a touch of impatience.

'Are you sure, love?'

'Yes. He was making writing, in a book. Making a story.'

Lucy ruffled the girl's hair and smiled. 'You daft thing. There wasn't a man, was there?'

'There was a man, and he was making a story.'

'What sort of a story?'

Claire sucked the end of her crayon and thought about it. 'A secret story.'

Lucy laughed and shook her head. She turned away to see Tom sitting at the table watching them.

'She's always been rather imaginative,' she said. Tom smiled.

'I mean,' Lucy frowned, 'you didn't go up to her room, did you?'

'You know I didn't,' Tom said quietly. 'I was with you the whole time.'

'I know . . . I know. Who'd be a detective, eh?'

She watched Claire go back to her colouring, squatting on the floor and carefully filling in an entire page of *Postman Pat* with black crayon.

'Listen, Lucy,' Tom said. 'I've decided I'm going back.'

'What do you mean?'

'I'm going back up to Norwich.'

'Why?'

'Well, there's the funeral to be sorted out, and your house. I don't like to just leave it, there's things to do ... and ...' Tom fell silent.

'You don't need to worry about all that, Tom. I can cope, I'm fine.'

Tom stood up and put away some of Claire's toys. 'I want to see what I can find out.'

'Don't be silly. What can you do that the police can't?'

'The bloody police think I did it!' With nothing left to tidy up, Tom began to walk aimlessly about the room.

'Oh come on,' said Lucy. 'They don't really. They're just, I don't know, that's how the police work.' Lucy went over to Tom, who was now standing at the window, and put her hands lightly on his shoulders. She gently rubbed his neck. 'They don't really think that, do they?' She meant it to sound like a statement, but it came out as a question.

Before either of them could say anything else the doorbell went.

It was Fiona, the girl from the flat upstairs, who had come down to look after Claire and Polly for a couple of hours while Tom and Lucy went out for a drink. Lucy fussed about explaining things, but Fiona was a professional; she'd had three younger sisters of her own and had spent her adolescence looking after kids. So much so that now she was a serious working girl she missed it.

'Have a good time,' she said at the front door as Tom and Lucy went out. 'I'll take drugs and watch video nasties with the girls.'

'It's funny,' said Tom as they crossed the road, 'I never really knew her before. It's funny how these things happen.'

'She's very nice,' said Lucy. 'It must have been great to have her as a big sister.'

'So I wasn't good enough for you?' Tom said with mock affront.

'I didn't mean that.' They laughed and walked on to the Heath.

Lucy had never really liked south London before; she'd always found it empty and exposed. It had wide streets and the cars always seemed to be just passing through on their way to somewhere else. Even Blackheath, though surrounded by large, elegant houses, had always felt somehow bleak and barren. There were no trees, just grass and emptiness.

But it was that very openness that comforted her now. Norwich was such a small town, isolated and turned in on itself, like a toy town. Here she could be lost; life went on around her. Perversely, she felt more relaxed than she had done for months. If only she could stay here for ever, and not have to return to Norwich and her old life.

'Don't go, Tom,' she said, holding tightly on to his arm and looking up at the purple sky.

'I just think I might be able to turn something up. It's probably stupid.'

'We don't have to stay here, you can have your flat back if you want.'

'It's not that. I like having you here. Bit of life about the place. I just . . . I'm feeling a little, you know, put upon. Police and that. I'm sitting around here twiddling my thumbs, and they're out ordering me a coffin.'

'I know you're under a lot of stress, Tom, but it's probably just delayed shock or something.'

'It's not shock, it's having the police suspect me. I didn't know what it was before, what they were getting at. But now it's all so obvious.'

'No, it's more than that. You know you didn't do it. And you've been coping so well for all of us, it's no wonder you feel upset. Why don't you take a holiday, a proper holiday?'

It was true. He looked terribly tired these days, old and worn out. He was pushing himself too hard, worrying too much about them all. She wished he'd just let go and relax. She couldn't understand what on earth he hoped to achieve by going up to Norwich.

'A holiday?' Tom said dismissively. 'I couldn't. Not with this hanging over me.'

'But do you really think that going up to Norwich is such a good idea?'

'My mind's made up, Luce. And you know what a stubborn bugger I am.'

'Yes.' He always had been. He'd been a quiet boy, a bit of a plodder, but he'd always got things done in the end, in his own way, and if his mind was set on something he'd do it. Like leaving home, after he'd fought with Dad that time. She'd begged him not to leave her behind, but almost the next day he was gone. She knew he loved him, but as a thirteen-year-old she'd found it all rather difficult to understand.

That was something he'd got from Dad, that stubbornness. Although with Dad it was different; it was a terrible, unquestioning resolve, the conviction that his way was right and everything else, everyone else, was wrong.

They came to a pub. It was large and noisy, packed with young people. Lucy went inside gratefully, soothed by the noise and bustle. 'This is nice,' she said.

'Are you sure it's all right? We can go somewhere less crowded, if you like.'

Lucy touched his cheek. 'This is fine,' she said.

Tom got them some drinks and they found a relatively quiet corner, where they leant against a shelf and watched the other drinkers.

'How's work going?' Lucy said after a while, raising her voice above the din.

'Fine. I tell you, all these years I've been thinking they'd fall apart without me. Thinking I had to work twenty-five hours a day, eight days a week, thinking I had to do everything myself. When in reality they were all relieved to see the back of me when I went up to Norwich.'

Lucy looked at Tom. His body belied his calm, sensible, tone. His eyes were bright, intense, and he was gripping his pint so tightly his hand was shaking.

'You know,' he said, 'lately, a lot of the things, a lot of my assumptions, things I've always thought, they're not true any more. I don't know if they ever were. Since I've stopped working I've had time to think. I've never had that before, never let myself have it. And there's so much I ...' Tom stopped himself. He looked slightly embarrassed, covered it by taking a drink, then suddenly became comically businesslike. 'Now, the funeral's next Friday,' he said. 'So I'll make sure the house is, you know, ready for you. It means you don't have to worry about anything ...'

A couple got up from a nearby table. Tom grabbed Lucy and hurried to secure the seats.

'That's better,' said Lucy, collapsing into the chair. 'God, I haven't done this in years. I never used to go to the pub with James.'

'I don't go much myself, it's no fun on your own. I hardly drink these days, as it is. Anyway, on Friday, what will happen, is ...'

'I know what'll happen, Tom. I've been through all this before.'

'What do you mean?'

'Dad's funeral, remember?'

'How could I remember? I wasn't there.'

'That's not what I meant. I know you weren't there, and I know why you didn't want to be there.'

Dad. The topic neither of them liked to discuss. But maybe here, in this neutral place ...

'I was wrong,' Tom said quietly.

'Wrong, how?'

'I thought at the time ...' Tom paused. 'I hated him so much, I wanted nothing more to do with him. But in retrospect I think if I could have just seen him lowered into the ground, seen them bury him, then I'd know he was dead for sure.'

'Oh, he's dead all right.'

166

'No. Inside me, there's something thinks he's still here. That's the something that needed to see the earth go over him. I didn't realize what an important part of funerals that was. To help us understand that someone is well and truly dead, and they won't ever be coming back.'

'Don't be silly, how could he come back?'

'Lately I've been dreaming of him. Dreaming that he's still alive,' said Tom, idly spinning an ashtray. 'He comes to me and tells me off for thinking he was dead, and all the old fear, all the old guilt, starts up again. You know, I think it'll be a good thing for you, the funeral; it's the next stage in coming to terms with James's death.'

'I am coming to terms, slowly. I'm sleeping properly now. Funny, I feel better than before even. With Dad it was the other way round, it just got worse and worse. But at least I was happy once with James. At least I feel I knew him, loved him, and I have the girls, they're a part of him I'll always have. Families go on. And James, whatever else he was, he was a good father.'

There. Dad again. Dad, Dad, Dad. He was always in the back of her mind. And with Tom around it was worse.

'Why were we so scared of him, Tom?'

'Dad?'

'Yes. He wasn't exactly cruel, was he? He never hurt us ... Except for that one time you fought with him. Why were we so afraid of him?'

'Because he hated us.'

'Did he? Maybe he just didn't know how to show his feelings.'

'He had no feelings.'

'Tom. We never really knew him, that was obvious at the funeral.'

'He wouldn't let anyone know him, he was too busy playing the big father.'

'There were people there I didn't know, friends of his I never knew he had. It was quite obvious he had a whole life separate to the one we knew about. Well, I suppose that was pretty obvious, really.'

'Why?'

'Because he killed himself, and he didn't leave a note, and none of us knew why he'd done it.'

'None of us cared.'

'That's not true, Tom. I know you never got on. I know it's easier for you to preserve this image. But we didn't know him. He was obviously a very sad man. Sad and lonely.'

'That was his fault,' Tom scoffed.

'He knew that. He must have known what a mess he'd made of things, what a waste it had all been. Why else does someone blow their brains out?'

'I was so happy when I heard,' Tom said. 'I went out and got very drunk. And I had to keep on drinking. I had to kill as much of my brain as I could, because I didn't want to start feeling sorry for him. I drank until I passed out. Hardly touched anything since. But up here,' he tapped his forehead, 'it's like I've kept on drinking ever since.'

'Maybe it's time you stopped. Maybe you should forgive him, maybe it would help. Maybe you should forgive yourself.'

Tom looked at her and a question appeared to pass through his mind. Then he looked back down at the table. 'Maybe. But I wouldn't want to give him the satisfaction.'

'He's dead, Tom, he doesn't know. He shot himself through the top of the head with a ...'

'Luger.'

'Yes.'

'His war trophy,' Tom said bitterly.

Lucy couldn't think of anything else to say, and Tom was staring gloomily into his glass, watching foam slowly slide down the side.

'What a jolly conversation, eh?' Lucy said, trying to cheer him up.

'I'm sorry, Lucy. I'm not exactly the life and soul of the party, am I?'

'Neither of us are.'

'But I'm glad you're feeling happier, at least.' Tom covered her hand with his own.

'Most of the time,' Lucy said sadly. 'I mean, I'm still prone to becoming a blubbering wreck, but I suppose that's a good thing, really. It's just, it would really help if I could know.'

'Know?'

'What happened. Who it was. There's someone out there. I don't want revenge, I just want to know. But it's like there was this invisible man, someone who didn't exist.'

'Someone the police think is me. As if he's hiding out inside me. That's why I have to go, I need to find out too.'

'But how? There's nothing there.'

Tom sniffed, scratched his nose. 'They might have missed something.'

'It's unlikely.'

'Why do you think they're so infallible? If they were perfect they wouldn't be suspecting me, would they? I mean, Christ, I feel guilty enough as it is, about pulling out that damned fork. They're just making it worse.'

'You've told them . . .'

'Of course I've told them. They've been over and over it. I feel like someone in a bloody Hitchcock film or something, the innocent man on the run from the police trying to prove his own innocence.'

'You make it sound terribly exciting.'

'It's not exciting, it's bloody tiring. It's driving me mad.'

'When will you go?'

'First thing tomorrow.'

'Good luck, then.'

'Thanks. Who knows, when I see you at the funeral this could all be sorted.'

'Who knows?'

TWENTY-TWO

Will was putting things back. He was dismantling his museum and returning the exhibits to their rightful owners. He'd already made five trips, replaced five photographs and mementoes. He hoped, in time, to return everything. Everything except the one thing he couldn't ever give back. Mullen's life. But these were parts of lives he'd stolen, and it was the most he could do.

He realized that it would be confusing for his people. They would have become reconciled to the loss of their possessions, and now they were turning up again in exactly the place they last remembered them, as if they'd never been away. But they could always put it down to magic. Yes, he was introducing a little magic into their lives.

He was trying to do it roughly in order. The first things he'd taken were going back first. He couldn't stick to this scheme rigidly, because he didn't have the time. One house might present itself for entry before another on the list, and he had to be flexible. But with the aid of his notes he made up a rough schedule from week to week. He'd done three in the first week, two in the second and now he was on his first trip of the third week. So far he'd been lucky, nobody had moved. He didn't know what he'd do when the situation arose, as it surely must do. He'd deal with that when he came to it.

Tonight was all set, and right now he was standing in the garden of the woman called 'No Justice'. She'd looked to be in her late thirties when he'd first fucked her house; she'd be maybe forty now. She had married, or at least had a regular man who appeared to live there with her. Will wasn't sure how well they were getting on, though; every night the man went out to the pub and No Justice stayed at home. He'd come back about half-eleven, drunk, and by then the lights in the house would all be off. Will had checked the house for the past fortnight as part of his nightly rounds; he'd even seen the man in the pub, laughing with his friends. The routine was set. He had nothing to worry about. And anyway putting things back was quick. Quick and easy, not like fucking. He was in and out in less than three minutes now.

Yes, it was all very different to fucking. He wore underwear for a start, pants and socks. There was no nakedness involved. The tracksuit trousers, T-shirt and jacket he kept; they were comfortable and unobtrusive. He was used to them and they made him feel safe. He'd been worried at first that they might trigger certain feelings and excitements in him, but he found that, as long as he wore the underpants and his penis wasn't hanging free, he could control himself. He also kept the surgical gloves, for protection. The notebooks, however, he left behind. He didn't want to risk a repeat of the disaster at the Mullens'. It wasn't difficult to memorize the relevant information for each expedition. He'd always been good at memorizing things.

No Justice lived in a small house on a quiet street off the Newmarket Road, closer to town than Will's place. In the early days he hadn't roamed very far afield, he'd stuck to the areas he knew well.

The house had a large garden, with access from the rear. It gave him cover and allowed him to see pretty well what was going on inside the house without having to stand out in the open.

From behind a large old tree with a hard shiny bark Will could see that tonight No Justice was watching television by herself again.

Not for the first time he thanked God and John Logie Baird for the invention that had made his job so much easier. People watching television stayed put. Perhaps they might go to the kitchen or the toilet, but generally they remained in one area. In fact No Justice was out of the room at the moment. She'd gone out a couple of minutes ago, it was probably the adverts. Will was waiting for her to come back into the sitting-room before he went in.

And there she was. She came over to the window, looked out briefly, then drew the curtains. It was nearly nine and growing dark.

Pub Man had left the house at about half-eight. So it was all clear. Will set off across the lawn. He knew the back door wasn't locked because he'd already tried it.

Soon, No Justice would have her photo back, and her bra, and it would be as if Will had never been here before.

He'd found the photo in the top drawer of a chest of drawers, the place where a lot of people keep their personal knick-knacks. It was a Polaroid. It showed No Justice standing with her back to a wall, naked to the waist. Her shirt was unbuttoned and hanging from her skirt and she was staring blankly at the camera. There was nothing erotic about the picture, it was almost clinical. The harsh colours and flat lighting gave it a strange, unnerving quality. You couldn't tell from the shot why it had been taken or what it meant.

It was because of this photo that he'd named her 'No Justice'. Her breasts didn't match. The left one – her left – was noticeably smaller than the other, which sagged slightly and seemed to hang at an angle, off to one side. The blank, impersonal expression made Will think of the statue of Justice on top of the Old Bailey, only the scales were unbalanced. She was tipped one way.

So she wasn't Justice, after all, she was No Justice.

He arrived at the door, opened it, slipped in and closed it all in one motion. Then he hurried down the hall and ducked into a doorway, just in case she'd felt the change in pressure and came out to look. She didn't.

He waited. He could hear the television, there was music and occasional narration. It sounded like a documentary, probably wildlife.

The hall was dark. It had a polished wooden floor and dark wooden bannisters up the wide staircase.

Look out for steps three, seven and nine, the notebook had said. He did and he hopped soundlessly up to the top.

Her bedroom was the first door on the right, thankfully not above the sitting-room with the television in it.

He went in and closed the door behind him.

It had changed since he was here last. It had been redecorated. It was now a pale, powdery blue instead of the previous pink. There was a smart new carpet, a new bed, and most of the furniture was in different positions. Luckily the chest of drawers was still there. He went over to it, turned on a little, white-shaded lamp and slid out the top drawer.

When he'd found it the photograph had been with a pile of others, a jumble of old ones taken over the years. They'd gone, though, and Will was about to just drop the picture in and leave when he saw the distinctive bright colours of a developer's envelope.

He opened it and took the photos out. They were recent holiday snaps. No Justice was in some of them and Pub Man was in the others. Funnily enough, she looked younger than in Will's photo, maybe because she was smiling. No. There was definitely something different about her. He flipped through, trying to pin down what it was.

And then he realized.

She was sitting on the sand, smiling up at whoever was taking the picture, Pub Man probably. She was topless, she had a nice tan and her breasts matched. They were both high and firm and round.

Christ. She'd had them fixed.

Will stared at the picture, fascinated. It made her look completely different. He was struck by the thought that everyone in his city was changing. His museum was just a record of a moment in the past, not the present. For it to be accurate he would have to go back into every house, over and over again. He would have to repeatedly get an update of births, marriages, deaths and plastic surgery.

But no, he was closing down his museum. It was all over.

He felt terribly sad. For a moment he'd pictured the two photographs side by side on the wall. Before and after. No Justice becomes Justice. Then perhaps another photo every year, following the woman to her grave, watching her new breasts sag and die.

Or would they? He didn't know about implants. Maybe they stayed young for ever. Maybe at seventy she'd have the breasts of an eighteen-year-old girl.

He'd never know. It wasn't fair. Why had Mullen spoiled everything? Why had he come into the room at that moment? Another twenty seconds later, another ten and he'd still be alive, and Will would still have his museum, and these nightly expeditions would be full of joy and passion and sex instead of regret.

But that was how it had to be now. Will's gratification had led to death. So now he had to put things back. The Fist was still waiting in the sky to swat him, but with every return he felt it move further away. It wasn't just that he was removing the evidence of past crimes, it was that he was doing the right thing. He must never cause pain again. Never fight back. Dad had been right. 'Hurt no living thing, no ladybird, or butterfly, or moth with dusty wing.'

But would it hurt to take this photo? Just this one small photo of the woman laughing on the sand with her new breasts . . .

Yes.

She was happy.

But he could leave her the negatives . . .

No. He was putting things back. He was giving now, not taking.

He was making the Fist go away. He just hoped that it wasn't simply drawing back to strike.

But if it did, he'd be brave, he'd take it and not complain. That was the only thing he would take . . .

But she looked so happy . . .

Shit. He came back to reality, he was taking too long. In and out, that was his rule. He mustn't get pulled back into the old life, into the life of sex and fulfilment.

Reluctantly he put the photo back in the folder and slipped the old one in beside it. She had her old self back now. It was up to her to dispose of it if she wanted. He no longer had a part of her.

A weight lifted from him, but it took a part of his heart with it.

He closed the drawer, took one last look around the room, turned off the lamp and went out.

He should have checked. He should have listened. He should have been careful, but the photograph had distracted him.

Justice was there, right in the middle of the landing.

Christ, it was happening again.

She said, 'Oh.' It wasn't a scream, more of a gasp of shock. She visibly jumped back.

'What are you doing?' she said, sounding shocked.

Will wanted to run for the stairs, but she was blocking them. She became more bold now, her fear curdled into anger.

'What the bloody hell are you doing?'

He said nothing and she slapped him very hard around the face. It was all he deserved. He'd violated her house, he'd stolen her photo. She had every right to hurt him.

'I'm putting things back,' he said sheepishly.

'What?'

'It doesn't matter.'

'Yes, it does. You're in my house.'

He slowly walked towards her, hoping she would move aside. She didn't, so he tried to brush past her. She grabbed his hand, twisted it.

'Hurt no living thing,' he said.

175

'What?'

'No ladybird, or butterfly, or moth with dusty wing.'

She twisted his hand harder.

'I'm going to call the police,' she said.

Will suddenly jerked his hand free, it was easy. She was left holding his glove. He pushed her aside and bolted down the stairs. As he raced towards the back door he heard the woman pounding down the stairs after him. But his need to get away was stronger than her desire to catch him and he was soon out the door, across the lawn, through the trees and into the road.

Shit, shit, shit . . . Not again. And he'd nearly given in this time. Stupid. He'd thought she was the Fist come down from the sky to crush him. She wasn't. She was just a woman with a new set of breasts.

Why couldn't they all leave him alone? All he was doing was trying to help. To put right what he'd done wrong. He didn't want to hurt them, they hurt themselves.

When he got home, the old bag was waiting in the hallway. He barged past her before she could say anything and went up to his room.

He didn't want to speak to her. He'd had enough of people.

He'd had enough of everything. It seemed in this world that whatever you did you couldn't do it right.

Maybe if you just did nothing? Just sat there and let it all happen to you. Maybe then things would work out. Because, sure as shit, if you ever went out and tried, tried to do what you enjoyed, even tried to help people, you simply got a hard time for it.

Sit there, sit still. Do nothing, say nothing. That reminded him of something. What was it?

Christ.

He laughed.

It was Norman Bates. *Psycho.* At the end of the film he just sat there and let the fly land on him. Showed them that he couldn't hurt anything. Not even a fly.

Psycho.

Well, that was a laugh. That was funny.

You shouldn't really take things too seriously ... You had to laugh.

Laugh and the whole world laughs with you.

And then he remembered he'd killed someone.

TWENTY-THREE

Tom was talking to James. But James wasn't being much help. Tom was trying to sort out how to find the Intruder but James seemed more interested in the fork sticking out of his neck. In fact, Tom wished James would bugger off and leave him alone.

When he'd arrived in Norwich at lunchtime, he'd had no clear plan of action. He'd hoped that just by being here, in the house again, something would suggest itself. He'd been nervous coming through the front door; there was a desolate emptiness about the place. Everywhere there were reminders of the absent, broken family. The children's rooms with their colourful decorations and unused toys. Lucy's room with its carefully made bed. And the kitchen, which held memories of a different kind.

The floor was scrubbed and gleaming, and there was still a lingering smell of disinfectant.

Tom had sat at the table and been overcome by a terrible, debilitating tiredness. He'd been unable to move. He'd remembered Lucy telling him of her own strange trances, and he'd wondered if there was something in the house, something haunting it that sapped your strength and stole your mind. He'd lost track of how long he'd sat there. He was paralysed; he couldn't get up to eat or even to turn the lights on. The room had become dark. Then, in the shadows, he'd seen something. As he'd stared at it, it had slowly taken on a shape. It was James, sitting on the floor, propped against the cooker, the fork sticking out of his neck.

'James?' he'd said. 'What are you still doing here? I thought they'd taken you away.'

'No. I'm still here. Why have I been left?'

'I don't know, James. I really don't know.'

And so they'd talked. But even now, no matter how much Tom told him the other things on his mind, James wouldn't shut up about the bloody fork.

'Can't you help me, Tom?'

'No. It's not a good idea, James. I'll hurt you.'

'Please . . .'

'For God's sake, James. I'm trying to fix things here, and you're not helping one bit.'

'Fix what?'

'Everything. I have to fix everything. You see, me and Lucy, we always looked after each other as children, and it's just in recent years we forgot that. We should never have got involved with other people.'

'Help me, Tom. Get this thing out of my neck.'

'You're not listening.'

'Pull it out.'

'No. I tried that before and it killed you.'

'This time it'll be different. Please, it hurts so much.'

'I mustn't. I can't. I can't help you.'

James began to sob. It was a pitiful sound, irritating and monotonous. Eventually Tom could stand it no more. He forced himself up and went over to his brother-in-law.

'Thank you,' James said. 'I knew you'd come. I knew you'd help me.'

'But I mustn't take the fork out.'

'Please, it hurts so much. It'll be all right. I promise it'll be all right this time.'

So he did it. He pulled it out and it happened again. The blood arced out, covering Tom. Then James cried out, 'Why have you done this to me?' and he disappeared.

Tom was still sitting at the table, it was still the afternoon; bright sunshine filled the kitchen. But the dream had disturbed him. It had been so real that even now he wasn't sure it hadn't actually happened. Whatever, he knew he had to get out of the house. It wasn't doing him any good at all.

Wearily he rolled the notebook and stuffed it in his pocket. It took a great effort to propel himself down the hall to the front door, but once outside he felt a whole lot better.

He took a deep breath, looked up at the big, pale Norfolk sky, then set out to wander the streets of Norwich.

Just as the Intruder had, he went out among the houses and the people and tried to understand the other man's impulses. Thinking that if he got to know him, he could find him, and then what?

The first thing was to find him.

As he walked aimlessly around and looked at the houses his mind wandered to the book.

I do not believe that a man can be truly happy unless he fully understands what he is and can act accordingly . . . How can it be wrong to be happy?

He imagined all the lives within the passing houses, all those people who somehow must be happy. It wasn't conceivable that you could have a whole city of people going around being miserable, and that meant that Tom was different. There was something wrong with him and he had to be cured.

Clive and his bloody therapy sessions hadn't been able to do anything for him. Maddie had helped, but then for some reason had abandoned him. What was he to do? He was to find the Intruder.

As he walked he recited whole chunks of the book to himself.

Somewhere within these words, within the very houses of the town itself he would find the clue, the one piece of information that would lead him to the museum.

The streets seemed so familiar; he'd read about them so much in the book. He peered in windows, stopped to stare at gardens. Was this house one that the Intruder had entered at some time? Had he walked along this pavement here? Had he crossed the road at this exact point? Then it struck him. Why not be sure?

In a newsagent's he bought a map of the town and looked up the addresses mentioned in the book. Then in turn he began to visit them, hoping that perhaps, if he retraced the Intruder's steps, they would lead him to the man. As he came upon each new house, he had an overwhelming sense of *déjà vu*, as if he'd lived there. The memories they evoked were so intense. He had to keep reminding himself that they weren't his memories, though, they were the other man's. These were his streets. The whole town was him. But it was frustrating. Where was his heart? Where was his museum? The map from the newsagent's wasn't the proper map; hidden beneath it was the real city and Tom had to find it.

The sky was growing dark as he came to Miss Fish's house. There were the net curtains, but there was no light on behind them to show what was inside. In fact there were no lights on anywhere in the house. Miss Fish, the teacher, must be out.

Tom walked down the alley at the side and came out by the gate in her back fence. It was partially open. He looked through and saw a small, tidy yard and her kitchen window. He could see the tall spouts of her taps standing up above the sill.

What if he were to go in there? Go up into her room just as the Intruder had.

He hesitated at the gate, his heart climbing into his throat. Then he heard footsteps in the alley and knew he had to get away.

He turned from the gate and headed back up the alley. In the semi-darkness of the passage between the houses he passed Miss

Fish. It was unmistakably her. The slim top half, the heavy thighs and legs, the wide hips. He smiled at her pleasantly and she smiled back. Then she was gone and he was out at the front again.

He realized that he'd been closer to her than the Intruder ever had. He'd brushed against her even. But it wasn't enough; it was her he'd found, not the man who'd written about her.

Miss Fish's was the last one. He'd visited all the houses mentioned in the book now, so he headed back towards Lucy's on the other side of town. As he trudged along, he realized how exhausted he was. He'd been walking for nearly four hours, and it was probably about another half-hour's walk to Lucy's from here. So he'd worn out his shoes, he'd been to all the places in the book, and what had he achieved?

Nothing.

But he'd missed somewhere, hadn't he?

He stopped walking.

There was one more house. One place he hadn't considered looking.

Lucy's house. The last entry in the book.

He ran the rest of the way. Before he knew it, he was standing in her front garden looking up at the house.

He took out the notebook and by the failing light he read through the last few pages. He'd never properly studied this part before; it had been too painful, too close. He'd felt embarrassed reading about his sister like this.

There was a page or so of mundane stuff, straightforward description, a bit about how the Intruder might get in. Then Tom felt the hairs on his arms stand up as he read . . .

It is interesting to note that the windows at the front are a recent addition, double glazing – to keep the noise of the traffic out, probably. The interesting thing is that they are exactly the same type as the ones Dad put in at Newmarket Road. He got them

cheap somewhere, like everything else. I wonder if they have the
same problems opening them as we do. The windows are one
of the things which attracted me to the house in the first place.

Newmarket Road. The Intruder had given his address. Not the number, admittedly, but still a description of his house. The windows. It had been there all along and he hadn't seen it. Suddenly he was filled with a surge of energy. He would find him, and he would find him now.

There wasn't enough light out here to read any more, so he went inside and studied the street plan in the kitchen. Newmarket Road looked fairly long, going from the city centre right out to the ring road a few miles away. It was too far to walk so he'd have to take his car.

When he got there, all he had to do was check the windows on all the houses down the road. There were problems, of course; the writer could have moved from the house he was describing. But what had he written? *'I wonder if they have the same problems as we do.' Do*, not *did*. The implication was that the writer still lived in his childhood home. Also, of course, there could be other houses with similar windows. Though he felt that the way they were described meant that they weren't very common. They'd stood out for the writer, they should stand out for him.

He looked at the keys on the table and was overcome by tiredness again. The excitement had drained him. He felt as if he couldn't get out of the chair. His head was like a rock; his neck barely able to support its weight. He stared at the scratched wood of the table-top, following the lines back and forth as they intersected. He was a bird high above the city, looking down on it. There was Lucy, there was the Intruder, there was James, there was Tom, there was . . .

He jerked his head up.

This was ridiculous. He had to get some rest. He looked out of the window. It was too dark now, anyway. There would be no point in traipsing all the way across town if he wouldn't be able to see anything properly when he got there.

He yawned and stretched. He felt stiff all over.

'Come on,' he said and hauled himself up off the chair.

He only got as far as the sitting-room. He couldn't face the stairs.

He sat in an armchair, willing sleep to come, but it wouldn't. He'd lost count of how many nights it had been now. Objects in the room seemed to move all around him in the darkness. Out of the corner of his eye he'd catch something jump a few inches, but if he looked directly at it or turned on the light it would return to where it had been before. At some point James came back as well, complaining that he was cold and whinging about the fork that he'd somehow got back in his neck. But Tom knew better than to talk to him and simply ignored him. In time he grew fainter and fainter and eventually dissolved altogether.

At last the sun came up. The sky brightened and at six o'clock Tom was in the car heading for the Newmarket Road.

He recognized it when he got there; it was the main route into town from London and the west. It was wide and busy. The houses were large, old and solid-looking, generally set back behind generous front gardens. Mostly they still kept their original features and windows, though one or two had been obviously modernized.

He realized his best chance of finding the house was to walk. He parked on a side street and made his way back to where the road started. He double-checked the sign, always best to be meticulous. And there, opposite, was the hospital, built of the same red brick as much of the rest of Norwich. This was good. A clean start.

Before he'd left he'd studied the windows at Lucy's house. He'd even drawn them as well as he could on a blank page of the book. He quickly looked at his sketch again to make sure the image was firmly placed in his mind. He was ready.

He began to walk.

Somewhere on this road the Intruder lived. All Tom had to do was check every house until he found him. It was a long road, but he had time. All the time in the world.

Then, when he found the house, he would need to watch it, see who came in and out, identify the Intruder. As far as he could tell from the notebook he lived alone with his mother, but he couldn't be a hundred per cent sure of that.

Don't jump ahead. Find the house first. One thing at a time.

One house at a time.

He soon discovered that he could tell at a glance whether the windows were the ones he was looking for. But it was still slow work, as he had to cross the road now and then to get a look at a house that was hidden by trees or a tall hedge.

House after house passed by. Unlike the city-wide meanderings of yesterday, today he had a purpose, a route. Today he could see the real map with Lucy's house on it, and all the other houses, and this road, and somewhere on this road the Intruder. The city had taken on a shape, a meaningful form. He felt all the streets leading here, to this house with the metal-framed windows. It all made sense. The further he walked down the road, the nearer he felt to the house. Closer and closer. He and the Intruder were converging.

Five minutes, ten minutes, twenty minutes, half an hour, and then he stopped.

There it was.

A large house with pointed gables, and that same red brick again. But it was the windows he was looking at. The windows which were completely out of character, metal-framed, double-glazed, ugly. To make sure he checked his sketches again. Yes, they were definitely the same. He made a note of the number. He felt excited, but then he told himself that he still had to check every other house, in case there were more than one with these windows. Although he couldn't imagine anyone else actually wanting a set like these; they looked so out of place on the once elegant Victorian house. But he carried on walking, carried on looking. Though casually now, savouring the knowledge of that building and what it might contain. Delaying the conquest of its hidden secrets.

Twenty minutes later, tantalizingly near to the end of the road, his heart sank as he found another building with the same windows. A wide, squat affair with a busy car park out front. There was a modern, square extension built along the ground floor, and it was here the windows were. As he looked closer he saw a sign by the front door and he went nearer to investigate.

It was a doctor's surgery.

He wondered if that was a good or a bad sign. There had certainly been nothing in the book about living above a doctor's, but it was always possible. He looked up at the top floor, the windows were different here, they were only double-glazed on the ground-floor extension, the surgery part. He cursed. He didn't want these complications. Things had been going too well.

But it wasn't so bad, was it? Only two houses so far. He just had to hope there weren't any more.

He was soon out of town, and thankfully the houses ran out before he discovered any more cheap metal double glazing.

Two, then. Only two. The map was near completion. The map was a system, the city was a system. He had to have a system now. He had to have a plan, one thing after another. Reasonable. Logical.

Right. Well, of the two his first choice was definitely the house rather than the surgery. It felt right. So that was the one he would watch first and if he was wrong, well, then he could watch the surgery. He didn't have to rush. He was still ahead of the police. Be calm, be organized.

The first thing was to get his car. He'd already discovered that he couldn't park on Newmarket Road itself, but he remembered another smaller road opposite the first house. He could maybe wait there and keep an eye on things. Yes, that was the sensible thing to do. He felt happy. He was doing the right thing. He had a nice, simple plan. This was good. He was alive again.

He managed to find a parking space that had a clear view over to the front door and he settled in to wait.

People passed by, walking along the wide pavement in front of the the house. Several times Tom sat up, his heart racing, as he thought he'd seen his man, but nobody stopped and went in. In fact, nobody went in or out until just after four, when a young woman with red hair strolled up to the front door and let herself in. She was too young to be the mother. She looked about Tom's age, maybe Lucy's, quite attractive, in a short skirt and baggy top. Perhaps she was the Intruder's girlfriend; perhaps they were even married. Tom held on to that hope, he so wanted this to be the house. He was ready and waiting.

Fifteen or so minutes later a bus pulled up and a mob of school-children got off. They were rowdy, shouting at each other, dressed in casual clothes, jeans, trainers, tracksuits, and several of them carried fluorescent backpacks. They dispersed. All except for a couple of boys who stood talking quietly, scuffing their feet. Then these two split up, one heading off down the road. The other went up the short drive to the house.

Tom was deflated. He'd allowed himself to imagine the Intruder might have a wife, but a son? No. He was being stupid, acting on impulse. Just because he wanted this to be the house, he was trying to twist the facts to fit it. But it was no good.

The surgery, then? The house above the surgery. Why not?

He started the car and drove off up the road. It was like he was driving through tar, everything seemed so slow now. Everything was a struggle. Sitting inactive for so long had sapped his energy. And he'd wasted all that time, watching the wrong house. He'd been a fool.

It seemed an interminable drive, but eventually he pulled up opposite and parked. Then he fixed his eyes on the building and sat unmoving.

The next thing he knew a switch had been thrown and it was the middle of the night.

He woke stiffly, and it took him a moment to remember where he was.

He had to get out of the car to stretch. He looked at his watch in the light from a street lamp. It was two-thirty in the morning. He'd been asleep in the car for ten hours. The surgery was dark. He groaned and rolled his shoulders. He felt terrible. Dried out, old, pathetic.

He climbed painfully back into the car, started the engine and headed off back to Lucy's. When he got there he crawled up the stairs into her bedroom and stripped to his underwear, too weary to undress completely. He pulled back the duvet and flopped on to the mattress.

He spent the next three days in bed, drifting between wakefulness and sleep as if the two had no boundary.

TWENTY-FOUR

Lucy had always found Tom an infuriatingly slow driver. Slow and irritable. Which was why she'd tried to persuade him not to come back to London and collect her and the girls for the funeral. But he'd insisted, and now he seemed to be worse than ever. He was swearing and shouting at the other drivers and crawling along at a dangerously sedentary pace. She knew it was pointless saying anything to him, it'd only make him twice as bad. She tried to take her mind off it by sitting in the back and keeping the girls amused. They would really have been much happier on the train; three hours in the car was too long. They were all very soon in as bad a mood as Tom.

By the time they arrived in Norwich all the peace she'd found in London had gone, and the four of them were a frayed and touchy mess.

Halfway up the path to the front door she exploded. Polly had deliberately walked into a flower-bed and trampled a group of begonias. Lucy grabbed her by the arm and yanked her back. She shook her violently and yelled at her for being a stupid little girl. Polly was too shocked to react for a moment, then she opened her mouth and began to wail.

'Oh, do shut up!' Lucy said. 'Mummy's getting a terrible headache.'

But she knew it wasn't just the journey, or the kids' behaviour.

She was nervous about entering the house. She'd only been back once since James's death, the next day; she'd had to come in to sort the place out and pick up clothes and things. But she'd gone through it in a daze, without thinking, and afterwards she hardly remembered being there at all.

This time was different. This time she was coming home.

As it turned out it wasn't too bad, she didn't break down or anything.

Tom had made a real effort. There were flowers everywhere and food in the fridge. There was a lived-in air about the place that helped make it feel less desolate.

She got the kids some tea, but she couldn't stay in the kitchen where they normally would have eaten. She told the girls that for a treat they could eat in the dining-room, like grown-ups. The girls' excited chatter kept her mind off things through the meal and their bath afterwards but, as she took them upstairs to get ready for bed, Claire asked where Daddy was and the whole fragile façade collapsed. She realized she would have to try and explain to them what she had attempted, only halfheartedly, to do before.

She waited until they were both in their pyjamas, then sat them on her bed with her.

'Listen,' she said. 'I've got to tell you something very sad.'

'What?' Polly asked, smiling.

'It's about daddy.'

'Where is he?'

'Your Daddy is dead,' Lucy said, trying to keep her voice calm and even.

'What does that mean?' Claire looked at her seriously.

Lucy wished they'd had some pets which had died and could have been used as examples, but James hadn't allowed pets.

'It means he's gone away,' she said, and knew immediately that it was inadequate. But she ploughed on. 'Gone away to a place he can never come back from.'

'Why?' Claire bit her lip. Polly was staring at her intently.

'Tomorrow we're going to go to a place where they put dead people. His body is going to be put in the ground for ever.'

'What do you mean, his body?' Polly said in her bossy manner.

'They put him in a box—'

'But you said he'd gone away.'

'His soul has gone away.'

'What's his soul?'

'It's a ... it's a spirit, like a ghost.'

'Ghosts are dead people.'

'Yes, and Daddy's a dead person now.'

'Does that mean he'll be a ghost? And come back to haunt us?'

'No. He'll never come back. You'll never see him again. Daddy was a good man. Only bad men become ghosts.'

'You said Daddy was a ghost.'

'Like a ghost,' Lucy snapped, then told herself not to be so silly, this was no time to lose her patience. 'A good ghost,' she said gently. 'He's become an angel.'

'An angel?' Claire, who had been listening quietly, trying to understand, picked up on this. It struck a chord within her. She evidently knew about angels.

'Angels live in heaven,' she said, proud of her knowledge.

'Yes, love, and that's where Daddy's gone, to heaven.'

Claire started to cry. 'Why's he gone? Why?'

'A bad man made him go there.'

'A ghost?'

'No, a bad man. He made Daddy die, and now Daddy's gone, and he's never coming back.' Lucy had started to cry now, and in no time at all the three of them were a bawling, tear-drenched bundle, hugging each other on the bed.

Luckily the effort of crying exhausted the girls, and when she eventually got them to bed they went straight off to sleep. She didn't know if she'd helped, or just scared and confused them with her talk of angels and ghosts. She wondered again if taking them to the funeral was a good idea, but what Tom had said to her about understanding the finality of it all had seemed to make sense. She didn't want them to think for the next few years that Daddy might be coming home some time. They'd get over it okay, they were young, they'd soon forget. And if that meant she had to be blunt with them, then so be it.

Once she was sure they were asleep, she went back to her room, tidied herself and straightened the bedclothes. Tom had been sleeping in the bed, but tonight he'd have to sleep on the sofa-bed downstairs.

When she went down she found him watching television in the sitting-room.

'Are you okay?' he asked.

'Yup, I'm fine. Just had a good old cry with the girls.'

Tom smiled reassuringly. He looked tired and thin, his eyes dark, sunk into his pale skin.

'Do you want a drink?' she asked him.

'No, no, thanks,' he said, smiling again. 'Keep my mind clear, you know?'

'Mm.' That was just like Tom, self-denial, keep everything battened down. She poured herself a large, neat vodka and slumped into an armchair. 'I'm not really looking forward to tomorrow,' she said, taking a sip.

'No,' said Tom. 'But it'll soon all be over.'

'I've decided I'm going to stay down after. I can't hide for ever. We've got to get on with things. There's school and ... I think I'll look for a job of some sort. I don't want to sit around here feeling sorry for myself.'

'What will you do?'

'I don't know, maybe go back to insurance or something. It doesn't matter, really.'

'What about the house?'

'It was our house. We bought it together, the girls were born here. I'm not going to let some ... anyone ... take that away from us.'

'You always were the strong one. I pretended I was looking after you, but you held it together.'

Lucy looked at Tom. His eyes were shining, almost feverish-looking. And there was something about him, something desperate. She'd felt it before. There was a desperate, guilty eager-ness about him, a need to please. She hadn't asked him what he'd been up to in the last few days and he hadn't offered, so she wasn't going to pry.

She pulled herself up out of the chair. 'I'll go and make us some-thing to eat.'

'No, you sit down,' said Tom, jumping up. 'I'll do it.'

'Tom, no. You've done more than enough. I want to do some-thing. Stay here and watch the telly.'

'I wasn't really watching it ... I ...'

'Tom, please. Relax.'

'Okay.' He threw up his hands in a gesture of defeat and sat down. 'You're the boss.'

Lucy took her drink through to the kitchen and topped it up with tonic and ice, then drank it as she prepared dinner. It helped her face things. It was difficult not to be drawn back to memories of that last dinner, but she forced herself on. Somehow James's death had woken her from her strange enchantment and now she had the energy to make herself do things. With each fresh achievement she felt stronger, more in control, happier. Tonight the meal, tomorrow the funeral. Then get the girls ready for school. Buy them clothes, get a job.

Yes, she'd been shocked back to life and she intended to enjoy it this time.

They ate in the kitchen, and it was all right.

But as it was, when she finally went to bed she couldn't get to sleep for ages. Then, just as she was dozing off, she was woken by

Claire screaming. She went in to her, and the poor girl was gabbling about ghosts and bad men.

'I saw him, Mummy, I saw him!'

'Who?'

'The bad man. The ghost.'

'No, dear, it was just a dream.'

'No, I saw him, he was in my room. It was the bad man, it was Uncle Tom.'

'Uncle Tom's downstairs.'

'Not that Uncle Tom, the other one, the bad one.'

'No, dear, it was a nightmare, a bad dream.'

Then Polly came into the room, rubbing her eyes.

'I've woken up, Mummy,' she said.

'Come along, back to bed.'

'Don't leave me,' Claire moaned.

'Would you like to sleep in with Polly tonight, darling? In her bed?'

'Yes.'

So she took them both into Polly's room and tucked them in. They eventually drifted off and she sat with them for an hour, watching over their troubled sleep.

She went back to her own bed, but it was no use; she was wide awake now. In the end, at four o'clock she gave up and went downstairs to make herself a cup of tea. But as she neared the kitchen door she heard someone talking, and froze. There was someone in there.

It wasn't possible. It couldn't be happening again.

Then she recognized the voice and relaxed. It was Tom. She opened the door and went in. He jumped.

'You're as bad as the girls,' she said. 'Everyone's seeing ghosts tonight.'

'You startled me.'

'I'm sorry. Who were you talking to?'

'No one.'

'I thought you were on the phone or something.'

'No. I was just ... reciting a poem to myself. I couldn't sleep.'

'Me neither.'

He seemed happy to see her and they sat and chatted for a while drinking tea. Tom still seemed upset that the police suspected him, but she tried to reassure him that even if they did, they couldn't possibly have any evidence to prove it. She told him he mustn't let it get to him, and he kept insisting that he was fine.

Slowly the sky brightened. Lucy had the feeling that they were all alone in the world, the only people up. It was quiet and very peaceful. But she began to shiver as the cold got into her and Tom put an arm round her shoulders.

It wasn't enough.

'I think I'll go back to bed,' she said.

'Will you be warm enough there?'

'Yes. What about you? Will you be okay?'

'Don't worry about me.'

'Goodnight, then, Tom, and thanks for everything.'

'No, thank you, Sis.'

She kissed him. 'I'll see you in the morning,' she said and went upstairs.

She got back under the duvet and lay there, watching the light seep through the curtains. Half an hour later there was a gentle tap on the door. It was Tom.

'I'm cold,' he said. 'I'm so cold.'

'Oh Tom,' said Lucy sadly, and with that Tom got into her bed.

He held on to her tightly and she stroked his head, cradling him like a child. Before she knew it, she herself was a child again. She was dreaming of whiteness. Flowers. White flowers. She was thirteen years old and back in Minehead. She and Tom were building a little hut in the garden out of branches. It wasn't their real garden, though, this garden was huge and overgrown, an untidy jungle. Nothing like the neat, little, ordered thing her father had created. She hid in the hut with Tom, and she saw that the walls were entwined with flowering bindweed. As she watched, it grew up between the branches, until the whole hut was covered with it, and they were in a house made of flowers. It was warm and cosy in there and the two of them lay in each other's arms, submerged in a glowing, green, underwater light.

And then Dad appeared, and started pulling the weeds down.

'No more bindweed,' he said. 'We have to get rid of it all.'

And he tore the weeds away until a new, bright, blinding light broke through the walls and roof. And she heard herself crying, crying out a name in fear, her own name. In panic she struggled up from the depths of sleep, but it was only Polly, calling out to her, and she knew it was time to get up.

She felt strange dressing for the funeral. Her black dress was her party dress.

Weddings and funerals, they were the only times you dressed up. It was as if they were just pieces of theatre. She wore black tights and black shoes, and she did her hair and put on make-up. She even wore a hat, one she'd bought for Dad's funeral and which had been in the box ever since. She couldn't help thinking, as she studied herself in the mirror, that she looked glamorous. Black had changed its meaning in recent years, had become fashionable. It seemed so inappropriate now. Really for a funeral she thought you should wear something ugly, something horrible that you wouldn't be seen dead in, purple loons, or a knitted poncho or something. But then James had always liked her in this dress. The few times she'd worn it, he'd looked at her admiringly. So maybe, maybe he was somewhere now watching her and would admire her again.

She dressed the girls in matching dark blue dresses, their party dresses as well. And they got excited putting them on. Claire once again asked where they were going but Lucy didn't want to try and explain it all again, so she ignored her.

'All set, then?' Tom asked as the three of them came downstairs.

'As set as I'll ever be.'

Tom had on a smart black suit with black tie. He was the only one who looked properly sombre and serious.

'Let's go, then,' he said briskly, and they left the house.

As it turned out, the funeral passed mercifully quickly. Lucy had so much on her mind trying to keep the girls in order that she paid scarcely any attention to the dreary vicar and his over-rehearsed sentiments.

At the grave-side, however, as they lowered the coffin into the ground and a couple of people half-heartedly tossed on some earth, Claire asked what was in the box and Lucy began to cry. This set the girls off, and Tom led them away from the grave.

As they walked between the grave-stones Lucy heard a series of whirring clicks and looked up to see someone she didn't know taking pictures. She was too surprised to be angry. Anyway, it just added to the air of theatricality. They could all look at the pictures afterwards and imagine they had really been there, and weren't just pretending.

Back at the house afterwards everyone tried to be jolly and philosophical, the noisiest group being James's workmates from the insurance company. 'Life must go on ... Let's enjoy ourselves, it's what he would have wanted ... I feel most sorry for the girls ...' But she did manage to have a good talk with James's parents, who had come down from Peterborough. They were both very small and old, quiet and faintly embarrassed beneath their grief.

They talked about old times, and the children, and what James had been like as a boy and Lucy felt better for it. The old couple wanted to leave early, however. They didn't really know anyone else here. Lucy walked them out to their car, relieved to be out in the fresh air.

'You must bring the children over,' James's mother said through the open window. 'Come and stay. You will, won't you?'

'Of course I will.'

'Good. Family is so important. We mustn't lose touch.'

'Maybe this will bring us all closer together.'

'I hope so, dear. I was so happy for James when he met you. I know that you made him very happy, and I'm glad he died happy.'

'Yes,' said Lucy and a lump came into her throat. Hold on to the lies, she thought. We can change the past. Remember the happy times.

She was too emotional to say anything else and James's mother realized it. She squeezed Lucy's hand quickly, then turned to her husband. 'Come along, Robert, let's get home.'

Lucy waved as they drove off, then heard someone behind her.

'Hello.' It was a big man with a rather self-conscious manner. He had a wine glass in one hand, he offered the other one for her to shake.

'Hello, Mrs Mullen, we've not met. I'm Bob Arnell.'

She shook his hand, but the name didn't register.

'I used to do the classes with Jim.'

'Classes?'

'The karate.'

'Oh, of course, I'm sorry.'

'That's all right. As I say, we've not met before.'

'You're the ... the policeman?'

'For my sins.' Bob smiled. 'I just thought I wanted to say hello. Meet you, and that. James used to talk about you a lot.'

'Oh, I'm sure he didn't.'

'Well. You know, like. It's just a shame we couldn't have met under better circumstances. All the lads miss him. He was a good laugh, old Jimmy.'

She tried to imagine James having a good laugh with the lads, but couldn't. It wasn't the James she'd known.

There was an awkward silence. Lucy tried to think of something to say.

Bob looked at his shiny black shoes and shuffled.

'Erm,' said Lucy, 'I don't suppose you'd know, I mean . . .'

'What's that?'

'The police. Do they know anything? Is there anything new?'

'Well, it's not now a case I'm on. Different department. That's, er, DI Hapworth. I'm mostly, you know, petty crimes, burglaries and that. But, well, you know, the lads talk. And, well, it's daft really. Usually, you see, murders . . . You don't mind me talking about it like that, do you?'

'No. James was murdered, I don't mind you saying so.'

'Right, but as I say murders are usually the easiest cases to solve. It's not like Agatha Christie, you know, the perfect crime. There's usually a, you know, clear-cut motive, a handy suspect. But in this case . . . Poor old Hapworth and Snack are running around like a couple of blue-arsed flies, er, if you pardon my language.'

'What about my brother?'

'I beg your pardon?'

'They seem to think my brother might have done it.'

'Well, I, I wouldn't know anything about that. As I say, it's not my department. I, er, I'm sure, you know . . .'

'You can tell them – tell them from me, he didn't do it. I know Tom, he didn't have anything to do with it, he tried to help.'

'I'm sure he did. Listen, I'd better be pushing off. If you ever want to ring me, if you ever want to talk about it, or about anything, ask me anything, you know? I'll try and do what I can. I'll make inquiries about your brother for you, I'll—'

'Thank you.'

'As I say, I'm sure it's nothing. I'll ring you. Here's my number.' He passed her a printed card with his name and telephone number on it. He waited for her to say something else, but she'd finished with him. In the end he smiled sheepishly and wandered off back indoors.

Lucy knew why he'd talked to her, why he'd been so friendly; it was the black. She was that old cliché, the sexy widow. He probably imagined she'd been wearing black stockings.

She smiled. She had to admit it was good to feel sexy again. Even if it was so horribly out of place at her husband's funeral.

Weddings and funerals, they were both the same. For their different reasons they made everyone feel sexy.

'Life must go on . . . Let's enjoy ourselves, it's what he would have wanted . . .'

She sighed.

The sexy widow returns to the wake.

TWENTY-FIVE

Tom had only bought the local paper for something to read while sitting in the car watching the house. So he was shocked when he opened it and saw a picture of himself. It had been taken at the funeral; Tom looked almost comically manly and serious, walking along with an arm round Lucy, who held a tissue up to her eyes. The two girls were clinging to her dress and looking up at her face. There was a formality about the composition, a staged look to it. The whole thing was like one of those ghastly Victorian morality paintings.

Tom looked very old. He wasn't used to seeing photographs of himself and had never enjoyed having his picture taken. It was disorienting finding this one here in the paper. Other people appeared in newspapers, not him.

He read the short article. The gist of it was that the killer had still not been caught; he was still roaming the streets of Norwich, a potential threat to all decent law-abiding families.

But the real reason for this photo being here, so prominent, was obvious. It was a lovely, emotive image.

Tom experienced a mess of feelings, so tangled that he couldn't even begin to sort them out. He knew there was pity in there, and anger and inadequacy, but there were others, darker, stranger. There was something that felt like lust, for instance, even perhaps a wild kind of joy.

He couldn't read the rest of the paper. He carefully folded it and put it in his jacket pocket. Maybe he'd show it to Lucy later, maybe he'd just throw it away. But for now he didn't want to think about it. He didn't want to think about anything.

It had been a help, getting things ready for the funeral. After his collapse and his days in bed, he'd felt weak and unmotivated. Yesterday had put him firmly back on his feet and he was glad to be out again now.

When he'd finally forced himself up out of bed he'd spent a day just wandering around the house trying to eat. Then he'd managed to make some phone calls and sort out the final arrangements for the funeral. The need to do that was what finally made him take a hold of himself.

The next morning he'd come back to the Newmarket Road. He realized that the other day he hadn't been thinking straight. He'd made it all seem so much more difficult than it needed to be. But now he was refreshed and clear-headed. First of all he'd gone up and down the road five times before he was completely sure that there were only the two buildings with Lucy's windows. Then he'd gone straight into the surgery and talked to the receptionist.

He'd told her he was trying to locate the people who lived upstairs and she'd told him he must have the wrong address because it was just offices. He'd pressed her but she was sure of it.

So that had been that.

He'd watched the other house for a while, but the only people he'd seen were the young woman with red hair and the schoolboy.

Perhaps they were visitors, perhaps they were friends. Whatever the case he hadn't got any further and then it had been the funeral.

Today was the first opportunity he'd had to come back. This morning he'd arrived in time to see the woman leave the house but he hadn't caught sight of the boy.

He'd gone and got the paper and then, as he was getting back in the car, the woman had returned. Now, after seeing the picture, he decided that he had to make a more positive approach. He couldn't just sit here for ever wasting time, particularly if this was the wrong house. And if it was the right house he had to find out very quickly what had happened to the Intruder.

Yes. Keep moving. Things fell apart if you sat and brooded for any length of time. He'd known that all his life; keep busy, keep your mind fully occupied at all times. Work so hard that when you went to bed you slept and when you woke you worked more. No time to yourself. No time to think. Keep busy. Never stop.

He looked in the glove compartment and found a leather folder of car documents. The folder looked suitably official, so he got out of the car and tucked it under his arm. He tightened his tie and adjusted it in the reflection in the car window. It was a routine he'd carried out countless times before, when visiting clients. This would be no different. Calmness, confidence, authority and a brisk businesslike attitude would carry him through. He flattened his hair, then crossed the road to the house with the metal-framed windows.

He rang the bell and in a few moments the woman opened the door. It was his first chance to see her close up. She was considerably shorter than Tom, and maybe a couple of years younger. She was conventionally pretty with a round, pale face and large eyes. Her red hair was thick and curly.

'Hello,' said Tom, before she had a chance to do or say anything. 'I wonder if your husband's in?'

'No.' The woman smiled politely and moved to close the door.

'It's all right,' said Tom with a grin, 'I'm not a salesman or anything. But I do need to speak to your husband. I wonder if you could tell me when he'll be back?'

The woman stared at the doormat. 'My husband's dead,' she said quietly.

Was this why he hadn't seen the Intruder? He'd died. That would explain a few things.

'Ah, I'm very sorry. It's just he was in touch with us about—'

'He died two years ago. Now what do you want, exactly?'

'Oh, this is terribly embarrassing, I do apologize. It's our, you know, our computers. I didn't mean to ...' Now what? Press on, don't think. 'So is it just you and your son living here?'

'Look, until you tell me who you are and what you want ...'

'I'm from the insurance company.'

'What insurance company?'

'It seems there's some, some money owing you. Now, your son is—'

'What money?' The woman glared at him provocatively.

'Perhaps this isn't a good time.'

'You're not from any bloody insurance company, are you? What's this all about?'

'I'll need to go back to the files,' Tom mumbled. 'In the light of your husband's ...' He began to back away from the house. 'I'm sorry to have bothered you ...'

He pulled a document from his car folder and pretended to study it. It was a letter from the AA. The woman stood in the doorway, watching him shuffle off, until he was back on the pavement.

He waved limply, trying not to catch her eye, then turned and walked briskly away in the direction of town.

So the husband was dead, the boy's father. It didn't make sense. Two years ago. But it had to be the house, it had to be. Unless they'd moved. No. He'd been so sure, everything pointed to that big Victorian house. But there was no man there. Dammit, of course, the Intruder was the woman's boyfriend. But that wasn't right. The notebook talked about a mother. It talked about ...

He stopped.

There was an explanation.

It could work one way.

The boy.

If the Intruder was the boy.

But that was impossible.

Why? The notebook was the sort a boy uses at school. And the writing.... What if the writer wasn't an awkward adult but was, instead, an unusually intelligent schoolboy?

Yes, a boy could pass through the streets without drawing any attention to himself. And most burglars, weren't they kids these days?

A boy. The Intruder was just a boy. Parts suddenly made sense and fitted together. The Intruder had a face; it wasn't a monster's face, it wasn't a freak, it was the face of a schoolboy.

He hurried across the road and up a side-street, then he doubled back on himself and approached the car from the other direction so that there was no danger of the woman seeing him return.

He got back in the car, took out the notebook and read it again, every word. As he did so, he could clearly imagine the boy writing it, could picture him concentrating, studying, sneaking about by himself, lonely and secretive, a quiet, introverted little boy.

He felt suddenly very sorry for him. There was no way he could have killed James on purpose. He must have felt awful afterwards, with no one to turn to. It was too much for a child to have to try and deal with.

Tom knew what it was like to be a lonely, awkward child. He remembered when he'd left home at fifteen how alone he'd been. After that terrible final fight with his father, when he'd gone to live with his Uncle Willy in London. Nothing was said about it. Uncle Willy had been kind but didn't understand. He had no children of his own. Tom had felt completely isolated. He was separated from Lucy, from his admittedly few schoolfriends; he had nobody of his own age to talk to.

He'd gone to work, mixed with adults, pretended he was like them. He had tried to forget about his own youth. He stopped being that miserable child and became a brisk, sensible adult. He'd started to build this shell about himself. I am a normal man, he told the world, in command, capable, reliable, ordinary in every way.

How early we get fucked up. It wasn't fair.

But the boy knew different; the boy had come to terms with what he was. He'd discovered how to be in some way happy, at least until ...

Until it had all gone wrong and he'd killed James.

The boy was the one, all right. He'd show bloody Inspector Hapworth. He'd show Lucy. He'd get it all sorted out. But he knew he'd have to make completely sure if he wanted to tell anyone.

Come on, Tom. You've always been thorough, always meticulous. You need proof.

And the only way to do that, short of confronting the boy in the street, was to enter his house, just as he'd entered other people's. That made good sense; he had to go in and see for himself. Find the museum that the boy had written about in the book. That would be all the proof he needed.

Just as he decided that he had to become an intruder himself, he looked up to see the woman leaving the house carrying a shopping basket. She locked the door and walked briskly off down the street. It was a sign. It was telling him he was doing the right thing. The house would be empty, the boy hadn't returned yet.

Go now, go quickly.

He left the car and for the last time crossed over to the house.

The boy had told him how to do it; move fast and purposefully, don't look furtive, look like you were supposed to be there. He ignored the front door and went round the side. There was a back door here. He knew it was too much to hope for but he tried the handle anyway.

It was open.

Another sign.

Go on. Don't hesitate, go straight inside.

But what if she came back?

Don't think about it, just go in.

There. He was in, and the door was closed behind him.

A flood of adrenalin washed through his system, it made him feel light-headed and slightly sick.

He was in a kitchen, a perfectly ordinary kitchen with fitted cabinets and modern appliances and a smart stripped-pine table. There was a pile of letters on the table, and next to them a yellow Post-it note.

WILL
gone to town back by six, mum
p.s. there is cake in fridge

He picked up the letters and flipped through them. They were bills mostly. He looked at the names on them: Emma Summers.

So the boy had a name, he was no longer the Intruder, he was Will Summers. It suited him better.

Finding the name was another sign, like the woman leaving the house and the door being open. It was all easy, he was meant to be here.

Now to find Will's room and the museum.

He left the kitchen and went into the hall. Then he stopped dead. He could hear music from somewhere.

He strained to listen. It could be coming from next door. It was muffled, distant. He could hear violins; it sounded classical.

He started upstairs, treading softly, moving slowly, and the music grew louder.

It was in the house. It was definitely coming from upstairs.

That meant there was someone in.

Will.

Of course he'd sneaked in without Tom seeing him. He'd come into the house as if he were a burglar entering a stranger's house.

Shaking with nervous excitement, Tom looked back at the front door. He had to get out, now. Come back when he knew the place was empty. He started to creep back downstairs.

Then once more he stopped himself.

No.

The boy always went in when there were other people. It was how it had to be. He had to go up, now, find the boy.

He had to.

He had to find the boy who had written, 'I AM HAPPY NOW.'

TWENTY-SIX

Mrs Harrison from next door had offered to look after the girls for the morning, to give Lucy a bit of time to spend by herself and get settled in properly, and Lucy was alone in the house for the first time since that night. In fact, it was the first time she'd been alone anywhere since then. She'd always had the girls with her, or Tom. It was the next hurdle she had to get over. There was no use in hiding from things, avoiding them and hoping they'd go away. She'd spent the last couple of years doing that; she'd retreated into a sort of dream world. It was a horrible thing to admit, but James's death had helped her. God knows what would have happened to the two of them if he'd lived, if they'd tried to carry on with their marriage. It was dreadful that James had died, she felt desperately sorry for him and would have given anything to have him still alive, but he was dead and that meant that a difficult decision had been taken out of her hands.

It was good now, thinking over happy times when they'd first been together: the birth of Polly, their first holiday with the girls, their first weekend away without the girls, James's promotion. It all seemed so long ago, almost as if it had happened to someone else, or it was something she'd seen on television. She kept her mind off the bad times, the nights they didn't talk, the way James changed and became coarser, bigger, manlier. Her growing revulsion at his touch which would occasionally give way to an uncontrollable, animal passion which left her confused and angry. And the trances. She was so glad she no longer found herself coming to in a strange place with no idea how she'd got there.

She had bad dreams still, but at least she understood them. They were dreams of that night, and she supposed that was only to be expected. It was her mind trying to come to terms with things, trying to purge itself of the poison. She was almost grateful for them, because they showed her that she did care, that underneath her protective shell James's death had affected her deeply.

But the sad thing was, she loved James more now that he was dead than she had done when he was alive. She tried not to dwell on this. It was natural that after an event like that, one's feelings would be sent a little haywire. Deep down inside she had a strong will to survive, and if that meant hardening her heart and shutting out certain emotions, if that meant being utterly selfish, then that was what she would do. Because it wasn't selfish, was it? To want the children to be happy.

She would get over this, and she would make sure the girls had a normal life, even if her own would be forever shadowed by the memories of that night and what had gone before it.

She went round the empty house from room to room, reclaiming it from the murderer, the man who had come in and tried to steal it from her. She was taking it back. She wouldn't be scared. She wouldn't be feeble.

She was also reclaiming the house from Tom's over-meticulous tidying.

He seemed to spend his whole time tidying up. As soon as anything was touched he straightened it. Lucy liked a certain level of mess, a realistic untidiness. James had never understood that with two young girls it was almost impossible to keep a small house looking spotless, unless you could afford cleaners and nannies and servants and God knows what.

She relived all the memories from all the rooms: the time Claire had been sick over the sofa and it had taken them weeks to get rid of the smell; the time the iron had shorted in the back room and if she hadn't found it just in time the whole house would have gone up in smoke; the time, early on when she'd made love to James on the stairs, when he'd come in from work and she'd been so horny she had him right then and there; the week they'd spent decorating Polly's room, putting up the Winnie the Pooh wallpaper and the alphabet murals; the sense of achievement when they'd finally had their own bedroom done, with fitted cupboards and proper curtains and a decent carpet. This was their house, their family home.

Afterwards she lay on their bed, staring idly up at the ceiling. But this time she wasn't in a daze; quite the opposite, she felt buzzing with energy, alive. It was almost as if all those lost moments were coming back to her, like an amnesiac regaining her memory. She was filled with a sort of collage of all the times she'd spent in this bed with James, from the good to the bad.

And now she missed him very much. She missed having his arms around her, missed having him warm the bed for her, missed having someone there to turn to when she woke up.

It had been strange when Tom had come in the night before last. They hadn't spoken about it. It had comforted her a little, but it had disturbed her as well. It had stirred up difficult memories.

She put it out of her mind again now. She couldn't confront everything all at once, nobody had to be that strong.

She sighed and ran her hands over the soft cotton of the duvet cover.

Their bed. Her and James.

It would always be their bed.

And would she always be alone in it?

Well, one day she'd maybe find someone else, she was still relatively young. Thirty-three wasn't old these days. Having children relatively late had kept her youthful. James had wanted to wait until they were sure they could afford it and he was properly settled in his job, so she didn't have to work. They'd wanted to do it traditionally, for the family. She realized now that had probably been a mistake. When you spent too long by yourself with kids you became a zombie. She had to have her own life.

Well, no more zombie. The girls were old enough now to be looked after by others. She was going to return to the world, take up where she'd left off.

She'd find another man all right.

Just as she decided this the doorbell rang and she laughed.

She checked herself in the mirror and went downstairs.

Through the frosted glass of the front door she could see the large shape of a man. It wasn't a shape she recognized.

She opened the door and there stood the policeman, Bob Arnell, looking just as uncomfortable as he had done yesterday.

'Morning, Mrs Mullen. I should have rung, really, but I was in the area and I thought you ought to get it from the horse's mouth.'

'Get what?'

'I've now got some good news for you. Well, I suppose it's good. Well, it's news, anyway ... Er, shall I come in?'

'Yes, of course, I'm sorry.'

He was a big man, tall and bulky, and he filled the hallway. He was dressed in a nondescript suit that was slightly too small for him and he smelled of aftershave and mothballs.

She took him through to the kitchen and automatically put on the kettle.

He sat down at the table and the room seemed half its normal size.

'What sort of news is it?' Lucy asked, getting two cups from a cabinet.

'We've found your man.'

'My man?'

'Yes, the bloke that ... You know.'

Lucy stopped what she was doing and turned to the policeman. 'You mean you've found the man who killed James?'

'Yes. Well, when I say found him, he's not exactly caught yet. But it'll only be a matter of time, I should think.'

'But you know who he is?'

Bob nodded.

Lucy felt like a very tight spring inside her had suddenly been released. The effect was both exhilarating and tiring at the same time. She sat down and for a few moments said nothing, letting it sink in.

'What . . . ?' she said at last. 'Who is he?'

'It's a funny story. Well.' He looked self-consciously at Lucy. 'Perhaps funny isn't the best word. It was your talk with me yesterday, you see? Set me thinking. I thought, you know, it can't be much fun for you, all this—'

'That's been the worst part of it. The not knowing. There was this nameless, faceless killer. And then, Tom being under suspicion.'

'Quite. And I thought, we can't have this. I'll have a look into it.'

'Who found him? Who found out?'

'The thing of it is, Lucy, about a week ago, ten days, I was investigating a B and E, that's breaking and entering. Only it was a peculiar case. Turns out this chap had gone into this woman's house while she was still in there. He didn't take anything, as such, so we don't know what his intentions were. It didn't look like rape, because when the woman found him – she caught him at it, see? – he ran off. Didn't try to attack her or nothing. Didn't try anything on. And what stuck in my mind at the time was that he must have known the woman was in there, and he must have had it all planned, because he was wearing these, like, rubber gloves, like doctors use.'

Lucy was bursting to ask questions, to get on with it, to find out about the man, but she saw that it was important to Arnell to tell the story his way, to show off to her, so she kept quiet.

'And the thing was, he was just a kid, you see?'

'A kid?'

'Young lad, fourteen or fifteen. He could have been up to anything.'

'A boy?'

'Yes. Now, burglaries and that,' the policeman went on importantly, 'are difficult to follow up, there's not usually much we can do. But this woman was in some distress, so I promised I'd do all I could, and I must say I put more effort into it than I would normally have. And I got to thinking, what if this kid got his kicks from going into folk's homes while they was in there? Women, and that? Not necessarily to do anything, as such, but as a sort of dare thing. And I've asked about, and turns out there's been a couple of cases in the last year or so of people reporting that someone had been in their house while they was there and taken things, just little things. Somebody had seen someone leave out the back, another had lost a favourite ring, quite a valuable one, though apparently you wouldn't know it to look at it. And, of course, we hadn't really followed them up, not petty burglaries. But, as is often the way, one thing happens and suddenly a pattern emerges. What if this boy does this quite a bit? But that was as far as we'd got, until yesterday, that is, when you cornered me.' He gave a little laugh. 'Gave me a hard time about your brother.'

'I'm sorry. But you can understand?'

'Entirely. But it, you know, it set the old cogs turning. Whoever had come into your place obviously knew what they were doing, but at the same time, conversely, it looked like they didn't know what they were doing. Otherwise, why come in while you all were in here? That was what had got Hapworth running round in circles. It didn't make sense, didn't fit a pattern. And, well, the only way they could get it to work involved your brother.'

'But that's ridiculous.'

'We know that now. But ... Well, anyway, as I say, I started thinking. And suddenly what had seemed to be two separate cases came together. What if this was our man again, our young lad? What if he'd come in to do whatever it is he does, and Jimmy caught him at it? A fight, the lad grabs the first thing that comes to hand, and ... Well, you know the rest. Accident, really. That makes sense, doesn't it?'

'Yes.' The kettle had boiled, so Lucy got up and saw to the tea.

'But, of course,' said Arnell, leaning forward on to the table, 'that was only conjecture, could be wishful thinking. We needed proof. Well, we had the glove, didn't we?' Arnell was getting excited; he was evidently pleased with himself. 'She'd got one of his gloves off him, see? The lady. So far the forensic from the two cases hasn't been compared, why should they? But when I take my case to old Hapworth, bingo! There's this powder on the gloves, makes them easier to put on, and they've found some on the fork, you know, the murder weapon ... So now we've got a picture and your brother's off the hook. I expect he'll be pleased.'

'Yes.' The understatement of the year.

'Well you can be the first to tell him, my love.'

'Yes.' Except Tom had gone out that morning before she was up and hadn't left a note, so she had no idea where he was. But that didn't matter because he'd be back soon enough, nothing was going to happen to him in the meantime. God, he'd be so happy, all that pressure taken off him. They could all finally relax.

She sipped her tea. 'But he's not caught yet, the boy?'

'Not yet, no. We don't know who he is exactly. But as I say, it's only a matter of time. He's still up to his tricks, by the look of it, and we can now go back over all the old cases, see if there's more of a pattern. You see, with an idea in our minds, we can sort out a method. I mean, he's just a kid. He can't have meant to do it. We'll ask around the schools and things. He'll come out of the woodwork soon enough. A kid can't handle a thing like that for long.'

'Poor boy.'

'I beg your pardon?'

'Well, I know he killed James, but—'

'I shouldn't go feeling too sorry for him. Kids these days are a bloody menace.'

'I know. It's just the whole thing is just a horrible accident. Christ, I don't know whether that makes me feel better or worse.'

'I just thought you'd like to know, I mean—'

'Yes, Bob. I am grateful. Thank you very much for coming and telling me. But the pointlessness of it all.'

'Happens all the time, you know? It's messy business, most of what we have to deal with. It's not like the perfect crimes, the perfect murders ...'

Lucy waited for him to say it, and he obliged.

'... It's not like Agatha Christie. It's random, it's stupid. The line between assault and murder is very thin, very arbitrary. I mean, I don't mean to appear uncaring, but this job, it's—'

'I know, Bob.'

'There's so much of it luck, you don't tell anyone, but there it is. Small things come together.' He stopped himself from going off again, and returned to being the policeman. 'Now, I expect Hapworth himself will be over later to tell you all this himself,' he said briskly. 'Official, like. I shouldn't really be here, to tell you the truth. Not my job. So you won't say anything, will you?'

'No, of course not. You were a friend of James's, and—'

'A friend of yours as well, I hope.'

'Yes.'

Bob smiled. 'Ha, old Hapworth'll probably claim it was all his work. But I, well, you was obviously worried about your brother, and as you say, Jimmy was ... Well, I've said all that.'

Lucy looked at him smiling manfully at her. Her black outfit had obviously had quite an effect on him. She'd always thought policemen were like doctors and vicars, forbidden to have affairs with the people they dealt with professionally. She'd never thought about policemen being interested in sex. But why not? Sex was lurking at the heart of everything else; why not crime detection?

Coppers. She'd never really even thought of them as real people. They were just men in uniforms doing a job which concerned other people, not her. God, it would be the ultimate rebound, picking up women after their husbands were murdered. Talk about vulnerable. Big strong man sorts it all out ... But Bob couldn't know, and she wouldn't hurt his feelings by telling him, that he was about as far from being her type as was possible. He was too large, too powerful-looking, too much a man. She found him about as attractive as the Incredible Hulk.

She wasn't on the rebound, she wasn't so vulnerable that she'd throw herself at just anyone as a means of comfort. She had time. She could be sensible now.

But there was no need to be rude to him. He'd helped her, for whatever reason, and she was touched by that. So she chatted to him for a while about the girls and James and then she gently eased him out of the house and waited impatiently for Tom to come home so she could tell him the good news.

She paced from room to room, excited and impatient. But there was something else, a new feeling, or rather a very old one, one she hadn't felt in years.

Happiness.

It was going to be all right. Everything was going to be all right.

Bob Arnell sat in his car and thought about Lucy. He hadn't lost it. She definitely liked him. And he liked her. He liked her eyes. There was something distant about them, something dreamy, which made her seem very unprotected. She had a nice figure, too; ordinary, but nice.

Not as nice as the other woman, though. The one who had found the lad in her house.

Now there was a body to die for.

He started his engine. He was going over there now. Ostensibly to give her an update on the case, but really just to see her again.

He grinned. He couldn't wait. He'd spent an inordinate amount of time on her case, which had been, after all, only routine to start with. In fact, the only reason he'd followed up the break-in at all was because of the woman. Oh, it looked good to tell people he'd had a hunch, like he was Sherlock bloody Holmes or something. But that was bullshit. It was her. Her body. He couldn't get enough of it.

God had blessed her with the most fantastic pair of breasts he'd ever seen.

TWENTY-SEVEN

Tom climbed the stairs towards the sound of the record. One flight, another, right up into the roof of the house. The music was very loud here. He followed it to a closed door.

He tried the handle; it wouldn't give. He knocked. Nothing. He leant against the door, testing its strength. It wasn't full-sized and the frame looked fairly flimsy. This part of the house was obviously a loft conversion, and not a very good one at that. He pressed his full weight against the door and the frame creaked, gave a little.

'Will?' he called, then louder, 'Will?'

Nothing. Just strings; violins and cellos.

He leant against the door again. Maybe it was stuck? No. It wouldn't budge. He knocked harder, thumping on the thin wood with the side of his hand. Still nothing. He put his shoulder to it and shoved and it popped open. He saw that it'd been locked but the lock hadn't held.

The room was empty. But somebody must have turned the lock and put on the deafening music. Tom eased the volume down slightly, but left the record playing.

The window was shut, so the boy couldn't have got out there.

Tom looked around. It was an anonymous room. There was a single bed, a rug in the middle of the wooden floor, a bedside table with a history book and a glass of water on it, a chest of drawers and a wardrobe. The wardrobe looked out of place, it was too near the window. He saw there were tracks along the floor where it had been moved. He had a closer look. The wardrobe was on castors. He looked at the space where it had been before and noticed some kind of panel in the wall, papered to match the rest of the room. There was no handle, though. He knocked on it; it was hollow. He pressed it and it sprang open. He lifted it clear of the opening and looked in.

The boy, Will, was there, cowering at the far end of a small, dimly lit space.

It was the museum.

Tom crawled in and pulled the panel shut behind him.

The arched roof was very low, and Tom couldn't easily move in the cramped den. He shuffled his way towards the frightened boy until he was crouched opposite him.

The boy looked at him with big, round eyes. 'What are you going to do?' he said. He had a slight rasp to his voice, which was on the verge of breaking. It sounded nasal and grating.

'I don't know,' Tom replied. It was true. He hadn't thought any further than this point: meeting the Intruder, confronting him ... and then?

He showed the boy the book. 'Did you write this?' he asked.

'Yes. Are you the police, then?'

'No,' said Tom. 'I'm married to the sister of the man you killed.'

'What?'

'I mean, she's my sister ... He was married to my sister.'

Will began to cry.

'Don't cry,' said Tom.

'Sorry.' The boy sniffed and wiped his nose. 'What are you going to do?' he asked again, and again Tom didn't know. He waited for the boy to stop sniffing.

'You didn't mean to kill him, did you?' he said finally.

'No. He attacked me,' said the boy, the words coming out in a rush as if he'd been holding them in, waiting to tell someone. 'I was trying to defend myself. I was only in the house because—'

'I know why you were there.' Tom held up the book.

'I've changed,' the boy said eagerly. 'I've been putting things back. I've nearly finished. Here ...' He scrambled over to a shelf and fetched something which he handed to Tom.

Toothbrushes. Four of them.

'From the house,' the boy explained.

'Why have you been putting things back?' Tom asked, turning the brushes in his hand.

'To apologize.'

'Does it make you happy?'

'I beg your pardon?'

'Putting things back, does it make you happy?'

'Look,' Will said desperately. 'I shouldn't have done it. I shouldn't have been in the house. Then it wouldn't have happened ... What are you going to do to me?'

'I don't know.' Tom looked at Will. Just a boy. Almost the same age as Tom had been when he left home, after the fight.

'Are you ... ?' Will said quietly. 'Do you want to punish me for what I did to your sister's wife. Your wife's brother ...'

'My brother-in-law.'

'Yes.'

'You made my sister very unhappy.'

'I'm sorry.'

'I love my sister.'

The boy nodded. He was very tense, watching Tom, waiting.

Tom looked down at the notebook, ran his fingers over the cover, tracing the outline of the skier. He opened it and turned the pages.

'You see,' he said, 'you wrote in your book, "I am happy now".' He looked up at the boy who was frowning at him. 'You are happy. You were happy, until ... the mistake, the accident.'

'Yes.'

'Tell me.'

'What?'

'I don't know. You're just a boy. How could you know?'

The stuffiness of the room was giving Tom a headache, he felt grimy in his heavy jacket.

Will licked his lips. Not taking his eyes off Tom for a moment.

Tom felt the newspaper in his pocket. He pulled it out and showed Will the photograph.

'Look. Look at this picture. That's me ... and Lucy, my sister. Those are her children, my nieces. My family. Always, when we were younger, I looked after Lucy. But, when it came to it, I couldn't help.'

'I'm sorry.'

'Stop saying you're sorry,' Tom shouted. He closed his eyes and pressed his palm against his forehead.

'When I was your age I was fucked up,' he said. 'I was miserable. I thought it would all change when I got older, when I grew up and left home. I thought that when I could just get on with my own life things would be fine. But it got worse. I just became more miserable.'

'I see.'

'No, you don't.'

'I'm trying,' Will said. 'But I don't usually do this sort of thing. I don't know what you want me to do.'

Tom grabbed the boy by the shoulders and shook him, banging his head back against a rafter. 'You know what to do. You know what to fucking do ...' The boy looked startled. 'Because it's you.'

'What is?' Will said, gasping for breath in his panic.

'I don't know. I don't know what I was thinking of. I should never have come here.'

Neither of them spoke for a long while. Tom could hear their breathing, loud in this small hot space. He felt foolish. What was he doing? Stuck here in this stupid little hidey-hole, talking nonsense with a bloody schoolboy. It wasn't dignified. He had to pull himself together before he lost it completely.

'You see, Will, the thing is,' he said at last, 'I get angry. I get so fucking angry ... And I read in your book, you wrote in your book, "I am happy now".'

'Yes. I remember.'

'But what did you mean?'

'Well, just ... that. I was happy.'

'Is that all?'

'Yes. I think so.'

'Oh Christ ...' Tom pressed his forehead again. It felt cold to his touch.

'I just wrote it,' Will said. 'All I did was what would make me happy, that's all I did.'

Tom grabbed him by the shoulders again. 'You don't understand. You lied to me. I thought you knew something. But you're just trying to humour me, aren't you? Trying to make me happy, to ...' He stopped, suddenly overwhelmed with claustrophobia. The boy seemed huge, filling the space like a spider. Tom couldn't look at him. He gripped his hands together, squeezing them tight, and closed his eyes. He felt a coldness in the back of his head, like ice, a growing white spot of rage. What must the boy think of him? An incoherent shambling mess of a man. He was supposed to be an adult, for Christ's sake. He was old enough to be the boy's father.

He had to explain, he had to make the boy understand.

'You see, the police think it was me, not you. And in a way it was me, because I was the one who pulled the fork out. But the thing is, I'm glad he's dead. You see? Ha! When I saw him there, thick and squat and smelling like an animal, touching Lucy, holding her ...' Shit, what was he saying? He was only making things worse. He should have been better prepared. He had to marshal his thoughts. Come on, Tom, be a little more businesslike here. But that white spot in the back of his mind was confusing him. He was just getting angry again. And now some bloody child was sitting there feeling

223

superior to him. He could picture Will, grinning at him, mocking him. Fourteen years old and he had it sorted. It wasn't fair.

'Please,' said Will. 'I want to make it right.'

'Shut up!' Tom yelled and he slapped Will round the face with the back of his hand, making his teeth clack together. 'You can't make me right. How can you presume to make me right?'

'I didn't mean that, I meant the other man, Mr Mullen.' Will looked sadly down at where blood had spotted his white shirt. 'Will you go now?' he asked and began to cry.

'I'm sorry,' Tom said. 'But, you see, Mr Mullen, James ... I just ... I shouldn't have come. I'm tired. Look ...' He took from his pocket a crumpled piece of paper. It was Maddie's letter. 'I used to think this was the secret. I used to read this and think everything was going to be all right. But it was lies. It was ... wrong. Then I thought ...'

Will tried to say something.

'Listen!' Tom snapped. 'When I read your book, when I read those words, when I read—'

'Please go away,' said Will. 'You're frightening me. I'll do anything you want. I'll go to prison if you want, but leave me alone.'

'No! You will tell me the secret. You will do as I say!'

'There isn't any secret. I'm just a boy. Now leave me alone. I don't know how to help you.'

'You will help me, boy.' Tom hit him again, harder than he meant to; beneath his nose, which seemed to collapse and slide upwards.

That was twice. What was he doing? He'd hit the boy twice. A man shouldn't hit a boy. It was just like ... Jesus, come on, concentrate on the matter in hand. Which was ... ?

Which was Will. Yes. Which was the Intruder. He looked at him. He sat quite still now. His head erect, pressed back against the rough wooden beam. Blood came down from his nostrils and a bubble formed at his lips. It slowly grew then popped. He stared at Tom and began to mutter something. Tom couldn't make out what he was trying to say, but the last two words sounded like 'dusty wing'.

'I don't know what you're talking about,' Tom said. 'But please just listen now, don't make me angry, don't interrupt. Because if I lose my temper, then everything falls apart. You understand? That's why I've failed in everything. All my life I've failed. Because all my life I've been carrying around this anger inside me. My father put it there, and I mustn't ever let it out. I'm sick. Like syphilis. My father was sick, and he gave it to me. I must never get angry. You understand? There's a white area, in the back of my mind, you see? And it's filled with anger, that's all it is, and it's always there, waiting for me, and the rages come up and it's like the whiteness will take me over. So I have to fight it. I have to resist it. It's dead. It's a dead white place. So you do understand?'

Will stared at him unblinking.

'Say you understand. If you would only understand, then you could tell me how to be happy. That's all. That's why I'm here. I know it sounds stupid, but I only want to be happy.' Tom stopped and smiled. Yes. It was that simple. And it made him happy to be able to say it.

He heard the music through the wall, a great surge of strings, and he remembered what the tune was, Vaughan Williams, Variations on a Theme by Thomas Tallis. It was all so typically English.

Yes, he was happy. He felt it up his spine, a delirious, electrical happiness.

He laughed. 'It's as simple as that,' he said.

Tom looked at his hand, there was blood on it.

He looked at the motionless boy, staring at him with blank eyes, and an awful realization struck him.

'Jesus Christ,' he said. 'What have I done now?'

PART THREE

PART THREE

TWENTY-EIGHT

Tom stood in his flat, switching the light on and off. On and off. On and off. He was hypnotized by the sudden changes from complete blackness to bright light. On and off. On and off. It was like watching a film, frame by frame. And, because it was frame by frame, it was very slow; nothing seemed to happen at all. Each picture looked the same as the last. A chair, a desk with papers on it, a waste bin, the corner of the carpet, the angle where the two magnolia walls met. On and then off. The room and then darkness. The world and then nothing.

He'd been on his way out, about to leave the flat for the first time since he'd got back from Norwich. He'd got as far as his front door, then he'd switched off the light. He'd thought it was about six o'clock and had been startled and confused by the sudden darkness of late night. In the darkness he'd become suddenly afraid. It was nothing he could put his finger on, just a vague, all-embracing fear. So he'd switched the light back on, and he'd seen the corner of his room, and that was somehow more frightening.

So he'd turned the light back off. No, that was worse. So, on ... Then off, then on ... Better this slow, tedious film about nothing than a return to any kind of reality.

Suddenly there was a 'plick' sound and the bulb gave out. Now it was black, with no chance of any light. He began to shiver; sweat formed under his clothes, cold and greasy. He stared at the curtains and slowly, as his eyes adjusted, a faint rim of light appeared around them. Then the curtains themselves dissolved until they showed up as a lighter patch against the darkness. He relaxed. In London it was never really dark.

And so the world began to reappear. It was a half-world, colourless, faint, made up of varying depths of grey. It was comforting, like a dream world, without substance. He was safe for the moment. Safe until the sun came up in the morning.

He slid to the floor and hid there, breathing heavily and looking around the room. Objects, parts of objects, were coming into existence; the arm of a chair; half the rim of a bowl on the low table; a length of flex leading to the unseen lamp; the foot pedals of his Yamaha . . .

If it wasn't for the fact that his broken hands hurt, he could imagine that this was everything. But the rhythmical throbbing of his blood as it pumped into his wounded flesh was a constant reminder of what else there was. Hard as he tried, he couldn't forget what he had done that afternoon.

He sat still, with his back against the wall in exactly the same position as he'd sat in the boy's secret room. Rigid, unable to move, paralysed by what he'd done. Then as now, he'd lost track of time. He'd looked at Will's lifeless face, willing him to move, knowing he never would. For a minute or so blood had slowly dripped from the boy's nose. Then the trickle had slowed and dried, forming a congealed stalactite of blood that hung from the chin. He'd stared at that little red nub as it had darkened to brown, and then to black, consumed with terror. Terror of himself and terror of what might happen to him now.

All his life he'd lived as quietly and as normally as he could, knowing that if he ever let go of his self-control something like this would happen.

And now it had.

It was ironic, really. A month ago, if you'd showed him and Will to the world, what would the world have thought? What would they have thought of someone who, for his sexual kicks, went into other people's houses while they were occupied and masturbated? And what would they have thought of a nice, respectable man with his own printing business who kept himself to himself?

Well, they'd have been wrong.

His head had suddenly become filled with whiteness, and, in the grip of a wild fury, he'd attacked the museum with his fists, the same fists that had killed the boy, smashing them against the brick walls, against the beams, against the shelves. At last, too exhausted to continue, something like rationality had returned and he'd looked at his hands. They were shattered. He couldn't move his fingers, they were crooked and fat, the knuckles black and swelling. But there had been no pain yet. A numb, automatic kind of consciousness had taken control, as if he were outside himself, watching a character on the television. You must do this. You must act now. You must get away from there. You must save yourself . . . Look behind you!

The first thing he'd told himself to do was hide the body. But where? It would be a terrible risk getting it out of the house at this time of day. He'd thought of waiting until nightfall, maybe wrapping it in a rug, or something. But that was even more of a risk, because the boy's mother would be returning soon.

He'd thought and thought, and then the idea had come to him. It had seemed right at the time. But now he wasn't so sure. He realized that he'd been thinking too much of the boy and not enough of himself. It was a temporary measure, very temporary, and a sentimental gesture that would count for nothing.

But it was done.

He'd buried the boy where he would be happy, where he belonged.

Moving the body out of the museum had been the hardest part. It wasn't just his useless hands.

Will had still been sitting upright, resting against the sloping beam of the roof. Tom had tried to shift him but the back of his head was stuck to the rough wood, his hair smashed into the furry splinters, wedded like Velcro to the beam. He hadn't realized he'd hit him so hard. He'd tugged at him and he came free with a ripping sound, leaving behind a scrap of hairy, transparent scalp.

He'd wrapped his hands in a couple of sheets of the newspaper he'd brought with him, to act as gloves, then opened the hatch and lined the floor with more of the paper. He'd put another couple of sheets around the boy's sticky head and dragged the body out of the museum. The corpse had been horribly heavy and awkward. Bits flopped about and got stuck, and his clothes got snagged on a nail head, but at last he'd got him into the middle of the bedroom.

Then he'd wrapped him in a shroud of newspapers and he'd taken him away and buried him where he could watch over his world for ever.

Ha.

For ever?

Tom doubted it. The boy would be found sooner or later. Sooner, probably. And that meant Tom had to sort himself out, make plans, make sure he was safe. Make sure that if he had to go away he wouldn't leave anything undone.

And there was so much to do now.

So much.

Luckily he'd got out of Norwich without incident, though he was exhausted, filthy, stiff and in considerable pain. His hands had almost completely seized up. But what could he do about it? He couldn't go to a hospital. What would he say? How could he explain the state he was in? No, he'd have to live with it, hide the wounds, cover the dark, puffy fingers and pray that they would somehow heal.

On the way home he'd done something he hadn't done in years. He'd gone into an off-licence, where he'd bought a bottle

232

of whisky and eight cans of strong lager. He'd fumbled for the money with his broken hands. The patient Asian man behind the counter had probably thought he was some hopeless drunk. Normally Tom would have been mortified. But what did he care now? What did it matter? He'd never been in here before, he'd never come in again.

When he'd got home he'd begun to steadily work his way through the drink. The lager was horribly sweet and the whisky made him gag; he'd never been a great drinker, but he'd persevered until he was spectacularly sick on the kitchen floor. Then, his head reeling, he'd poured the rest of the stuff down the sink and cleared up the mess as best he could.

After that he'd fallen asleep in an armchair, and when he'd woken he'd decided to go out and get something to eat, though he still felt sick. He knew he had to get himself together; getting drunk had been the end, an attempt to flush out the last of the shit. Now he was cleansed he had to get back to normal, work out a plan of action ...

Then he'd turned off the light at the door, then on, and off, and on, and off ...

And now here he was, sitting on the floor in the dark, no closer to his normal self and no closer to a plan than he had ever been.

It wasn't fair. He'd so wanted to get things straight, to fix his life, and how had he gone about it? He'd killed someone.

Brilliant.

Tom wept. He could so clearly see the boy sitting there, waiting for him in the museum, so small and frightened.

Yes, waiting for him, as if he'd almost wanted Tom to do it. After all, he'd shown him the way, hadn't he? First the book, left for him in Lucy's kitchen. The book with the message. The book that contained the clues to Will's secret place. Had the boy really planned it all? Was everything that had happened supposed to happen? Had the boy been a sacrifice?

Come on Tom, that's madness talking. You killed him and there is no excuse.

The whiteness was still there, inside him, and in his despair he gave in to it again. But it was different this time, not the whiteness of rage but the whiteness of clarity, of a bright light. He could see his room very clearly, more clearly than ever before. Each object stood out painfully sharp, as if lit from within. And then he realized that it wasn't just this room; he could see through to the bedroom, to the kitchen. The whole flat was transparent.

He looked around, laughing. He could see out through the walls into the street outside, over on to Blackheath, the houses round the Heath, the whole of London. He could see every minute detail of it all, illuminated by the whiteness. Tears of laughter were pouring down his cheeks; he hurt from it. And then he turned his face up to look at the sky and written across the stars, as if they were nothing more than a huge join-the-dots puzzle, were the words:

I AM HAPPY NOW

He pulled back into the flat, filled with a wild elation. He got up off the floor and went to the wooden chair by the desk. He picked it up; it weighed nothing. There was no pain in his hands because it was as if the chair didn't exist. Well, it didn't, did it? These things didn't matter, physical things. He broke the chair easily, and still his hands didn't hurt. He looked at them. They were glowing, beautiful hands, nothing like the twisted things he'd had just now. He flexed the fingers. No pain.

The boy had given him these hands so that he could use them to do what must be done.

He threw the broken pieces of the chair against the bookshelf. They floated in the air in slow motion. Then he swept his hands across the top of the desk, brushing aside the carefully ordered documents, the letters to be replied to, his personal accounts, a brochure from a prospective client. They rose up into the air like birds taking flight.

He laughed. It had happened, the boy had given him a new life. He had been right to embrace the whiteness. Why had he spent his whole life building these structures to keep the world out? Well, now he had to smash it all down.

He picked up the lamp stand and used it like a club to destroy the room. He'd always thought he'd liked this room, his own little hiding-place, but he now realized he hated it. It was a prison, a sham.

As he twirled the lamp through the air, light streamed out behind it, white sparks trailing it like fireworks. A sparkler, that's what it was. He wrote his name on the room with fire, as the lamp pummelled and sliced and crushed. He saw his electric organ and he crashed the lamp down on to its keys. He struck it again, and he must have hit the power switch, because now sounds came from it, horns and strings, a flute, a church organ. And then a rhythm joined in, a beating of a drum. Then singing. Christ, that was too much to ask for. Only perhaps it wasn't singing? No, come to think of it, it was shouting. And that wasn't a drum, was it? No, it was someone knocking on the door.

'Tom? Tom?' A woman's voice. 'Are you all right? What's going on?'

And it was dark again. Who was this? Who had come here? Was it Maddie? Was it Lucy?

He dropped the lamp and, stumbling over unseen debris, went to the door but didn't open it. One of the keys had stuck on the organ and a note sounded monotonously.

'Who is it?' he asked.

'Is that you, Tom?'

'Yes . . .'

'It's Fiona from upstairs. Are you all right?' Fiona the baby-sitter.

'Yes, the bulb's gone . . . I tripped in the dark. I knocked against something.'

'It sounded like a full-scale war ...'

'No. Sorry to disturb you.'

He could picture her there on the other side of the door, in her night things. He could see her anxious face and he felt terribly superior to her. What did she know about the whiteness? What did she know about happiness? Why not put her out of her misery right now? Why not open the door, bring her in, show her the meaninglessness of physical things? Then put his hands about her neck and squeeze the life out of her. Free her from all this. Take her to the same place he had taken Will.

Yes.

He put a hand to the door-handle and gripped it. A searing pain shot up his arm and into the back of his skull. He groaned, pulled his hand away and cradled it against his chest, biting his lower lip in agony.

'Tom?'

'It's okay, Fiona. It's okay, I'm all right. I'm sorry if I woke you.' He couldn't do it. He didn't have any hands.

'You're sure?'

'I'm sure. Goodnight.'

'All right. Goodnight.'

He waited. He couldn't hear if she had gone away. So he waited a long time, resting his ear against the smooth wood of the door. There was silence. Silence in here. Silence outside in the street.

Eventually he opened the door and looked out. She wasn't there any more. He blinked in the light of the hall; it bounced around the white walls and off the shiny black-and-white-tiled floor.

He looked at his watch. It was half past one.

So what? What meaning did time have any more?

He pulled the watch off, dropped it to the floor and carefully ground it into the tiles with his foot. He felt the glass snap and cave in.

When he was sure it was no longer working, he picked it up and turned to hurl it into his flat. Then stopped. The light from the hall fell into the room, showing him a scene of utter chaos.

There was broken furniture everywhere, books pulled down, glass smashed, the walls gouged. When everything had been in its place, it hadn't looked like much. But now, strewn and shattered around the flat, it was like an overflowing rubbish tip.

He went back in and carefully closed the door behind him, shutting off the light and hiding the devastation. He picked his way back over to the droning organ and began to play. The machine was badly damaged, some of the keys were silent, others stuck, the stops wouldn't work properly. But it was enough. He sat and made up a song, random, meandering, and he hummed along tunelessly, lost in the darkness.

Then the phone began to ring, as it had done every couple of hours or so since he'd got back. Miraculously it had been undamaged in the assault. He went towards the shrill sound of the bell and lifted the receiver.

He heard Lucy's voice.

'Hello ...? Hello ...? Hello, Tom, can you hear me? I don't know if you can. I can't hear you, but if you're there ... I don't know, maybe there's something wrong with your phone. But if you are there and you can hear me, don't hang up. I've got something very important ...'

Tom hung up.

He was crying, overwhelmed with self-pity, and pity for Lucy.

What a family they were. Unlucky. Poisoned. Whenever they tried to do anything positive, it ended in disaster. Well, he knew for sure now that the last thing he must do, after sorting everything and everyone else out, was to sort his family out. He owed that to Lucy. He knew that he was probably done for, the end was near for him. So he had to fix Lucy and the girls. Make sure they would be all right, safe from the poison, safe from the vile influence of their father. Safe from the man who, as a last cruel trick, had put a bullet through his head without leaving a note.

Well, Tom would leave a note. He'd leave more than a note, he'd explain everything. Everyone would know. All the loose ends would be tied up. He was going to finish it and he was going to do it properly.

His father was lying in the ground, strangled by bindweed. And Tom would make sure that Lucy and the girls wouldn't get tangled in the weeds themselves.

That was easily done, that was the last thing to do. The first thing was to see Maddie, who had started all this.

TWENTY-NINE

Maddie watched Peter turn over a page of *Time Out*. It was the food page, she saw, new restaurants in London.

'Is that it, then?' she said. 'Is the conversation over?'

'You tell me. It's up to you, really, isn't it?' Peter said without looking up.

'Why? Why is it up to me?'

'You started it, love.'

'Don't call me love.'

'I'd be quite happy not to call you anything. I was trying to read this magazine, actually.'

Maddie snatched it out of his hands and hurled it into the armchair across the room. Peter gave a little clap. 'Bravo,' he said.

'Peter, one of these days I'm going to kill you.'

'I don't doubt it for one second.'

'Why can't you ever take anything seriously?'

Peter shifted round on the sofa and looked at her. 'Maddie. We've had this conversation a hundred times since you came back from Norwich. A thousand times since we got married. A million. And it's always the same. You accuse me, I admit it, you attack me, I apologize, you don't forgive me, I get pissed off with you and I think about seeing someone else ... Quite frankly, I am bored to tears with it.'

He was right, really. They'd been arguing ever since Peter had got

239

in from work. He'd showered, changed, they'd eaten, and all the time the rankling, circular conversation had rambled on. Now it was nearly nine and she'd as good as wasted three hours. It was like biting your nails; you knew it was wrong, you hated it, but you couldn't stop.

'But you're not going to do anything about it, are you?' she said.

'What?'

'You're not going to stop seeing other women.'

'No, Maddie, I'm probably not. You knew who I was when you married me. You must have loved me then, or at least liked me enough to want to marry me. So why try and change me?'

'I didn't think I'd have to change you. I thought you'd want to change. I thought you'd want to settle down, show some commitment. I thought perhaps you'd want to prove to me you love me.'

'I love you. There. Proof.'

'Oh, piss off.'

'But the thing is, Maddie, I do love you ... Whatever that means.'

'Whatever that means.'

'I'm just pathologically incapable of not being attracted to other women. I can't help it, I like women. I like the way they look, I like the way they walk, the way they talk. I like—'

'You're pathetic.'

'You're probably right. I'm weak and selfish and pathetic. So how can I act any differently than I do?'

'That's a ridiculous argument.'

'When I first did it,' Peter said casually, as if he were talking about going shopping, 'when I first cheated on you, I thought I'd do the decent thing, tell you about it, try and discuss it. And you attacked me. So the next time I tried to keep it secret, I tried to lie to you, but you found out anyway and you attacked me again.'

Maddie stared at him, sitting there so smug and self-satisfied. 'Just once,' she said, 'just once, I'd like you to lose your temper. I'd like you to stand up to me, fight back, argue, anything! So I'd feel bloody justified in knocking all your teeth out.'

Peter smiled at her patronizingly. 'Look. I've said I'll try this time. I'll really try. And the thing is, I don't really enjoy it with the others. Every time I say to myself, "What am I doing? Why am I doing this?" And it makes me realize how much I'd rather be with you ...'

'And that's supposed to make me feel better, is it?'

'You make it very difficult sometimes.'

'That's right, it's all my fault.'

'I didn't say that, Maddie. I accept full responsibility. What I said was, I will try. I will try to behave.'

'And when you try, things are great.'

'I know.'

'We're both happy and I remember why I love you. But then, every time, you turn around and spit in my face.'

'Try not to take it personally.'

Maddie began to laugh. After a while Peter smiled and shook his head. 'I'm sorry,' he said. 'I'm sorry, I'm sorry, I'm sorry. For everything. I admit it was stupid bringing Laura back here when you went away, it was beneath contempt. But, well, to tell you the truth I was desperately lonely.'

'You're nothing but a big kid, Peter. It's just instant gratification with you, isn't it?'

Peter threw up his hands in an 'I surrender' gesture and tried on one of his cute smiles. 'As long as you're there,' he said, 'I'll be here. But when you go, when you're not here ... I just go all to pieces. Maybe I should just get a T-shirt printed saying "SORRY".'

'No. Just talk to me. That's all I want.' Maddie retrieved the magazine from the chair and gave it back to Peter. 'Well, it's not all I want. I'd obviously like you not to do the things you have to apologize for in the first place. But when we're like this, communicating, it's good. It's how it should be.'

'Yup ... Christ, look at this. They've recommended that new vegetarian place in Clapham. That was the worst meal I've had in years.'

241

Maddie turned from him. She looked round the elegant white room with its expensive furniture and its lack of clutter. Everything neatly in its place. It was like a film set, or a museum display or something. There was no life to it.

'Maybe we should have children,' she said quietly.

'Hmm?' Peter didn't look up from his magazine.

'Nothing.'

'No, what did you say?'

'It's all right, nothing.'

'You said something about children . . .'

'For fuck's sake, Peter, if you heard me the first time, why did you pretend not to?'

'I wasn't sure exactly what you said.'

'Yes you were.'

'You want children?'

Maddie said nothing.

'But you've always hated children, the idea of children.'

'I don't know. I'm not getting any younger. And us . . . I really don't know how we can carry on without them. We'll be teenagers for ever. We'll never grow up. You'll never have any responsibility.'

'But we've always said we can live very comfortably like this, just the two of us. We've always said . . . I mean, maybe if we got better-paid jobs, and—'

'But we never will, will we? There'll always be excuses. You're always going to be a lecturer and I'm always going to be a magazine writer. But other people have kids . . . Poor people.'

'Ha! Too bloody right.'

'And I suppose we're not like that, are we?'

'No need to be sarcastic. No need to take the piss.'

'That's good, coming from you.'

'Listen, Maddie? Do you want kids? Seriously? Do you?'

'I don't know. I want something. I can't go on like this for ever.'

'Okay. If that's what you want.'

'Oh for God's sake. I don't want you to say it just because it's what you think I want.'

'Christ!' Peter threw up his hands in exaggerated despair. 'What can I say? I can't do anything right for you, can I?'

Maddie said nothing. She tried to picture the flat with children running round it and couldn't. She tried to picture Peter holding a child and couldn't. She tried to picture herself breast-feeding one and the idea seemed so ludicrous, so bizarre that she actually laughed out loud.

'Good joke?' Peter asked.

'Not bad,' Maddie said and got up. 'Do you want a drink?'

'Mm, lovely.'

She went through to the kitchen and opened a bottle of wine. She was just pouring out a couple of glasses when the phone rang.

'Hello?' she said, putting the cold plastic of the receiver to her ear. 'Maddie Fisher.'

'Oh, hello. This is Lucy. Lucy Kendall.'

For a moment Maddie couldn't place her. Then it came to her at the same moment as the woman explained.

'Tom's sister. In Norwich.'

'Of course, yes. Hello. How are you?' She asked it automatically, then remembered that the woman's husband had died so she probably wasn't feeling too great.

'Oh, you know . . . I'm okay, I think. Holding up, just.'

'Good.' Maddie couldn't think of anything to say. But what did Lucy want, anyway? She was trying to put her and Norwich and Tom out of her mind.

'I'm sorry to bother you, Maddie.'

'Listen,' said Maddie, looking through to the sitting-room where Peter was sitting reading the magazine. 'Can I take your call on the other extension?'

'Of course.'

'Okay, I'll put the phone down. Don't hang up.'

She replaced the receiver and picked up the drinks.

'Who's that?' asked Peter.

'Work,' she said, giving him his wine. 'I'll take it in the office.'

She went through to her office, thinking they wouldn't have room for an office if they had children, and sat at her desk. As she picked up the phone she looked at her word-processor screen. She'd been working on an article earlier and hadn't switched it off.

'Hello, Lucy?' she said.

'Hello. I'm sorry about this.'

'That's all right, I wasn't doing anything.' She wedged the receiver between her chin and shoulder and saved the article to the computer's memory.

'It's just, I got your number off the police.' Lucy sounded nervous. 'I hope you don't mind.'

'Oh. Well . . .'

'I didn't know what to do, you see?'

'No, it's all right.' Maddie absent-mindedly called up one of the games on the machine, Tetris, and sat there manipulating the falling shapes while she talked.

'The thing is,' said Lucy. 'I wondered if you knew where Tom was.'

'Tom?' Maddie glanced at the door. It was shut. Peter couldn't hear. As she looked back at the screen she saw that she'd messed up the game and would have to start again.

'Yes,' Lucy went on. 'He left here a couple of days ago . . .'

'He was in Norwich?'

'He'd come up for the funeral. And he left, didn't say anything, no note or anything. And I need to get hold of him.'

'To tell you the truth, Lucy, I haven't seen him since, well, a week . . .' Maddie tried to remember exactly how long it had been. 'Two weeks . . .'

'Oh.' Lucy sounded deflated, tired. 'Are you likely to be seeing him? It's just that I've got something I need to tell him and I don't know where he is.'

'I don't think I will be seeing him, actually.' Maddie jumped as Peter put his head round the door. He said he was popping down the pub and did she want to come. He said it in the tone of voice which implied that she probably wouldn't want to and that would suit him just fine. She obliged him by saying no.

She was alone in the house now.

'I'm sorry about that,' she said. 'But there shouldn't be any more interruptions now.'

'That's all right.'

'Listen, Lucy' – Maddie rotated a 'T' shape and slotted it into place – 'I might as well tell you. It's finished between Tom and me.'

'Oh.' Again that deflated tone.

'We didn't say anything at the time. It was all a bit embarrassing. But I'm married, Lucy.'

'I don't understand. Tom didn't say, I mean, you're not married to Tom?'

'No. God, no. Not Tom. That's the thing. Norwich was . . . a sort of dirty weekend.'

'I see.'

'Least that's what it was supposed to be. And, well, everything that happened. It made me look at things, what I was doing, with Tom. And, well, I decided it wasn't right, it wasn't what I wanted.'

'I see. Yes. I'm sorry to have bothered you.'

'It's all right. To tell you the truth, it's good to have someone to talk to about it. I haven't been able to tell anyone. I tried to explain to Tom, but he was under stress, I suppose.'

'That's it, Maddie, that's why I need to get hold of him.' Lucy sounded suddenly animated and excited. 'You see, the thing is, the police have found out who attacked James.'

Maddie froze. Had they finally proved it was Tom? God, what must the poor woman be going through?

'Yes, it seems there's some teenager been going round getting into people's houses while they're in them.'

'What do you mean?'

'And James must have surprised him, and ... Well, you know the rest. So, you see why I have to let Tom know. I mean, I don't know if you knew.'

'Knew what?'

'That the police actually suspected Tom.'

'No,' Maddie lied. 'No, I didn't know that. But they don't suspect him any more?'

'No. Of course not.'

Maddie felt a great relief, but it was mixed with painful guilt and something else. Her suspicion of Tom had made it easy for her to get rid of him, to sidestep that particular complication in her life. It had been a good psychological tool. She realized, now, that she had actually wanted Tom to have done it, so that she had an excuse, a reason to run from what her relationship with him offered and threatened.

Now things weren't so simple. Now she realized she had probably hurt Tom. She, who had accused Peter of thinking only about himself, hadn't really stopped to consider Tom's feelings. Tom who was so vulnerable. She swallowed. Her throat was tight. Poor Tom, what had she done to him?

'Oh, Lucy,' she said. 'I'm so glad. But he's gone missing?'

'Well, it's only been a couple of days, but—'

'You've tried phoning him, I suppose?'

'Yes. Loads of times. I think his phone might be out of order. You couldn't, I mean, I know it might be awkward for you, but you wouldn't go round to his flat and see if he's there, would you?'

'I don't know, Lucy. I really don't know. I've been trying to keep out of his way.'

'I understand.'

'I hope somebody does, because I don't. I'm fighting here to keep my marriage going. Since Norwich, I've realized that it's what I want, me and Peter, and I'll do anything to – God, this must all seem so trivial to you.'

'No. I understand. James and I had our problems like anyone else.'

'Yes. Look, Lucy, obviously I will go round there. He must know, he needs to know.'

'If he's even staying there at all.'

'I'm sure he is.'

'Thank you, Maddie. And I hope you get things worked out. I know how important it is to be happy in a marriage.'

'Thanks, Lucy. And ... Well, do you mind if I ask you a question? It might seem rather strange.'

'No. Not at all.'

'Well, do you ever regret having children?'

'No. Not for a moment. Specially after what happened to James. A family is such a marvellous thing.'

'Yes. Well, thanks.'

'Do you think Tom's all right?'

'I'm sure he's fine,' said Maddie, but she didn't believe it. Last time she'd seen him he'd been a little crazy. He might have done anything. She'd told herself at the time it was because of his guilt at attacking James. But now ... Maybe Lucy didn't know about his rages, about the therapy. And her own treatment of him hadn't helped. But there was no need to worry her.

'He'll be fine,' she said kindly. 'Don't you worry.'

They said goodbye and she hung up.

She looked at the screen and saw that, without thinking, she'd surpassed her highest score, gone well beyond any point she'd ever reached before. And with the realization she panicked and fucked up, and the 'Game Over' sign came up.

THIRTY

A man answered the phone. Tom assumed it was Peter. He sounded cold and terse, as if he didn't like being disturbed, didn't like talking on the phone.

'Hello,' said Tom. 'Can I speak to Maddie Fisher, please?'

'She's not here.'

'Do you know when she'll be back?'

'Later.'

'It's quite important I speak to her. Do you know where I can contact her?'

'You can't contact her, she's at a meeting.'

'What type of meeting?'

'Look, who is this?'

'It doesn't matter.'

Tom hung up. He knew where Maddie was. He'd remembered. But he got out his diary to make sure. Yes, there it was, neatly written under today's date. 'Session. Clive's place. Brixton.' He checked his watch; they would have only just begun, he could be there in less than half an hour.

As he left the flat he noticed a pile of mail on the little table by the front door. He skipped through the envelopes, bills mostly. Bills which, in the past, he would have paid as soon as they'd arrived. But not any more. They didn't matter any more.

There were a couple of other letters that looked like they might be personal, but they didn't matter any more, either. There was even an unstamped envelope with just the word 'Tom' on it. He remembered now: sometime during the day someone had come to the door, rung his bell. They must have left it.

Well, fuck them. Fuck them all. He was done with all their shit. He was moving on.

He took the letters outside and stuffed them in a bin.

Driving to Brixton, he imagined the scene at Clive's. The whole sorry bunch of losers sitting around on Clive's chairs that didn't match, and the old sofa whose springs had gone. And in the centre of the loose circle was Maddie. He pictured her glowing, like a Madonna in an old painting, picked out in a shaft of light, impossibly beautiful. The other figures dark, dull, worshipful.

He knew what he'd do. He'd go in, walk up to her, take her hand and lead her out of there without saying anything. Then they'd go to a pub, like they had done that first time. They'd drink and he would talk to her, he would tell her all about himself, all about his life. He'd explain everything to her, he'd unburden himself of a lifetime of secrets. And she would love him again.

The roads were fairly clear and he made good time. Clive's basement flat was in a row of large terraced houses, and he managed to park out the front. He locked the car and stood on the pavement looking down at the light that spilled into the well at the bottom of the concrete steps leading to Clive's door. Behind that door, at the centre of that light, was Maddie. He realized he was very excited. The excitement both frightened and exhilarated him. For so many years he'd tried to quash any feelings like this. And now his life was becoming a wild and unpredictable ride.

He started down, each step taking him closer to her.

He rang the doorbell and waited. In a few moments the door was opened and there stood Clive. In corduroys and a jumper, blinking behind his glasses. He frowned when he saw Tom, then changed the frown to a smile.

'Tom, come on in. We didn't expect to see you again.'

Tom pushed past him. 'I'm not staying,' he said flatly.

The door to the sitting-room was open. He carried on through without waiting.

What a depressing scene it was. They were all there, all the same sad, old faces. Staring dully at him. Ian the hooligan, Jane the victim, old Mr Bentley, and the couple he still thought of as the new couple, though by now they were probably old hands, the Maxwells.

No. Not all the old faces. Something was missing. Tom looked round the group again to make sure. It wasn't possible Maddie wasn't there.

Clive came into the room.

'Look who it is,' he said.

'Where is she?' Tom asked.

'Who?'

Tom didn't reply, but left the room and searched the rest of the flat, which comprised a kitchen, a bathroom and a bedroom. He strode from room to room, throwing open doors and switching on lights. Clive scurried after him. In the bedroom he spoke.

'What is it, Tom? What are you looking for?'

'Where is she? Where's Maddie?'

'Maddie? Maddie doesn't come any more. She stopped coming when you did. I thought—'

'What did you think?'

'Nothing.'

Tom looked around Clive's bedroom, with its untidy book-shelves and framed Wassillie Tingle posters, then sat down heavily on the bed and rested his head in his hands.

'Will you stay, Tom?' Clive asked.

'No. I have to find her. I don't understand it. Peter said ... said she was here.'

'I can assure you she's not.'

'Christ. She must have lied to him. She must be somewhere else. With ... someone else.'

'Come on, Tom, I've got to get back to the others. Why not join us?'

Clive didn't say anything else. He left Tom sitting there and went next door to the sitting-room. After a while Tom heard voices. Conversation.

He wondered what to do. There was no way he could find Maddie now, but he'd so wanted to talk to her. He'd prepared himself to confess, and now there was nobody to confess to. He wearily stood up. Go home, get some sleep. Carry on tomorrow.

There were more bookshelves in the corridor; this tiny, dark flat was like a nest. And there in the sitting-room was a family of frightened little bunnies. He put his head in the door to say goodbye and Clive spotted him.

'It's good to see you back,' he said.

'I'm not back. For God's sake, Clive, can't you tell? I'm beyond all this now, I don't need you or—' He looked round at the blank, lifeless faces.

'Okay, point taken. If that's how you feel.'

Tom looked at Clive. For a moment he thought he saw genuine regret.

'Yes. That's how I feel. I am happy, Clive, and you'll just have to accept that.'

'Good. I'm glad. And what about Maddie? How is she?'

'I haven't seen her for a while, that's why I thought she was here. I wanted to talk to her.'

'What about?'

'Oh, leave it, Clive. Don't try to drag me into one of your bloody sessions.'

'I was just asking.'

Tom realized he'd been drawn into the room, he was standing in the middle of them all, just as he'd pictured Maddie earlier.

'I'm going,' he said.

Clive got up and touched his arm. 'It really is good to see you again, you know, Tom. And I really am happy for you – that you're happy.'

Tom turned round and grabbed Clive by the shirt front. 'Don't touch me, Clive,' he said. 'Don't ever fucking touch me.'

'I'm sorry, but really there's no need.'

Tom shoved Clive away and he toppled back into an armchair. A ripple of tension passed round the room. Old Mr Bentley smiled.

'I'm sorry,' Tom said. 'I'm a little confused. I do things, I expect them to go one way, and they go all to hell.'

'You can't control the world, Tom.'

'I'm not trying, I just want to be able to control the small part of it that affects me.'

'Things don't always go as we plan ...'

'Oh, shut up! Shut up! I don't want any of your bloody platitudes.' Tom felt very tired, weighed down by the oppressive atmosphere, the stink of failure rising from these people. 'You can't do anything for me, Clive. Maddie could if she was here. She'd understand what I was going to tell her.'

'What?'

Clive stood up and Tom hit him with his broken hand. They both yelled. And Clive ended up back in the chair again.

'What was that for?'

'For everything.'

'Don't do that, please.' It was Jane, grey Jane.

'I'm sorry,' Tom said. 'I didn't mean it.'

Clive's nose was bleeding. He was holding it.

'Put your head back,' said Mrs Maxwell, and he did.

'Pinch the top,' said Jane.

'What's the matter with you, Tom?' Clive said, his voice strangled.

'It's none of your fucking business.' Tom felt like weeping. He'd made a bloody fool of himself and he'd fucked up his fingers again.

'Maybe you'd better go,' Clive said.

No. If only somehow he could explain.

He moved towards the door, then stopped.

Why not?

'All right,' he said. 'All bloody right. I'll tell you what's the matter with me. That's what you want, isn't it? What you've always wanted. Yes, I'll tell you, Clive … All of you.' He felt lighter; there was some hope after all. Why not tell them?

But he didn't know where to start. He felt suddenly very embarrassed, painfully self-conscious.

'All my life …' he said falteringly, then stopped. There was an electric silence in the room. He took a deep breath and carried on. 'All my life I've been … I haven't been … I …' He saw Bentley turn away and yawn.

'All right, listen. My father was an army man. My mother was German, I never really knew her, actually, she died. I was only three, my sister was one. That's what I'm telling you about, my sister, Lucy. You see? That other stuff's not important. Except, I suppose what I mean is, all we had was him. And he hated us. You see? He never once showed us any affection. Lucy and me. He treated us like, I don't know, his men – in the army. He never touched me. I was terrified of him, we both were. He never shouted at us, but he would talk coldly, intense, with a deep bitterness and resentment, with hatred. You don't know what it's like to grow up like that. It destroys you, it …' He paused. He had them now, they were fascinated. It was his moment. Then someone spoke. It was the hooligan, Ian.

'So what?' he said.

'So what? I'm trying to tell you how my father fucked me up, and you—'

'My father used to bugger me,' said Ian.

'What?'

'Yeah, up the arse. It's the first thing I remember.' He stared at the carpet and spoke in a lifeless monotone. The others were looking at him now, it was the most words he'd ever spoken. Clive was open-mouthed.

Tom felt a twinge of anger. 'Please, Ian,' he said. 'This is my turn.'

'We're not interested,' Ian said and someone sniggered.

'Shut up, Ian. This is important.'

'You shut up,' said Bentley. 'You boring fart. Ian's story sounds much more juicy.'

'I'm not surprised you like his story,' Tom snapped. 'I'm sure you love the idea of young boys being sodomized. Is that what turns you on, eh? Sex with kids?'

'Come on, Tom,' said Clive.

'Bollocks. I wouldn't put it past him to have done it himself.'

'Yes,' said Bentley quietly. 'I have.'

'Oh Christ,' said Tom.

'My girl,' Bentley said, his voice almost a whisper. 'My little girl . . .' He began to cry now.

Tom felt the anger begin to breed inside him. He was losing it. This one chance to open up and unburden himself was being hijacked.

'It's the same!' he shouted. 'I mean, not sexual . . . This was mental. This was cruelty of a different kind.'

'My dad said he loved me,' said Ian. 'When he was doing it. I'd have preferred him to hate me, if it meant he'd leave me alone.'

'Please.'

'What's your problem?' asked Mrs Maxwell.

'I've told you, it was my father.'

'My little angel,' wailed Bentley. 'What did I do to her? She killed herself, the poor little thing.'

'Oh shut up, you stupid old git!'

Silence fell.

'Right,' said Tom. 'I want to tell you about the one time he did hit me. The only time he ever did. The only time I even remember

254

him touching me. He attacked me. Punched me twice. I was only fifteen. I left home, came to London, lived with my uncle. He was a printer, he—'

'Oh do be quiet,' said Bentley and Tom snapped. He stormed over to the old man and smacked his head back against the wall. Bentley's eyes widened with shock. Clive ran to them and grabbed Tom from behind.

'For God's sake, Tom,' he said, 'calm down. All of you, calm down. This is going too far.'

Tom wheeled round and confronted Clive.

'Why?' he said. 'This is what you wanted. To find out all our secrets. To open us up like mussels and dig out the soft flesh. Prod the raw nerve. Isn't that what you wanted?'

'It has to be controlled. This is crazy.'

'Of course it's crazy! We're all fucking mad!'

'You're definitely fucking mad,' said Bentley and Tom turned on him again, pressing him up against the wall. He put his face very close to the old man's, stared into his frightened eyes.

'You want some smut, Bentley? You want some filth to go home and wank over? You want to know why my father attacked me? Do you? You want to know about my sister? My thirteen-year-old sister?'

Bentley stared at him. Looked right inside him. And he knew.

'I didn't mean to do it,' Tom said, letting him go.

'We none of us meant it,' said Bentley.

'No! I'm not like you.'

'Yes, you are. We're all the same.'

'Be quiet, all of you,' Clive shouted. 'This has gone far enough. We'll all start to say things we don't mean if we carry on like this. It's not healthy. There must be some control.'

Bentley began to laugh. Ian joined him, then Jane, then the Maxwells.

No. There was so much more he had to say. So much more. He

hadn't even got to the part about killing someone. But there was no chance now, they weren't interested in him. To them he was just another sad fuck-up.

He ran from the flat, chased by their laughter. He ran out into the fresh air, scrambled up the stairs and fell against his car, gasping for breath.

'Maddie,' he called. 'Maddie, help me!' There was only silence. 'Lucy, help me! I don't know what to do.'

He crawled into the front seat of his car and curled up under the steering-wheel. He was back there in bed with Lucy, holding on to her in the darkness, disappearing into bliss and whispering her name while she stroked his hair and told him what to do.

THIRTY-ONE

Emma Summers looked at herself in her son's bedroom mirror. She looked old, worn out. Her red hair, usually her best feature, usually so full and shiny, hung limp and lifeless. She pushed a stray lock off her pale forehead. There were spots growing there. Spots at her age. But it wasn't surprising. She'd had enough.

She left the mirror and went to Will's bed. She gently ran her fingers over his duvet cover. It was cold. The bed hadn't been used for six days. The whole room felt cold, unused.

Ever since Will had disappeared she'd come up here every day, as if his room might give her some clues to where he was. And every day the room was the same, cold and empty. Abandoned.

She hardly slept at all. Even though she had the phone right by her bed, she felt that if she was asleep and it rang and she didn't wake in time to answer it she might miss him. So her sleep was shallow, troubled by anxiety dreams. Every time she woke she looked at the clock and it was half an hour later, twenty minutes. Then, every morning, she waited by the front door for the postman, and every day it was the same. Nothing. He was gone.

The first time the police had come she'd been pathetically grateful, naïvely trusting in their omnipotence. But they'd told her as gently as they could that there was really not a lot they could do. Obviously they'd try, but every day teenagers went missing. And she couldn't lie to them, couldn't pretend that they'd had a blissfully happy home life. She told them the truth, that they rarely spoke, that he was secretive and kept himself to himself. She told them about him, but not herself. She didn't tell them that she had no idea how to get through to him and let him know that she loved him desperately, that he was all she had in her life.

No, she didn't tell the police that, and neither did she tell them about Will's secret room. They didn't need to know about that. That was between her and Will. Not, of course, that she'd ever let Will know that she was aware of its existence.

She remembered the first time she'd found it, she'd come up here to clean Will's bedroom. He hated her to do it and always kept the room locked, said he liked to clean it himself. He was like that about everything; she tried to look after him, but he wouldn't let her. He resented her. So when he was out at school she sneaked up here with a key of her own and carefully tidied the bits he'd missed; the dust on top of the shelves, dirt behind the wardrobe, grime on the light switch. And she'd straighten his bedclothes and rehoover the carpet, and sometimes just sit and talk as if he were there, ask him things, share things with him, pretend they were a normal, happy family.

Then one day, cleaning behind the wardrobe, she'd noticed the tracks along the floor, then the line where the wallpaper didn't quite match. She'd shifted the furniture and discovered the panel.

Inside the little space she at first hadn't known what it meant. But she'd read the books, seen the objects, and understood. Her son was a housebreaker, a thief. That's what he did when he went out, on tiptoes as if she couldn't hear him. That's why he crept around so secretive and sullen.

She never went back there, never opened the panel again. She'd respected his privacy. After all, he did well at school. His teachers said he was specially gifted, Oxbridge material, and if he needed this secret outlet she wouldn't interfere. Besides, she knew that if she did say anything he'd only resent her more.

The secret room had, of course, been the first place she'd looked after he didn't come home that night. She'd been surprised to find it virtually empty; the objects were mostly gone, though the books were still there. She'd hoped he'd given up this strange activity. But as the days passed, she began to worry that he'd run away, taken the stuff with him and left her for good.

What about the broken doorframe, though? As if someone had forced Will's bedroom door in. And what about the man? The shifty, nervous man who'd come to the house that afternoon with the nonsensical story about insurance and had then scurried away. What had that been about? Had he been a burglar, perhaps? Seeing if anyone was at home? Had he broken in while Will was in there, broken into his room, and found him . . . ? And then what? Burglars didn't kill people, did they? Not in Norwich. And then, if they did, surely they didn't take the body with them. The police didn't think so, they reckoned this was an unlikely story.

They didn't think he'd been kidnapped, either. No note. No reason.

They'd taken some photographs of Will away with them. She didn't think they'd be much use, as she didn't have any recent ones of him. He wouldn't let her take his picture any more. The only ones she could give them were of him aged twelve.

But she'd thanked them and felt confident in them, and wished them luck.

The first time, anyway.

The second time was different.

This morning an Inspector had come, Hapworth, with a Sergeant Arnell. And they'd given her quite a grilling. Did Will have any friends? Did he hang out with bad types? How was he doing at school? Had she noticed any changes in him recently? She hadn't understood their approach, wasn't sure what they were on about. In the end she'd asked them why they were acting as if Will were some kind of suspect rather than a victim. And they'd told her.

They were looking for a boy, a young man who went into people's houses while they were in them. The boy had got into a fight in one of these houses and killed someone. They hadn't needed to spell out to her that they thought the boy might be Will or one of his friends.

So of course she'd exploded. How could they think such a thing? Her son had disappeared! He wasn't a murderer... Like something out of a film. Phrases which sounded meaningless coming from her. It was all so unreal. And in the end she didn't think they'd been any more convinced than she was.

At last they'd gone and now here she was, alone in his room, more depressed than ever. Because now she couldn't ask them for any more help. She knew the truth; he'd run away. He'd done this thing and run away. The police had gone from being her saviours to her enemies.

How had Will become like this? She didn't know. She didn't understand people. She'd always thought of herself as being a bit stupid, really. Pretty but stupid. So, as with everything else, she blamed herself. If something went wrong in the family it was the mother's fault, wasn't it? And now she'd lost her husband and her son.

Both her fault.

True, Robin's death had been an accident, and a senseless one at that, but she'd lost him long before then. Now she had to face up to it, she had to admit that she hadn't known how to get through to him any more than she had done Will. She had to admit that in the end she'd slept with his best friend out of a sort of desperate loneliness.

Alan had even deserted her too. Soon after Robin's death. He couldn't handle it. Couldn't handle the possibility that now Emma was single she might want to marry him.

She looked around the room. There was so much evidence here of the men she'd lost. The double glazing Robin had put in, which didn't open. The bad carpentry. Will's clothes. Will's schoolbooks.

Will's secret room. It overwhelmed her. She'd never made a mark in this house. It was their house, not hers. She always felt like an intruder here, a stranger, a ghost in somebody else's home.

And now she was the only one left, rattling around this huge, empty house. A house in which she used two, maybe three rooms at most. Will was gone, she knew that now. He'd killed that man and run away, and she'd lost him.

But she'd still wait by the phone; she'd never give up hope. One day he might ring. One day he might send a letter, just to let her know he was alive and well. He could look after himself, he'd proved that. If only somehow she could have proved to him how much she cared. She'd do anything to prove it now. But it was too late. Too late.

'Will,' she said out loud, 'I know you can't hear me, but I did love you. You just never let me.'

There was even his smell here to taunt her, that vague cocktail of odours unique to a boy's room. If anything, it was stronger now than before. Maybe he'd left a sock somewhere, or an uneaten sandwich. Though she hadn't found anything when she'd searched the room.

Maybe it was just her imagination? Some deep, sad nostalgia creating aromas from nothing. But whatever it was, there was no point in torturing herself. She had to get on with things . . .

What things?

Nothing really mattered any more now that he was gone.

But she forced herself up off the bed.

Shopping. Yes. Get the shopping done.

She still shopped for two, it was a betrayal not to. What if he came home and there was nothing for him to eat? As it was, the house was filling up with food. She hardly ate any more. But getting out was a relief, turning her mind off, wandering the anonymous aisles of the supermarket in her daily ritual.

She left the room and pulled the door behind her. It wouldn't shut properly and bounced away from the broken frame. As she fiddled with it, trying to make it stay closed – Will always liked his door shut – she noticed that, for some reason, the smell was stronger out here. Indeed, when she thought about it, it seemed to be coming from the other side of the stairs, not Will's room at all.

She leant close to the loft door and sniffed. Yes, it was definitely coming from in here. She opened the door and was hit with a rancid waft of warm air.

She grimaced and turned the light on. There was something in here rotting.

She looked around the room; she hadn't been in the loft for ages. Everything reminded her of a past life. A lost life. There was Will's old cricket bat. There was a box of Robin's tools. And, with a stab of guilt, she noticed his shotgun locker. That beastly gun of his which she should have turned in after his death. She'd been meaning to do it ever since, but had never got round to it. It held very potent memories for her. In her mind it had come to stand for the gulf between them. She remembered, when he'd first got it, he'd tried to get her interested. He'd taken her shooting and she'd come home deadly bored and with a sore shoulder.

How many other things were there in here that would remind her painfully of the past? Old things of Robin's, old things of Will's.

There was the Subbuteo set she'd given Will and he'd never used.

'God, Mum. Don't you even know I don't like football?'

There was his first bike.

There were the suitcases they'd used on their last family holiday.

And there was Robin's old trunk. When they'd moved into their first little flat together, he'd fitted all his belongings into it.

But where was that bloody smell coming from?

Tentatively she sniffed again. After the initial blast the trapped air had dispersed somewhat, but there was still a distinctly unpleasant odour in the room.

She followed her nose and it took her to the trunk. There was a smaller suitcase on top of it and a box of ancient magazines. She pulled them off. The stench here was very powerful; it stung her eyes. It reminded her of the time they'd come back from abroad and found Will's pet gerbils starved to death. The whole house had stunk.

She opened the lid.

The hot, foul air that escaped almost made her throw up. She rocked back and grunted and screwed up her face.

She steeled herself and looked into the trunk. There was a layer of crumpled newspaper, stained and smeared with something brown like excrement. Covering her nose and mouth with her hand, she pulled the newspaper away.

She knew before she saw it what she would find underneath.

Now she was sick.

She knelt, bent double, choking and sobbing, screaming through the gasps.

Cruel. How could anybody be so cruel? To leave him there. Her son. To leave him like that . . .

His face. She tried to remember his face, to blot out the black-ened, swollen face in the trunk. What had he looked like? She couldn't remember. Surely she couldn't have forgotten him so soon? Now she'd never see his face again. She tried to picture it, she willed it to focus, but another face came into her mind. A different face. An older face. Why was it there? Where had she seen it? It was a man's face.

Then she remembered.

It had been on one of the sheets of newspaper. A photograph. But why had it imprinted itself so strongly on her mind?

She held on to the picture, used it to pull herself up from the floor. Used it to force herself on. She sorted through the pile of discarded newspaper and then she found it.

In the picture the man led a woman through a graveyard. Two small children held on to the woman. But she wasn't interested in the woman and the children, just the man, because she recognized him. He was the same man who had come to the door that day. And then she read the caption and everything became clear to her.

She could read Will's books to find out the rest.

THIRTY-TWO

It was quiet here, a contrast to the busy main road at the end of the street. There was no one around. An amber street light flickered slightly. Tom walked up the steps to the front door. There were two bells. He read the names and found Maddie's. There was an entryphone. He pressed the button with a painful, gloved finger and leant close, ready to speak. He heard Maddie's voice, distorted by the machine but still beautiful.

'Hello,' he said, trying to control the excitement in his voice. 'It's me.'

'Who's me? Me who?'

'Tom.'

Maddie didn't say anything but she was still there; Tom could hear the hiss and buzz of the machine. Then it went dead. He waited. Perhaps she'd misunderstood. Perhaps she hadn't heard him properly. He raised his finger to ring again, when through the pebbled glass he saw a door open inside the house at the top of a flight of stairs, and a figure came down.

Maddie opened the front door. She looked tired.

'Hello,' said Tom.

'Tom, what are you doing here?'

'Can I come in, Maddie?'

'No, of course you can't.'

'What do you mean?'

'This isn't a good time, Tom. Listen, I'll ring you, okay? But go home now.'

'I can't, Maddie. I've come to get you.'

'Come to get me? What are you talking about?'

'Us.'

'There's no such thing,' she said wearily.

'Maddie, just let me in. I can't talk out here.'

'No, Tom, please ... Just go.'

The door at the top of the stairs opened again. A man in glasses stood there.

'Maddie? Who is it?'

'It's nothing, Peter. It's okay ...'

'Hello, Peter,' said Tom, and he stepped inside past Maddie.

The hallway was painted sky-blue, ragged with grey and white to give a sort of cloudlike effect. It hadn't been very delicately done. Tom found it rather ugly.

Maddie came in behind Tom but kept the door open.

'This is Tom,' Maddie said. 'He works for – he was just passing.'

'Why are you lying, Maddie?' Tom asked. 'What's the point?'

'Oh God,' Maddie said quietly.

'Erm ...' Peter said at the top of the stairs and Tom looked up at him. 'I'm not exactly sure what's going on here. You two seem to be ahead of me.'

'Tom,' Maddie said, 'go now, please go.'

'No,' said Peter affably. 'You must stay, Tom.'

Tom looked back at Maddie, who was still holding the door open. A car passed by outside. Maddie looked very beautiful. Then he looked back up at Peter, holding his own door open. Two doors. One behind, one ahead. Behind was dark, confused; ahead was light, peace and understanding; a big white sky.

He started upstairs. He heard the front door close behind him.

Inside, their flat was stylish but comfortable. Whoever had painted the hallway hadn't decorated in here. The walls were white and there were paintings and shelves of books. Grey carpets, small, geometrical rugs. Wall lighting. A beautifully restored Georgian fireplace.

'This is a nice flat,' said Tom.

The television was on and there were the remains of a meal laid out on a low black table. Peter put the plates on to a tray and took them through an archway into a kitchen. Tom saw modern appliances, a wok, enamelled iron pans.

Maddie came in and looked at Tom with a mixture of what appeared to be sadness and anger. She leant against the doorframe with her arms folded. Peter returned from the kitchen with a bottle of wine.

'Drink, Tom?'

'Oh, for God's sake, Peter,' Maddie snapped. 'Do you have to be such a cunt?'

Peter raised an eyebrow and looked at her with an expression of mock affront. 'My dear, I was just offering our guest, a drink.'

'I know perfectly well what you were doing.'

'What was I doing, dear?'

'Oh, shut up.'

'I won't have a drink, thank you, Peter,' Tom said. 'I've given up.'

'Really? How interesting, Tom.'

'Yes, I think it's important to keep a clear head.'

'I'm sure it is, Tom.'

'I just came round, Peter, to pick up Maddie.'

Maddie snorted.

'I see,' said Peter. 'Fine. Well, I'm glad you told me.'

'This is ridiculous,' said Maddie.

'I couldn't agree more,' said Peter. 'Who is this person?'

'He's just a friend, someone I met.'

'Maddie and I are lovers.'

Peter started to laugh, a hard, bitter laugh. Maddie shouted at him to stop.

'Well, this really is a pathetic scene. My noble, holier-than-thou wife and her halfwit lover.'

'I beg your pardon,' said Tom, 'but there's no need to be rude. The simple fact of it is, Maddie and I love each other. She doesn't love you and you don't love her.'

'We don't love you, you don't love us, and they don't love him.'

'I'm sorry?'

'I was finishing your conjugation for you.' If it had been meant as a joke it hadn't come out as one.

'Maddie?' Tom said. 'Is all this strictly necessary?'

'Necessary?' For the first time there was the hint of real emotion in Peter's voice. 'You waltz in here and tell me you want to take my fucking wife away with you ...'

'It's all right, Peter,' Maddie said. 'Let me just talk to Tom. This is all just a bit of a misunderstanding.'

Peter laughed again and poured himself a large glass of wine.

'We can talk in the car,' Tom said. 'Come along, let's go.'

'Look, mate, Mr bloody Tom whoever you are, why don't you just fuck off out of it, okay?'

Peter held on to Tom's sleeve and tried to pull him towards the door. Tom yanked his sleeve away, spilling some of Peter's wine. 'Not without Maddie,' he said patiently.

'Look, can't you get it into your thick skull that Mrs Fisher isn't coming with you? I don't know who you are, or who you think you are. But I'm tired of all this. And I'd like you to just leave my house, please.'

Tom felt a twinge of anger now. A brief flash of white. It wasn't supposed to happen like this. Why did Peter have to be so obstructive?

'Maddie, for the first time in my life,' he said, 'I've got everything sorted out. I can see a straight path ahead of me, clearly sign-posted. This is the first thing I have to do. Fix things up, get back to how we were before. Anyone can see that's the correct thing for both of us to do.'

'Shut up, Tom,' said Maddie. 'Both of you, just shut up and stop acting like a couple of kids. Now, Tom, I don't know where you got the idea that I love you. Anything I might have felt for you has long since passed, and you must know that. So why don't you just go home? And I'll give you a ring and we'll talk about this sensibly.'

The whiteness of the walls was creeping into the back of Tom's brain. Why was Maddie saying these things? What was she trying to do? It didn't make any sense.

Of course, Peter. She was pretending for his sake. She didn't want to upset him, make a scene. But the simplest way to do this was to do it now, quickly, not give him a chance to react.

'Come with me,' he said and, just as Peter had led him, he now led her towards the door. Then Peter put a hand on his shoulder from behind and Tom turned back round.

He hit Peter in the side of the face. He spun away into the table and his glasses came off.

'Jesus Christ,' Maddie said and went over to her fallen husband. She turned from him and glared at Tom. 'What the fuck do you think you're doing?'

But Tom was squeezing his hand, trying to make the pain go away. The pain that gripped his knuckles and coursed up and down his fingers.

But at least the pain held the whiteness back.

Peter got up and groggily manoeuvred himself into an armchair. Maddie fetched his glasses and put them back on him. Peter held his jaw and moved it gingerly. He wouldn't look up at Tom. Maddie stroked his hair back off his face.

'Will you come now?' Tom asked.

'No, Tom, it's over. I would have thought that was blatantly obvious. Now get out of here before I lose my bloody temper.'

'But he can't stop you now.'

Peter finally looked at him. 'Are you a fucking madman, or what?'

Tom clenched his teeth. Was it possible? Was it possible that he might be mad? He'd changed, he knew that much. He knew that things hadn't been like this in the past. But he wasn't mad. It surely wasn't mad to want to be happy, to want to sort your life out, to throw off years of guilt and repression.

No, he wasn't mad. It was everyone else. It was Maddie and Peter. He suddenly looked round the room; it felt horribly small and cramped. It was an alien place. A place he didn't belong. A white place. He advanced on Peter, then bent down and gripped Peter's head in his aching, swollen hands. He was vaguely aware of Maddie tugging at him, trying to pull him away. He took no notice, she was dissolving into the whiteness along with everything else.

He looked into Peter's eyes. They were scared but he was trying not to show it. Tom held him like that and stared at him for a very long time.

'I'm not mad,' he said. Then he laughed; a thought had just struck him. 'The Americans say "mad" when they mean angry, don't they? "Don't make me mad! Don't make me mad!" I'm not mad. I'm not angry. I'm happy. You see? And nobody's ever going to stop me from being happy again. Do you understand? Not you, Peter, you won't stop me. Because I'm following the signs. Following the map.'

'You're hurting me,' said Peter. 'My head.'

Again Tom felt someone grab hold of him. He threw them off and they went away.

He felt like he could squeeze Peter's head to pulp. If he just pressed harder his eyes would pop out, his brains would squirt from his ears, his tongue come out of his mouth like toothpaste from a tube.

'Peter,' he said quietly. 'Peter, are you happy?'

'Jesus, you're hurting me.'

'I mean, apart from that. Are you happy?'

'No ... Not at the moment, no. Ow! Yes, yes, I'm happy, I'm very happy, I've never been happier, you are making me so fucking happy.'

'You're lying, Peter.'

'Please . . .'

'I can make you happy, Peter. I know the secret, I was given it . . . Do you want to know?'

'Yes.'

'It's . . .' But Tom couldn't remember. He had thought it was so clear and now he couldn't remember. What was the secret? If he could just remember it. Suddenly a searing pain lashed into Tom's back and he fell to the ground, releasing Peter. He looked up. Maddie was standing over him holding a poker.

Then she disappeared.

Everything went white.

Tom was floating in the white world, peaceful and relaxed. He reached out for something to hold on to. He felt something warm and soft. It felt good to him, it comforted him. He held on to it tight and it passed its warmth into him. He wanted to hold on to it for ever.

Then a fly buzzed, it hit his arm. He let go of the warm thing with one hand and swatted the fly. A brief spray of red fell through the whiteness. He smiled, and held back on to the warm thing.

He heard vague sounds, they floated around him, mumbled and incoherent. He wondered what they might be. The sounds became louder now; they were trying to tell him something. He strained to listen, to make sense of them and he realized they were calling his name.

'Tom,' they said. 'Tom . . .'

'Yes?'

'Stop it, Tom . . .'

'Stop what?'

'Stop it, Tom . . .'

'Stop what?'

'Tom.'

He wondered if he ought to look, try and see what they were

271

warning him against. He opened his eyes and peered into the whiteness. A shape began to form. It was a beautiful face. It was Maddie's face. He smiled at it. It spoke to him.

'Stop it, Tom!' it said.

'Stop what?'

He was holding Maddie's face up, holding it by the neck. And he was shaking it, flopping it backwards and forwards. More shapes came into focus. He saw a white wall with a faint red smudge on it. The smudge flicked on and off. No, it was being hidden by Maddie's head as it swung back. He was reminded of a rough wooden beam with a scrap of scalp on it. He looked again at the face and suddenly it screamed at him.

'Stop it! Stop it! Stop it! It's me, Tom, it's Maddie. Stop it!'

He let go of Maddie's neck and she slid down the wall. He felt very cold, sick. He was shivering. He saw Peter lying on the carpet, bleeding from his nose, which looked broken. He looked down at Maddie. She was weeping, rubbing her neck.

'Maddie,' he said, 'what am I doing?'

'Go away, Tom. Go away and never come back.'

'What? Why? I don't understand.'

'Neither do I, but please do it, darling, please go away and never come back.'

Tom turned from her, walked to the door. He took one last look back; Maddie had crawled to Peter and was cradling him in her arms.

Then he did as he was told.

He went away and he never came back.

THIRTY-THREE

'Tom, where are you?' Lucy came suddenly awake.

'I'm in London.' His voice sounded strained, tired.

'But where have you been?'

'I'm all right, Lucy, I'm okay. Don't worry about me.'

'I've been going crazy here, Tom. Where are you? Are you at your flat?'

'Yes.'

'I tried ringing, but the phone kept getting cut off, as if someone was answering it then hanging up.'

'It's been out of order.'

'Well, why didn't you try to ring me, then? Get in touch somehow?'

'I am ringing you,' Tom said, vainly attempting to sound light-hearted.

'I mean before now, Tom.'

'I did. I did try a couple of times, you must have been out.'

'You can't have tried very hard.'

'I've been busy. Doing things.'

'Tom, you disappeared. Didn't you think I might be worried? You can't just ring up now in the middle of the night and tell me everything's fine.'

'I'm sorry, I didn't realize it was late. What time is it?'

Lucy looked at her watch. 'It's half past three, but that's not the point ...'

'I'm sorry. Look, I'll ring back tomorrow.'

'No, don't hang up. I'm awake now.' She took a deep breath, tried to get rid of her resentful tone. 'Oh God, I'm so relieved to hear your voice. I thought something terrible had happened to you.'

'No, I'm fine.' He sounded very close, as if he were calling from the next room and not all the way from London. She wondered if it might be because it was so late, fewer people on the line or something. But she had no idea if phones worked like that.

'But where have you been?' she asked. 'What have you been doing? You left right after the funeral, and that was days ago.'

'There were things I had to do.'

'And you're sure you're all right?' It felt intimate, lying here in the dark with his voice in her ear. Like the old days, when they'd comforted each other.

'Yes, yes, I'm fine,' Tom said dismissively. 'Listen, Lucy, there are things I've got to do still. I've got to—'

'God, I nearly forgot. The police came round, they've found the person who did it.'

'What?'

'Well, they've not caught him, but they know it wasn't you.' There was silence on the other end, and she became aware that, far from being clear, the line was, in fact, filled with a universe of hisses and crackles and far off electronic noises. 'Tom? Tom? Are you still there?'

'Yes, I'm still here.'

'They know who it is, darling. That's the main thing, isn't it? I wanted to tell you before, but ... I mean, isn't that fantastic?'

'Yes,' Tom said flatly. 'Yes, that's great.'

'You don't sound terribly pleased. I thought you'd be pleased.'

'Of course I'm pleased. It's great news. I'm just tired. Listen, I rang to say I'm coming back up to Norwich.'

'You left all your stuff here, I didn't know what—'

'That doesn't matter any more. It's just stuff. Stuff. I've got to sort this whole bloody mess out once and for all.'

'But it is sorted. They know it's not you ...'

'I don't mean that mess, I mean the other, us, our family.'

'What do you mean? I don't understand. You mean wills and things? James's death ... ?'

'Wills? Will.'

'What?' Lucy wondered if Tom was drunk.

'I'm sorry, Sis,' he said with his serious voice. 'You're right. It's all the same mess really, isn't it?' And then he laughed, though she had no idea at what.

'If you say so,' she said.

'Christ, Luce, this has got so bloody complicated.'

'But it's all right. Don't you see? You're in the clear. It's just a matter of time before they find the boy. Oh, I didn't tell you, did I? It was just a boy. A young boy. And it's only a matter of time before they find him.'

'That's why I'm coming up.'

'What do you mean?'

'It doesn't matter. I'll explain when I get there. I need you, Lucy, I need you so much.'

'Well, I'm here. I always have been. You're the one that keeps going away.'

'Never again, though. I understand things now. Lately I've been learning some things, and it's all very clear. Where before it was, I was, like fighting through ... Er. I'll be up tomorrow.'

'Tomorrow?'

'Yup. Tomorrow afternoon sometime, maybe evening. I have, a couple of things to do here before I leave. But the thing is, I'll be there with you soon. You and the girls. They will be there, won't they?' Tom sounded suddenly anxious. 'They are there with you?'

'Of course they are.'

'Good. Because I need to sort you all out.'

275

'I've missed you, Tom. I was so worried. Can't you tell me what happened? Where you've been?'

'I've been down here in the flat. It's nothing very exciting. I had to leave that morning, day after the funeral. There were some problems at work. I didn't want to worry you with it. I came down—'

'I rang your work, they said you'd not been in.'

'No. I got it sorted. I had to see someone else about something, a client. It was connected with work. You see . . . ? Look, don't ask me all these questions. Can't you just accept that I'm all right and I'll see you tomorrow and talk to you then?'

'Okay. I'll look forward to it. I love you, Tom. I'm so glad you're all right.'

'And I love you too, Luce. That's why I'm coming up. We'll be happy in the end, won't we?'

'Yes. We'll be happy.'

'And how can it be wrong to be happy?'

'It's not wrong, Tom. We will be happy, you and I. It's over, we can get back to normal. We can . . .' Lucy stopped. She realized the phone had gone dead. Tom must still have been having troubles at his end. But never mind, he was all right, that was the main thing. Through it all, her family had come out okay. Her brother, her daughters, herself. Everyone.

Then she realized with a guilty twinge that the thing they were coming through was the death of one of the family. James. Poor James. But it was like the last time, when Dad had killed himself. The grief had come later, much later. Over a year. At first she had just felt a sort of surprise, not really even shock, a numbness. She even sort of felt glad that she wouldn't have to put up with him any more. But as time had gone by sadness had crept in, realization that he was gone, that he was missing all this.

She assumed the same thing would happen with James. She assumed that she wouldn't keep on just forgetting about him altogether.

She put the phone back on the hook and looked over at the faint light of the sky through the curtains. She'd been fast asleep when Tom had rung, dreaming about something, something white ... The bindweed dream. She'd been having it more and more since the night before the funeral when Tom had got into bed with her. Each time it stirred painful memories. Memories she'd tried to put out of her mind since she'd been a child but which in the last few weeks had been poking through her flimsy defences. She realized now that it was time to let them in. They couldn't hurt her any more.

She closed her eyes and she was once more lying in bed with Tom. Not in this bed, not in the hut made of branches and bindweed, but in her bed at home in Mine-head. She's lying there ashamed, silent and hurting. Confused. Then the door opens, and there's her father. He looks at the two of them.

Does she scream? She remembers it as if she did, but she can't be sure. The scream could have been inside.

Her father advances to the bed with fury in his eyes. But it's not just fury, she sees something else, something more frightening. It's jealousy. Jealousy and betrayal. He pulls Tom from the bed. Sends him sprawling across the floor. Lucy holds the sheet up to protect herself; not to cover her nakedness, but as if it might shield her from the violence and the rage.

Her father and her brother are shouting now, yelling incoherently. One shouting in anger, the other in fear. Then, for the first time in their lives Dad hits Tom. He swings at his head, twice, with his big, clumsy, white hands. Tom is knocked down, but he stands up and rushes at his father with a great roar, his face scarlet and contorted with anger. He hits the older man; punches him hard in the face. Dad staggers once, stunned and Tom punches him again. This time Dad goes down. He flops back and ends up sitting on the floor. His face is bleeding and Tom stands over him, panting like an animal. Tom's fists are clenched and his whole body is shaking.

There is an awful expression on her father's face. It is the expression of a man who has suddenly lost everything. She has never seen him like this before and will never see him like this again. He is broken, sad. He looks from Tom to her, pleading, knowing that something has happened here this night between them that will change their world.

And then Tom bursts into tears and runs out. And the next day he is gone.

The memory ran its course and Lucy realized she was crying. But as she realized, the tears dried on her cheeks. It was no time to cry again, because now, at last, twenty years later, Tom was coming back, and it would be like the old days again. The memory had lost its power to destroy her. She would be strong. She could be strong.

After all, they were only children.

She was wide awake now, with no chance of getting back to sleep for a while, so she turned on the light and reached over to get her book off the bedside table. As she did so she saw the folder of photographs she'd picked up from the developer's that afternoon.

She sat up in bed and took the pictures out, smiling.

They were mostly of the girls. She'd been photographing them a lot lately. She wasn't a great picture-taker; they were just snaps, out of focus, badly framed, wrongly exposed. But she didn't love them any the less for that.

The girls were happy, grinning. Playing with toys out the back. Wearing Mummy's gardening gloves. Digging with an outsize spade. Covered in mud and laughing. And then she came to the one of her. Polly had taken it, had insisted she be allowed to take one of Mummy. In the end Lucy had let her, and it had come out surprisingly well. It was just luck, she supposed, but it was the best of the lot.

In it, Lucy was standing in the garden, the bindweed behind her.

It was the afternoon they'd ripped it all out, but this was before they'd started. She was standing there in the sun and behind her was this great swathe of green. While she'd been away it had nearly taken over the whole garden. She was wearing shorts and her legs looked surprisingly good. She'd had her hair cut recently and it looked much better short. In fact, she had to admit it, she looked pretty good in the picture; radiant, healthy and full of life. She leant over and pulled out of the drawer an old picture taken at their last wedding anniversary. She looked fat and pasty, her hair dull and tangled. She wasn't drunk but she looked bloated and bleary, like someone on drugs. It was quite a transformation. Death obviously agrees with me, she thought, and then told herself not to be so flippant.

She'd been asleep, all that time asleep, like a butterfly waiting in its chrysalis, and now she was awake. Awake at four in the morning!

So what? It was good to be awake. She didn't want to miss anything now. She'd been ill and had then been given back her life. So now she was going to live. That morning she'd gone down to the jobcentre. There hadn't been many jobs on display, so she'd talked to a friendly young girl about getting back into insurance. That was how she'd met James, working in London together. And when they'd decided to have children, they'd moved up here, to a more civilized environment. Ha! That was ironic. Here they were in safe little Norwich and James had been stabbed to death.

Well, that was just bad luck. There was going to be no more of that.

The girl had explained that these days computers were the thing and if Lucy wanted a serious chance of getting back into work she should really get some training.

'Okay,' she'd said, she would. Why not? If computers were what people used these days, she'd join them. Why bury your head in the sand? She had a good brain, she'd learn quickly.

So she'd gone off and organized it there and then; signed up for a two-week course. It was expensive, but James had been well-covered. She didn't have to worry about money for a while.

She was happy.

The only thing that had clouded the happiness of the past few days had been Tom's disappearance, and now he was coming home. Well, not home exactly, not his home. Her home.

He'd sounded odd on the phone, but it was late, she supposed, and he'd probably been drinking. She'd imagined all sorts of horrors in the past few days, but now she knew they were unfounded. She looked again at the photograph of herself. Happy. She smiled back at it.

'You're doing all right, girl,' she said and winked. She'd been talking to herself a lot since James had died. She wasn't used to being alone, having nobody there to share things with. She often caught herself babbling on to the girls about things they couldn't possibly understand. But what the hell? She looked at the strong, attractive woman in the picture, that's who she was talking to. A lot of people would probably like to talk to a woman like that. Yes. She could almost fancy herself in that picture. Polly was really pretty clever to have taken it, maybe she'd grow up to be a famous fashion photographer.

Maybe not.

She didn't want to press the girls, spoil them just because of what they'd been through. She wanted them to have thoroughly normal lives. She wanted them just to be happy, ordinary girls. No more dramas. Nothing like the life she'd had, with her mad father and her sad brother, and suicide and murder, and the other. She had to protect them from all that, she had to make sure her own experiences didn't seep through and affect them in any way.

And later on, if Polly wanted to become a photographer, well, then she'd let her. They could do what they wanted. They had their whole lives ahead of them.

As Tom had said, 'How can it be wrong to be happy?'

Wrong decisions, all his life, ever since he was fifteen. He shouldn't have left home, he should have finished it then and there. Well, there was still time, time to finish it before he made any more mistakes.

'The end,' he said, and round the bend ahead he saw a car coming the other way. He looked at the line of traffic again; there were still no gaps.

'And they all lived happily ever after.'

The other car was getting nearer. He pushed his foot down on the accelerator. Still no gaps. Maybe if he eased over he could squeeze through down the middle, the road might just be wide enough for three. He looked back at the oncoming car. It was a silver Cavalier.

'Happy now?' he asked. It was seconds away.

He saw that he was very close to the car on his left, almost touching it. They were both travelling at the same speed. He looked at the driver and the driver turned to him, close enough to talk, terrified. Tom grinned at him.

'You can't take it with you,' he said.

The other driver suddenly slowed, braking sharply, opening up a gap in front. Tom jerked his wheel round and shot into the gap. The Cavalier screamed by, its horn blaring.

Tom was laughing. The car behind was hooting now. Tom was tempted to slam on his brakes and have done with it, cause a pile-up twenty or thirty cars long. But instead he pulled out again and sped up the right-hand side.

'Happy days are here again!' He wasn't going to let his father tell him to drive slowly any more. He had to get to Norwich before it was too late. There were things he had to do before the boy's body was found. After that it would all be over, so he had to act fast. There was Lucy and the girls to see to, he had to make sure they were sorted before he was gone. They had to be safe, for ever.

Stupid, to misread the signs and fool around in London when he should have been in Norwich with his family.

Lucy understood. She always had done. He pulled back in coming up to a corner.

If the police didn't find Will's burial chamber, his mother would. He'd known it was only temporary, and he'd foolishly wasted time, he'd been sidetracked from his main purpose. Somebody or something had tried to blind him to it, had tried to keep him away from doing what had to be done. He knew who it was. It was all of them, they were all in it; it was like *Murder On the Orient Express*, everyone was guilty, Clive, Maddie, Peter, all trying to sidetrack him. But not any more. The boy had shown him, had opened his eyes. He had a purpose.

Happiness.

And that real purpose would keep him alive on this road, whatever he did.

As long as he learnt to tell the warning signs from the direction signs.

He didn't need any signs now, he knew this road very well. He'd ridden it four times recently. It went straight there, no turning off to right or left. Straight there, straight into the round, fat heart of Norfolk. The bulging belly on all the maps. Yes, now he would ride straight there, find Lucy, find the girls, find his family.

The road opened out into a short stretch of dual carriageway, and he raced ahead; eighty, ninety, a hundred, a hundred and ten. He'd had no idea the car could go so fast.

The dual carriageway came to an end and he nipped in front of a van. More horns. It reminded him of something. Of course, the Mexican song. He yelled the words out of his window ... 'La Cucaracha, la Cucaracha ...' Then he began to laugh. He'd left London behind. He'd left everything behind.

'Soon, Sissy. I'm coming home. Soon, darling.'

He was wearing dark brown driving gloves and, although they hid his broken hands, they did little to dull the pain. He could grip the wheel only very lightly and he changed gear with the palm of his hand. With time the pain seemed to be getting worse rather than better; it was spreading up his arms. Sometimes it got so bad it paralysed him. He'd stand holding his arms stiff and just wait for the agony to recede.

But now he wasn't thinking about it. He was part of the car, with one purpose. Get there, get to Lucy, get home.

He sped on, past car after car. Soon the trees gave way to open land and he passed through small towns, a blur, meaningless. Single lane, dual carriageway, by-pass, rolling forwards, coming home.

And then he was near the city, and he saw a sign. Wymondham Lodge.

And he turned off the road.

He had to put everything right before he ran out of time. He had to finish everything.

In ten minutes he was pulling up on the gravel drive of the hotel. It was eight o'clock and growing dark. Something flitted overhead; it might have been a bat, but could just have been a small bird. It was very quiet. There was only one other car in the driveway.

Tom got out, leaving his door hanging open, and went into reception.

There was no one there.

The place was unchanged. Frozen in time, stifling. The same spotless blue, monogrammed carpet; the same dark, polished wood; the same displays of dried flowers on the tables.

'Hello?' It was Phil – head honcho. He came out from a small office to stand behind the desk. 'Oh, hello, Mr Kendall. This is a surprise.'

'Hello, Phil.' Tom smiled at him.

'How are you? Are you staying? Do you want to book in?' Phil opened the register.

'I'm fine, thanks. And, no, I'm not staying.'

'What can I do for you, then?'

'Well, I was just passing and I thought I'd . . .' What? What had he thought he'd do? 'You see, I . . .' He couldn't remember now why he'd come in. He looked out through the open door at his car, as if there might be some clue there. He thought back. The hotel, Phil, the Wymondham Lodge.

Phil was smiling at him patiently, though with a slight frown.

'I saw the sign, Wymondham Lodge, and I thought …' Yes, that's right, there was the sign, he'd been sure it was a direction sign, but what was he supposed to do now he was here? The two of them stared at each other, faintly embarrassed.

'Are you busy?' Tom asked finally.

'Oh, so so.' Phil looked relieved to change the subject. 'Rooms aren't all full, by any means. Things are rather tight all over at the moment. As I'm sure you know. But there's always things to do … You know …' Phil trailed away.

'Yes, I can imagine,' said Tom limply, then they returned to uncomfortable silence.

Finally Phil said, 'Was there something you wanted?' and took up an 'I've got things to do' stance.

'Yes,' Tom said quickly. He looked at the manager, at his shiny bald head, his glasses, his ingratiating smile and it struck him. 'Phil,' he said, politely, 'this is a crap hotel.'

That made Phil snap to attention. 'I beg your pardon?' he said, still maintaining his smile.

'This hotel is crap.'

'I'm sorry, is this some sort of joke? I'm not with you, Mr Kendall.'

'The rooms are too small, they're badly furnished, the plumbing's a disgrace.'

'We've had no complaints, Mr Kendall, and quite frankly—'

'Shut up, Phil. The swimming-pool's more like a paddling-pool. The nets on the tennis courts have holes in them …'

Phil's smile had finally gone. 'With all due respect,' he said coldly, 'I really don't think this is the time for complaints. If you had any grievances you should have aired them at the time. Now, if you don't mind, I am rather busy.'

'Yes.' Tom looked around the lobby, there was whiteness creeping into it, the blue of the carpet was bleeding away. Phil was staring at him, his expression once more bland. But his pasty face had become deathly white.

'You listen to me, Phil,' Tom said, his voice coming out excited and high-pitched. 'When I came here with Maddie, I thought it would be the start of a new life for me. And when we got here ...' A vicious wave of anger struck him. 'Jesus Christ, Phil! The fact remains that these rooms are too bloody small!'

Tom saw himself reach out and take Phil by the throat. He saw the brown leather of the driving gloves take hold of his white, spotty neck. He saw himself squeeze and squeeze. Phil's eyes bulging. His tongue ...

'Good evening.'

A middle-aged couple came down the stairs.

Phil had spoken. He was all right. Thank God, Tom hadn't actually done anything. Now, if he could just concentrate on the couple ... But they seemed pale, distant, drifting as if in slow motion, like two ghosts. They went outside.

Phil turned back to Tom. 'Now Mr Kendall ...'

'I'm sorry, Phil.'

'Are you all right?'

'Yes. I'm sorry, I don't know what I'm doing here.' Tom began to back out of the lobby. 'I saw the sign and ... and I thought perhaps I'd left something here. Yes, that's it. Ha! Something ... something ... something of mine.'

Phil watched him all the way out of the door. His face betraying no emotion.

Tom went out into the night air and for a moment felt dizzy. He imagined he was seeing everything through the eyes of the bat, he was high up and everything was spinning away from him.

He slammed his fist on the car roof and screamed. He clutched his broken hand and began to cry. Phil came out of the hotel and stood in the doorway watching him.

'Are you sure you're all right, Mr Kendall?'

'I'm fine Phil, I'm fine. I just made a mistake, I shouldn't have come.'

He climbed wearily into the car, put on his headlights and drove away. The further he got from the hotel and the nearer to home, the better he felt. The whiteness faded away, the pain reduced to a dull cold throb.

Fuck them! They'd tried to trick him again. They'd tried to prevent him from getting to Lucy. But he'd seen past their ploy just in time. If he'd really attacked Phil, it would have all been over.

Come on. Come on. Don't be an idiot.

He had to keep his mind on his purpose, he had to concentrate, remember his goal.

He was coming home.

And then his hand wouldn't hurt any more. The whiteness would never trouble him again. He'd be painless and they'd all live happily ever after.

THIRTY-FIVE

Tom was different. Ever since James's death he'd been changing, and now there was a wildness about him, an unpredictability. Lucy looked at him sitting at the kitchen table rubbing his gloved hands, and she hardly recognized him.

Well, perhaps under the circumstances, it was understandable; James's death had changed all of them. It had put Tom under terrible strain being a suspect. Given time he'd settle down, and maybe cutting loose like this, letting rip a little, might be good for him in the long run. He'd certainly been guilty of being a bit stiff in the past. It surely wouldn't do him any harm to loosen up.

She handed him a cup of tea and smiled at him. 'You sure you don't want anything stronger?'

'Yes ... This is fine.' He took a delicate sip from the mug. 'You make a good cup of tea.'

'I was trained well, you know how fussy Dad was about his tea.'

'Yes. It stays with you, doesn't it?'

'I suppose it does ... some of it.'

'Not many people know how to make a decent cup these days, considering the amount of the stuff drunk in this country ... God, listen to me, I sound like him.'

'You worry about that too much.'

'Do I? I don't know.' Tom stared gloomily into his tea.

'Come on,' Lucy said, sitting down and touching his hand. 'Let's not talk about all that again. It's done with, it's all in the past now. We've got to get on with things. We can't have him hanging over us for the rest of our lives. He was just a man after all, just our father. Everybody has trouble with their parents.'

'No, Lucy. It's not as simple as that. You see, James was right.'

'What do you mean?'

'James knew it, he could see. He was right about our family. It's him, the old man, he poisoned us. Can't you see that? And he was poisoned, too, by his father, and his father before him. And you're right, too, it's not just us, it's all families, they're all poisoned, they're all fucked up.'

'They can't all be, they—'

'You can't escape. You can never escape from your childhood. Can't you see, Lucy? James was right. I am like him. He's inside me, a part of him in me, a part of his poison. It's with me, it always will be.'

'But, Tom, you can't think that . . .'

'I am him, Lucy, I am the old man . . . And you're him, and your children. He's in them, too. It's like the bindweed; you can dig it up and dig it up, but you'll never get it all out. If you leave just one tiny bit of root, it'll grow again from that. You can't dig it all out, we've all got bits of his roots in us and they're growing there and he's growing from them. As long as I live, I'll never be able to get rid of him. That's why I never married, Sissy, that's why I never had children of my own. Deep down inside I knew, I knew that I would just be carrying on. I would pass on the bindweed. We're a sick family, Lucy, we always have been, and we've always known it, you and I. Right from when we were young. We're crazy, Sissy. We're poisoned and we're sick, and we're strangled by bindweed . . . And we're fucked up.'

Lucy didn't know what to say. Looking at Tom now she could quite believe that he was mad, but she didn't think that agreeing with him would really help.

'You're just under a lot of stress, Tom. This has been a bad time, we'll get over it.'

'No. No, this hasn't been a bad time. Don't you understand? This has been the best time. I've woken up, Lucy, I've seen what it's all about.' Tom was beaming at her like some kind of deranged Moonie.

Lucy felt like she was going to cry. She had so looked forward to Tom coming back, to seeing him happy at not being suspected any more. She had wanted to tell him about the course she'd signed up for, about looking for work, about the girls, the photographs, the shelves she was putting up in Polly's room. She'd wanted to tell him about Sergeant Arnell who fancied her. She'd pictured the two of them sitting here at the table laughing at that. But it had all gone wrong. Tom wasn't better than before, he was worse. He was talking nonsense.

'What's the matter with you, Tom?' she asked.

'Nothing. I'm happy. I'm so happy.'

'You don't sound it.'

'It's not that sort of happiness.'

'What other sort is there?'

'It's so hard to explain. But everything that's happened has been for a purpose. To bring me here. Now. Knowing what I know now. I've changed, Lucy, I've become something different.'

'What?'

'I'll show you.' Tom carefully peeled off his leather driving gloves. Lucy winced. His hands looked broken. The fingers were crooked, bent at odd angles, stiff and swollen, horribly discoloured by bruising.

'God, Tom, what happened?'

Tom smiled at her again. 'He gave them to me. The boy. He gave me these hands.'

'What boy? What are you talking about?'

'Aren't they beautiful?'

'Don't talk like that, Tom. You're upsetting me.'

'Look at them glow. They're full of light.' He moved them slowly in front of his face, watching them with an enchanted look on his face.

'Tom. Please ... What have you done to yourself?'

'I do not believe, Lucy, that a man can be truly happy unless he fully understands what he is and can act accordingly ... How can it be wrong to be happy?'

'Your hands, Tom ...'

'I know how to be happy. I understand. I know what I've got to do finally.'

Lucy had to get out of the room, he was beginning to really frighten her. 'Well, that's good,' she said, trying to smile disarmingly. 'Because I know what I've got to do as well.'

'What?'

'I've got to check on the girls.'

She got up and left as quickly as she could. She didn't really need to check on the girls, but it was all she could think of, and perhaps if she left Tom alone for a while he might calm down.

The girls were both in the front room upstairs. They were sharing a bed, as Claire had been having bad dreams again. Lucy carefully went in and shut the door behind her. They were fast asleep. She thought of Tom and the bindweed and felt terribly sad for a moment. Then she looked at them, sprawled innocently in the bed, and they gave her hope.

'Don't you worry,' she whispered. 'Everything's going to be all right.'

And then she heard Tom coming up the stairs.

She closed the door and leant against it. She heard Tom call her name quietly and she didn't reply. She heard him approach the door. He knocked.

'Lucy?'

'Go away, Tom,' she said quietly. 'They're sleeping.'

'Are you coming out?'

'In a minute. Go downstairs.'

'There's so much more I have to say to you.'

'In a minute, Tom. Now be quiet or you'll wake them.'

'But I have to talk.'

'Can't it wait?'

'No.'

'But the girls.'

'It concerns the girls. I want them. Let me take them.'

A cold wave of dread passed through Lucy, making the hairs down her back and arms stand up painfully.

She locked the door.

'Please, Tom.'

'Why have you locked the door?'

'Please, Tom, just go away.'

Polly woke up, sat up in the bed. 'What's going on, Mummy? Who are you talking to?'

'No one, dear, go back to sleep.'

'Listen, Lucy, I did kill James.'

'No, you didn't. You're not under suspicion any more.'

'I killed him because he knew,' Tom said quietly. 'Oh yes, James knew it. James saw it, and look what happened to him. I killed him. I pulled the fork from his throat and it killed him. I didn't realize at the time, but I meant to do it, because I couldn't bear to have him know, to see us, you and I, and to see the sickness in us. Well, it's got to stop, Sis. We can't go on, we've got to stop it now.'

'Please, Tom, go away. I'm not listening.'

'I've got to burn the roots, sterilize the soil so no more weeds can grow. You've got to understand that it's the only way. The only way we'll ever be free of him.'

'What do you want, Tom? I don't understand.'

'Let me have the children, Lucy, let me take the girls. I won't hurt them, I'd never hurt them. I'll just take them away from this place, take them to where they'll be safe, safe from his poison.'

'Where, where will you take them?'

'To heaven, Sissy. I'll take the little ones to heaven. And we'll go too, all of us. We'll be no more. No more Kendalls, no more Kendall blood. No more roots.'

Lucy looked at Polly and Claire. They were both sitting up now, with wide eyes. She left the door.

'Come on,' she said quietly but urgently. 'Get dressed.'

'Why?'

'Just do as you're told.'

'Lucy.'

'Tom, for God's sake, listen to yourself. You're not making any sense.'

'I want to help you.'

'How? By killing us? What are you saying?'

'No . . . No . . . Well, yes. But it's not like that, it won't be like that. I won't hurt them, it'll be just like they're going to sleep.'

The girls were half dressed now, and she hurriedly helped them to finish, cramming small limbs into unhelpful sleeves and legs. 'Come on, get in there . . . !'

'It won't hurt. I know how to do it without hurting. I'll tell them they're going to sleep and they will be, and they'll be free.'

Lucy went to the window, fiddled with the clasp on the double glazing they'd had put in to keep the noise of the traffic out.

'And then I'll take you too, Sissy. And when it's done and I know it's done, and it's safe, and I'm the last, then I'll kill myself as well. It's simple, Luce, it's the only way.'

Lucy was trying to put his voice out of her mind. She had opened the clasp but the panel wouldn't slide, it was jammed in the runners, she could see no way of getting it open.

'Move, you bastard. Open!'

'Let me in, Lucy. Please let me in.'

'No, Tom. Just stop and think. Calm down.'

'I've thought. I've thought and I've thought, and this is the only way. We can't carry on the line, we've got to stop it here ... So open the fucking door, Lucy.'

'No.'

Lucy picked up a heavy suitcase, crammed full of the girls' winter clothes.

'Stand over here behind Mummy. Move away from the window.'

The girls did as they were told and watched as Lucy hefted the suitcase against the glass. There was a huge bang, but the window was unaffected. She swung again, but it was no good, the glass wouldn't break.

'Now, come along, Sissy. I don't want to get angry. I don't want to lose my temper. If I do it this way, while I'm calm and rational, while I'm sane, then it'll be all right. No one will get hurt, but if I get angry, if I go into the white world, then it won't be me any more ... And then it'll hurt, Lucy. It'll really hurt.'

'Tom, please, just go away. You're not calm now, you're not rational.'

'I *am* calm! I *am* fucking calm! Now open the fucking door!'

'No, Tom.'

'I'll show you how fucking calm I am.'

The door shook as Tom slammed something against it, then he yelled in pain.

'Now you've made me hurt myself, Lucy.'

'All right, Tom. All right. Just wait. I'm going to open the door, but only when I know you're not angry. You want it that way, don't you? You don't want to be angry. You don't want to hurt any of us.'

'No. No. That's what this is all about, I don't want to hurt you.'

Lucy noticed a big screwdriver on the floor next to the shelves she'd been putting up.

'Good. Good boy. I could always calm you down, couldn't I?'

'Yes.'

'When you were angry at night, I knew how to make you happy. Make you forget about him.'

'Yes. You knew, Lucy. You've always known. We should never have split up, you and I. We should have stayed together. Then none of this would have happened.'

'Yes.' Lucy went to the window. If she could get the screwdriver between the glass and the frame, maybe she could lever it out. She jammed it in and leant on it.

'Lucy?'

'It's all right, darling, I'm here.'

'Good.'

'Are you feeling better?'

'Much better. Not angry now ... Are you going to open the door?'

'In a minute. I have to be sure. Talk to me ... You talk, let me know you're all right. If I can hear your voice I'll know how you're feeling.'

'What should I talk about?'

'Tell me about being happy, Tom. Tell me about that.'

'I am happy now.'

'Yes, tell me about it.' The window gave slightly; part of it jumped free of the casing. A gap appeared between glass and metal. She pushed the screwdriver in and began to prise it loose.

'It was the book, you see? The boy's book. I took it. It told me how to be happy. It told me that I would only be happy when I accepted what I was, how I was, and I did accept it and I was happy. The boy taught me. You see, I'd always been scared of being angry, scared of what would happen if I gave in to it. Like that one time. That one time when I attacked Dad, when I had to leave you. I thought if it happened again it would be painful, like then. But the boy showed me that it wasn't the anger that was painful, it was Dad. It was his hitting me. The only time I ever saw him angry, the only time I ever saw him show any emotion of any kind. So it wasn't my anger I should be afraid of.'

The glass had shifted slightly, but would go no further. Lucy grabbed a chair and hefted it twice against the window. The glass just dropped back to where it had been before.

The girls sat quietly on the bed, not understanding what was going on.

'The boy died, Lucy, but he showed me how to live. And now I have to take us all away to safety.'

'To safety?'

'To where he won't be able to get to us any more. Away from here, away from this life.'

'Tom, Tom, don't talk like that again.' Lucy looked around desperately for something heavier.

'But nothing's changed, Lucy. I was just explaining. Now you said you were going to open the door.'

'No. No, Tom, I can't. I can't let you in.'

'You fucking bitch. They're my children. Give them to me.'

'They're not, Tom, they're mine.' Lucy tried with the chair again and she thought she heard a crack.

'What are you doing?'

She swung again and the crash of the chair against the window was followed by another thump on the door. Tom gave an inarticulate shout, and the door shook again.

The window stayed intact.

Lucy put her arms round the girls. 'You've got to be brave now.'

'Why?'

'Listen. When the door opens, as soon as it opens, you've got to run out, okay? Run past Uncle Tom.'

Polly looked at her with big shining eyes. 'It's not a game, is it?'

'No, dear, it's not a game. You must run past him and run out of the house. Go next door to the Harrisons as quickly as you can and get help. Tell them your Mummy's in trouble.'

'Where will you be? Will you come with us?'

'No, I'll wait here with your Uncle Tom.'

'But he'll hurt you. He's angry.'

'No, I'll be all right.'

The door shuddered again and one of the panels split down the middle.

'I'm frightened.'

'Yes, dear. But you must be brave. You've got to look after Claire.' Lucy picked up the chair. 'Remember, as soon as the door opens, you've got to run past Uncle Tom.'

'No. We won't go without you, we don't want to.'

'You will go! Or Mummy will be very cross.'

Another crash and the panel was half knocked out. Tom's hand came through the opening and reached for the key. His fingers were bleeding, and they smeared blood on the white wood of the door.

Lucy hit the hand with the chair and Tom screamed and pulled it back out. Quickly Lucy jumped forward and tried to yank the key from the lock. But it needed to be turned and Tom's hand came back through the opening and grabbed her forearm. She bit him and again he withdrew. The key turned and she pulled it out, then threw it across the room.

'Lucy. I'm angry now. You've made me angry. Why are you doing this to me? Your own brother? I only want to come in. Why can't you just accept what's right?'

'It's not right. It's not.'

'Damn you to hell!'

Tom must have thrown his whole weight against the door, because it cracked down the middle and the frame splintered.

'It's Uncle Tom!' Claire screamed. 'It's Uncle Tom!'

'Don't be frightened. You're not frightened, are you?'

Claire nodded her head.

'Be brave for me.' She held the chair in one hand and gave the girls a quick hug with the other.

There was another almighty crash and this time the door sprang inwards.

Tom came in.

'Go.'

Lucy shoved the girls.

Polly got past, but Tom grabbed hold of Claire and she shrieked. Lucy hit him with the chair and he let her go. She ran out.

Lucy stood looking at Tom, who was panting and clutching his shoulder where she'd hit him. Both his hands were a mess; they hardly looked like hands at all any more. There was a calm, blank look on his face, as if he was in a trance.

'I am happy now,' he said. 'I am happy now.'

Lucy said nothing, she stood and waited for him. The girls were gone. They were really all that mattered.

Tom took a deep breath and straightened up.

'I am happy now.'

He took a step towards her, and she didn't have it in her to hit him again. He was her brother. Despite everything she loved him. Poor Tom. Maybe he could do it without pain. Maybe it would be just like going to sleep.

He took another step.

'Happy now.'

He raised his broken hands and looked at her with black, mindless eyes.

'Sissy. My Sissy.'

Lucy took a deep breath and waited.

Tom took a last step, reached out his arms for her and placed his hands gently at her throat.

The room seemed to explode.

Tom gasped and Lucy felt a great force buffet her.

There was a flash and Tom leapt forwards, knocking her to the ground, covering her with his body. There was smoke in the room and a smell of burning. Lucy's face was stinging. She put her hand to it and it came away with blood.

Tom was lying still; she pushed him off her. His back was cut open and bleeding.

A woman walked into the room holding a shotgun. She had red hair and she was weeping.

She looked at Lucy and at Tom.

Tom was dying. Lucy kissed him gently on the cheek.

He opened his eyes and he was Tom again. But his face had grown young. He looked like he had done when he was fifteen. When she'd held him in her arms in bed and he'd relaxed, all his cares forgotten.

'Happy now,' he said, and smiled.